Nowhere Near Hollywood
by Mark SaFranko
Honest Publishing

All Rights Reserved
© Copyright 2019 Mark SaFranko
ISBN 978-1-9160043-0-6

Manufactured in the United Kingdom
Cover: Slava Nesterov, additional design by Tim Clulow

For Emmanuel "EJ" Juhel

"People know when you are trying to be something that you are not... This is a story about a man who tried to be something he was not; who wasted his time, and asked for and got a lot of trouble."

-- John O'Hara, *The Big Laugh*

"It was a sickness: this great interest in a medium that relentlessly and consistently failed, time after time after time, to produce anything at all."

-- Henry Chinaski, *Hollywood*

"The losers and the lost always seemed to make a beeline for me."

-- Max Zajack

NOWHERE NEAR HOLLYWOOD

MARK SAFRANKO

1

"You're going to do what?"

Gayle was propped up in bed reading a magazine on world affairs. She stared at me as if I'd just told her I was going to turn myself into a woman.

"I'm going to be an actor. If that bastard can do it, why can't I?"

Her jaw dropped open. She shook her dirty blonde hair.

"What in the world are you talking about, Max?"

"I was just down at the bar, and I happened to look up and saw Seamus Sean-Hughes on the TV screen."

"Who in the world is Seamus Hugh -- whatever his name is?"

"Sean-Hughes. He's one of the stars of this popular series, *Stoneman And MacDougal*."

"I think I might have heard of it."

"It's one of the top ten major network shows."

"Did you smoke any cigarettes?"

"No," I lied.

"I can smell it, Max."

"Come on, honey. I told you I quit."

I knew she didn't believe me, but I sat on the edge of the bed anyway. "So here's what happened..."

Gayle had wanted me out of the apartment. She said she needed some space, always a bad sign. I jumped into my heap and drove five minutes to the Top Of The Hill

Inn, grabbed a seat at the bar, and fired up a Marlboro, one of the stash I kept in the glove compartment. There were a few bodies scattered around, biker types, mostly, and construction workers. They were glued to the big TV set.

The bartender drifted over. He looked bored and fucked-off that he had to serve me.

"What's on tap?"

He reeled off a slew of brands.

"Budweiser." I wasn't in the mood for anything fancy or expensive.

He drew a pint and slid it in front of me. It was flat as an old tire, but it was cold.

I sat there thinking. I was thirty-four years old and had nothing to show for myself. I'd been writing for thirteen or fourteen years, and over that time I'd tried everything -- plays, novels, stories, music. I'd even been a professional for a couple of years, a reporter for a pair of daily newspapers and a regional magazine, but I'd been lousy at journalism because I didn't give a damn about what was happening in the world. The truth was I was a failure at everything I'd ever tried. Just making it through everyday life gave me fits. I suffered anxiety, panic attacks, fears and phobias. I lived in a state of perpetual depression.

Whenever I opened a newspaper or magazine I couldn't help but notice that some new young hotshot writer had made it big. Everyone gushed over what a great talent, even genius, had been discovered, and the masses agreed. But when I sent my own stuff out, it returned like a homing pigeon with the same note -- "No thanks." What was the key? I could never figure it out. Probably I just wasn't cut out to be a writer.

But for some insane reason I kept trying, kept planning. I made notes. I typed. Day after day, night after night, I sat there waiting for something great to happen. But I didn't know how to make something great happen, which all the young hotshots seemed able to do...

"That Seamus Sean-Hughes sure is a good actor."

The two muscle boys at the end of the bar were riveted to the big TV screen.

The name -- Seamus Sean-Hughes -- faintly rang a bell. I looked up. The actor they were talking about was burning asphalt behind the wheel of a red sports car. He was blond and tan but not very good-looking. At first I didn't recognize him. Then, slowly, the years melted away...

Seamus Sean-Hughes and I had once read for the same part: Stanley Kowalski, in *A Streetcar Named Desire*. At the time we'd both been attending a college in the middle of a cow pasture in western Pennsylvania. I'd become enamored with the theater. I landed parts in plays by Saroyan and Pirandello and Stoppard, but never thought seriously of trying to become an actor. Where I came from, there were no actors. Besides, actors, I'd already figured out, weren't exactly fountains of creativity. *The writer was everything.* He was the one history remembered. That's what I aspired to be: a genius, the divinely inspired maniac who produced great literature, real art, the master who gave puppets something to say. I wanted to be Tennessee Williams and Eugene O'Neill. I wanted to be Sartre. Above all, I wanted to be Dostoyevsky. I hadn't yet written a word, but I knew that a mere thespian, a mouthpiece, wasn't the equal of a genuine Prometheus.

I was the one who got the part of Stanley. Even though I didn't know what I was doing, I won raves for my performance.

Now there I was, sitting in a roadhouse full of nobodies who were gushing over a hack I'd once vanquished. How the hell had he made it from the cow shit to Hollywood?

"That dude must snag lots of pussy, huh?"

"Hey, if you looked like him and were in that show, you'd score all kinds of poon too."

Those two idiots were starting to annoy me.

"I once took a part away from Seamus Sean-Hughes," I said to the air.

The muscle boys turned in my direction. *"What?"*

I repeated myself.

The one sitting closest to me glanced at his buddy.

"Is that right?"

"I wouldn't kid you."

"That's really something. I once beat out Tom Hanks for a part in a movie, but I had to turn it down because it was my turn to drive the garbage truck."

The first guy started to laugh. Then his pal joined in. They both laughed really hard and couldn't stop.

The show ended and the credits rolled. The muscle boys tossed their drinks back and headed for the door.

"Have a good night," said one of them.

"Got a ride back to the asylum?" said the other.

Before they revved up their cycles I could hear them howling like a pair of drunken chimpanzees.

I looked around. I was the only person left in the joint. The bartender lurched towards me. He looked even more bored and pissed off than he did when I came in.

"What's it gonna be, chief? Another Bud?"

"No... Yeah, why not."

That was how it started.

"Actors, they get all the attention," I said to Gayle.

"Maybe that's the way to draw attention to my writing. After all, Sam Shepard and Woody Allen do both, right? Once people start learning my name they'll *have* to pay attention to my writing. Hey, it's America -- all things are possible. And it can't get any worse than it already is."

"I don't know, Max. Actors are props -- mannequins. You're a writer. The real deal."

"Says who? I can't even get a short story into some tiny piece-of-shit journal in Arkansas that no one's ever heard of. You read my mail lately?"

"Jesus, Max! I left Hollywood because I wanted to get away from that world."

It was a story I knew inside out. Gayle's ex had been a location manager for Zoetrope and had worked his way up. Now he was the executive producer of mega-hits starring the likes of Bruce Willis. It was a bit of a sore spot, that he was a somebody, and I wasn't.

"We're nowhere near Hollywood, baby. New York's different. There's supposed to be a thriving indie movie scene here. They need actors, right? It won't take all that much time and I'll go on writing. Hell, I'll write for the stage and I'll write for movies on top of writing stories and novels."

"What about your job? What about paying the bills? I don't know, Max. It's all the same -- Hollywood, New York, wherever. Those people are vile. I think you're just jealous of this Scott-Hughes guy."

"Sean-Hughes," I corrected her again.

"My God, what a pretentious name! See what I mean?"

"When I knew him he was Gerry Hughes."

"I don't know, Max..."

"I'm telling you, honey, actors are where it's at. They hold all the power. In case you haven't noticed, our *goddamned* president happens to be a second-rate B-film actor. What does that tell you?"

Gayle shook her head again.

"I just hate to see you... *debase* yourself, that's all."

"I've done more than my share of that already. I've written a couple of plays -- nothing. Three novels -- zilch again. My short stories go out, and if they're not returned before I even get back from the post office, they disappear into a black hole. And it's not like I started writing yesterday. This has been going on for years."

She had nothing more to say. The truth was the truth and she couldn't deny it. She rolled over, switched off the lamp, and went to sleep.

2

The first thing you do when you want to be an actor is get yourself a headshot. I checked the yellow pages. A photographer up in Morristown claimed to do "show-business" photos at a discounted rate. I needed to go discount. I called and made an appointment.

Henry Godaris Photography was located on the third floor of an ancient office building. There was no elevator, so I climbed all the way up there, thankful that I'd finally quit smoking cigarettes -- at least for the week.

Godaris was a twitchy little man with black hair and oversized tortoise-shell glasses who darted all around the loft like a cornered mouse. All the photos on the walls were of bland suburban scenes: family portraits, weddings, trees and flowers, even smiling dogs. Where were the performers? And why wasn't his gear already set up?

"How's business?" I said, trying to make conversation. He was fumbling with his camera and tripod and cursing under his breath. I got the feeling he was annoyed I was there.

"Don't ask! Awful! Just awful!" Godaris had a fussy voice. "And it doesn't help that I'm not feeling well."

"Sorry." I was beginning to regret that I'd shown up.

"It's my stomach. I've got a terribly nervous stomach, and the fact that business is bad doesn't help."

"I should think not."

"Come over here and sit on this stool."

Well, this was what I got for trying to cut corners. I did as Godaris ordered. He rummaged in some boxes, pulled out a white bed sheet and fastened it onto the wall behind me. Within seconds it came undone.

"God-*damn* it!"

"Ever taken a headshot before?"

"Just what do you mean by that? I'm a professional! But I have to tell you, this is a real pain in the ass. Especially since I have an office retirement party to shoot in a half-hour!"

Finally he was behind the lens.

"Don't move until I tell you to move!"

Snap, snap, snap.

He took thirty, maybe forty shots. He never told me to smile, or turn my head, or pretend to look like I was about to take a shit. But I figured that one out of forty had to be usable.

"That's it. That's all I can do with my stomach in the condition it's in," he said after fifteen minutes or so.

I slid off the stool. Godaris told me to come back in a few days and pick up the contact sheets.

When I walked out, he was kicking the bed sheet across the floor and complaining about how the Pepto-Bismol wasn't working.

I brought the contact sheets home and looked them over. I was wrong about finding at least one good photo -- they were all crap and looked nothing like the professional headshots I'd seen. Once in a while I got told that I looked like Frank Langella or John Larroquette, but I saw no resemblance whatsoever in Godaris's snaps.

I didn't look like anything: not a hood, not a leading man, not a character actor. I didn't know what I was *supposed* to look like, but in Godaris's shots I looked like someone who *wasn't me*.

Gayle wasn't impressed either, but since I'd already paid the photographer, I had to settle on one of them. I went back to the studio and ordered a box of fifty.

I was ready to go.

3

I began scouring the trades for a part, any part: commercial, industrial, stage, print, TV, film -- whatever. It was obvious what I was up against: I wasn't a member of any of the performers' unions, and unless you had a famous mother or father who could grease the skids for you, it wouldn't be easy to score a card. Me, I wasn't related to anyone. I'd have to settle at first for non-union work, which meant that I probably wasn't going to get paid. To get my feet wet and acquire some experience, I knew I would have to consent to anything that came along.

And how was any of it supposed to help me get noticed as a writer? It wouldn't. It was going to mean nothing but even more rejection. Maybe I was crazy, like Gayle always said.

There was an open call for a production of David Mamet's *Sexual Perversity in Chicago*. I didn't know the play, but I dug the title. With a title that included the words "sexual perversity," the show just might not be a bore -- like Shakespeare or Shaw. And there might even be some hot tamales in the cast. I read the ad again. They needed two guys about my age for a short run in a small suburban theater. It wasn't going to pay a stinking penny, but it was a start, and I needed something to slap on a résumé.

I signed in and dropped my headshot onto the stack left by the other wannabes. When no one was watching, I shuffled through them. My competition had all kinds of credentials. They'd graduated from drama programs at prestige universities, some with advanced degrees, they were professionally trained in everything from classical singing to stage combat, and some had experience in regional theater, Off-Off Broadway, even in television commercials and movies. I had nothing. What was I doing?

The strangest part of all was that I had no consuming desire to be a performer. If I wanted to perform, I wanted to do it on the page, to have people beg for my autograph, the way they once importuned Balzac for permission to "kiss the hand that wrote *Seraphita*."

I looked over the sides I was supposed to read. From time

to time an acne-scarred assistant came out of the theater, glanced at the sign-in sheet, and called a name.

"Epstein!"

"Logan!"

"Crenshaw!"

The actor in question would rise and strut into the theater, sometimes moving his lips with the words he was about to deliver. What a horde of fools we were, and I was king of them all.

On the other side of the doors there was lots of screaming and shouting, as if someone were pleading for his life. It was intimidating. I began to feel nervous. I stood up and faced the exit. If I split right now, no one would ever know I'd even been there.

"Maroski! We need you to read with someone on stage."

Shit. What the hell was that about? It must have meant that the guy inside was a cinch to win a part. And since there were only two parts for males in the play, what chance would I have? Now I was going to have to be better than someone else, and I didn't know if I was any good in the first place.

I tried to concentrate on Mamet's lines, but on account of the actresses flitting around, it was tough. They were mostly beautiful, and if not, then they were drop-dead gorgeous. Every one was dressed to seduce. Now I remembered why men wanted to be actors.

Mamet's scenes were funny, very funny. I was going to read for the part of a Jewish guy who's trying to talk his younger friend out of getting himself mired in a relationship with a girl he's shacked up with. I could relate to his words, especially when the character convinces a woman he meets in a bar to hop into bed with him. I was beginning to wonder why I hadn't written the play myself...

"ZAJACK!"

Well, this was it, the moment of truth. I tried to force my mind into a state of blankness. I got up and walked into the theater, down the aisle and towards the stage. In the third row sat a stout, jowly, middle-aged man and a chubby woman with dyed orange hair swept into a ridiculous bouffant. They looked at me as if I'd just dropped to earth from outer space. What the hell? Maybe I wasn't good-looking enough to be an actor. I certainly didn't have the looks of a handsome star, one of the "hunks" all the ladies adored. But I reminded myself that offbeat types like Gene Hackman and Dustin Hoffman had become sex symbols, and maybe I looked as good if not better than they did.

The acne-scarred assistant handed over my headshot to the heavy-set guy, who looked at the photo, then flipped it and was confronted with the threadbare résumé.

"It's been a while...I'm just getting back into it."

He nodded. The woman sitting next to him was still staring.

"So, let's see what you got."

I climbed up on stage, my heart going like crazy.

"How about the Bernie Litko monologue -- did you have a chance to look at that one?"

I started reading, trying to inject the words with life, the way I'd done with Stanley Kowalski fifteen years earlier. It was easy, really. You said the words like you meant them.

When I was through, he asked me to read a shorter speech by the same character.

"Thanks for coming in. We'll be in touch."

Despite the fact that it was my first in ages, I thought I'd read pretty damned well in that audition -- but it was only my opinion. Maybe the director thought I was awful. Maybe he thought I shouldn't have wasted my time. Maybe he even thought I was some kind of nut.

I waited for the telephone to ring with an offer. It didn't. After a while I stopped thinking about it. I had a job to deal with.

"I guess I didn't get that part," I mentioned to Gayle over our hamburgers one night.

"There are other parts. And you just started."

She wasn't wrong about that.

Then the phone rang.

"Max Zajack?"

"You got him."

"This is Les Altagash, the director of *Sexual Perversity In Chicago*. My wife and I both liked your audition."

"No kidding? Thanks."

"The role is yours if you want it. Rehearsals begin on Monday evening at seven. In the meantime, come on over and pick up the script."

I reported the good news to Gayle. "So what do you think?"

"How many times have I told you, I hate to see you wasting your time when you could be concentrating on your own work?"

"And have you noticed that my writing isn't exactly setting the world on fire?"

"It's just a matter of time, Max."

"You might want to believe that, honey, but so far there hasn't been the slightest shred of evidence that I have any talent as a writer. But on my very first shot as an actor I scored. Maybe I've been barking up the wrong tree all along."

"Now you sound delusional."

"You don't think I can pull it off?"

"Sure you can pull it off -- but why would you want to?"

4

The director, his assistant, that acne-scarred fellow by the name of William Chesterfield, the producer, Ida, who also happened to be Les Altagash's wife, and all of the actors sat in a room offstage and read through the play. Renee checked me out, I checked out Suzette, and Ida checked out both me and Dennis, who was the other male in the four-character piece.

I couldn't keep my eyes off Suzette. Jesus, she was one hot little wench, with her big eyes and tight ass. I wondered who she was screwing. The beauties are always screwing somebody.

We only had a couple of weeks to get ready before the show opened. I didn't know how else to do it, so I went home and rehearsed my scenes in the mirror. The dialogue came easy, because that was the way most guys talked anyway.

"So how'd you do last night?"

"Are you kidding me?"

"Yeah?"

"Are you pulling my leg?"

"So?"

"So tits out to here so..."

Etc.

The blocking was simple too -- Mamet wasn't complicated, he was all about what came out of his characters' mouths. As long as you fit the part and had his words down, you were okay.

One night after rehearsal I ran into Ida, who was outside puffing on a cigarette.

"You know, Max, you're a good actor," she said. "You could really go places in this business."

"What gives you that idea?"

"Well, you're good-looking. You've got great projection. And you have presence on stage... You know, I could help you along."

"Oh, yeah? How's that?"

"After Les took off on me and went and lived with a

floozy for a few years, I figured that what was good for the goose was good for the gander, know what I mean?"

I squinted at Ida through the twilight shadows. She couldn't possibly mean what I thought she meant. She stood about four feet ten and weighed in at two hundred and fifty pounds. A perfectly nice lady and all, but definitely not my type. Maybe, if we were stranded on a desert island, with no chance of ever being rescued... but probably not even then.

I made some excuse about having to get back to my job, then home to my fiancée and the dinner she was holding for me. It was all a bald lie: I didn't have to go back to work, I didn't have a fiancée, and Gayle had gone out with some of her friends, leaving me to fend for myself.

"Well, if you change your mind," she smiled, revealing a set of small yellow teeth. "And by the way, Suzette is too young for you."

"I figured as much. Thanks for reminding me."

Opening night. Suzette looked super fine in her tight jeans and red sweater, but I'd never let her know. The last thing beautiful women need is more compliments. They hear it all their lives, which transforms them into monsters. Lay back and stay cool -- after years of torment and anguish at the hands of the goddesses, I'd finally learned my lesson.

Suzette and Dennis ran lines in one corner, while Renee and I did the same in another. When we were through, the four of us drifted around backstage, growing more and more nervous and killing time. Near the props Suzette and I bumped into each other.

"I am *so* wired," she whispered in my ear. "Let's go somewhere and fuck!"

I was caught completely off guard.

"I'll give a much better performance if I work some of this excess energy out of my body."

"Okay," I heard myself say. This girl could work me all she wanted.

Sex: it was the only thing I ever thought about, all day long, every single day. Sure, there was writing, and jobs, and paying the bills, and the horrible and nauseating inevitability of death, but sex permeated everything. Even when I'd just gotten it, it was only a matter of minutes before I was thinking about how to get it again.

Gayle was out in the audience. We hadn't been together all that long, less than a year. From the beginning we'd had an understanding. She was sweet. Tolerant. She possessed a profound intelligence. After reading some of my work, she had an unwavering, irrational belief in my talent, which even I didn't have. Finding her was like discovering a rare, invaluable gem. But what I liked best about her was that she was soft around the edges, unlike so many other women.

Now here I was, following Suzette's delicious ass down the hall, about to betray Gayle for the first time. I'd once told her that "if Bo Derek backed me into a corner and demanded that I fuck her," there would be little I could do but surrender. How often would I have the opportunity with a babe who was practically begging me for it? I'd never been much of a liar to the women I was involved with, but maybe that would have to change. After all, most artists, from Mozart to Picasso, were despicable pieces of shit. Why should I be any different? It was life's fault, not mine or anyone else's.

And you only live once, I told myself. *What's one more lie? You can live with a lie, you've lived with many lies...*

Suzette took a sharp right, then another. We found ourselves in a small room filled with more props and other junk. She turned and threw her arms around my neck.

"Let's do it!"

She reached down and yanked on my belt. My cock jumped forward like a jack being let out of the box. I was just about to run my hand into Suzette's panties when the backstage PA system erupted into life: "PLACES, EVERYONE!"

Suzette let go and kissed me on the mouth. "Later!" She dashed out of the room. I heard her footsteps tripping down the corridor.

Damn, I cursed. But maybe it was for the best. Now I didn't have to pretend to Gayle that something hadn't happened.

I forced my dick back into my pants, tucked my shirt, hooked my belt, ran down the hall and assumed my position in the wings... me."

———

Before I knew it, the run of *Sexual Perversity In Chicago* was history. After all that frenetic activity, there was nothing.

I no longer thought about the show, but I kept wondering about Suzette, and how close we'd come, and how that too had ended up as nothing. Everything ends up as nothing. Life itself ends in a void.

A few nights later, the phone rang. It was Renee.

"Max! Want to meet Suzette and me for a drink? We'll have a little wrap party of our own."

"Where and when?"

5

They'd picked an Irish tavern up in Morristown, one of those places where you went to drink seriously. All three of us stood at the bar and knocked back beer after beer. For females, they were good drinkers.

Whenever the bartender said "Another?" the answer was yes. He gave me a wink whenever he stopped by, as if he knew something I didn't.

The actresses wanted to talk about the play, but there was nothing much to say about it. I kept glancing at Suzette, searching for some kind of sign. What we'd started backstage had not been resolved. But all we were doing now was drinking. Of course that was good, because it would keep everyone loose, and crazy things happened when you drank a lot. But I wasn't interested in drinking too much -- I was interested in something else.

A couple of hours disappeared. Renee didn't do it for me sexually, but she showed no sign whatsoever that she was going to split, and I wanted her out of the way so I could get my hands on Suzette. The problem was that I was picking up the vibe that Renee was interested in me too, Unbelievable. In life there's either too much or not enough.

We kept running up the tab and getting more and more drunk, but there was still that logjam.

"Yeah, I thought the play really came off..."

"The audiences seemed to love it..."

"You were great!"

"So were you...!"

It was all horse shit. We were just beating around the bush. Maybe there was going to be a threesome, which meant Renee would have to be along for the ride. She looked a little better the more I drank, but I still didn't go for her sharp hook of a nose and the size of her feet. Women with feet bigger than mine were a turn-off.

"Well..."

"Uh..."

"How about if we...?"

"One more for the road?"

Nobody seemed able to make a decision. Then, all of a sudden, the vibe was gone, lost in a blur of alcohol. We'd drunk too much and waited too long. The ladies reached into their purses and began tossing their money onto the wood.

"Bye, Max!"

"Bye!"

And they were gone. My lustful fantasy had vanished into the smoky air, and Suzette with it.

How had I managed to blow such a golden opportunity? Suzette had practically beseeched me to screw her and nothing, not a thing, had come of it.

The bartender scooped up the money around all the empty glasses. "Another?"

"Why not."

"What the hell happened, man? Those two were practically in bed with you."

"That's what I thought. But something went wrong. And I don't know what."

He shook his head. "Women. You can never figure out where the hell they're coming from."

6

I was already through with the amateur stuff. It didn't take long to figure out that it would lead to nothing. Besides, Max Zajack wasn't amateur material. After all, *once upon a time I'd taken a part away from Seamus Sean-Hughes.*

I tried a few open calls for films, but that was another dead end. One look at the lines of pathetic wannabes wrapped around the block outside a midtown audition space told me all I needed to know. I had better things to do with my time than stand around for hours waiting to be looked over like a head of cattle.

Acting was some kind of racket, all right. As usual, the big names came from famous or wealthy families and had studied at places like Juilliard, Yale and NYU. Or they'd been underwear models. Or they were married to other big names. Once in a while a Gene Hackman or Robert Duvall rose from the ruck, but it was rare.

There had to be a way to figure out how it worked, some avenue into the better projects, but what was it?

I reminded myself that I was nobody and nowhere. At the age of thirty-five I was just starting.

7

For a while nothing happened, but I kept sending my photo out. Finally the telephone rang.

"I'm calling on behalf of Peter Morganstein," announced a feathery voice. I couldn't tell whether it belonged to a male or a female. "Peter would like to see you for a part in his upcoming film."

Well now, this was something. "Can you tell me a little about it?"

"It's an independent film in the vein of Ingmar Bergman."

Okay, this was *really* something.

"How about the part? What is it?"

"Peter would prefer if you didn't know until he saw you."

Well, artists had their methods. If he was modeling himself on the great Swedish master, maybe this fellow Morganstein was the real deal. I was told where to go and when to be there.

I'd always admired Bergman, even if he was a white European maestro, and they were falling out of favor. Just when you thought all movies were cow manure, you caught *Fanny And Alexander* or *Summer With Monika* or *Winter Light*. Even when he was less than great, there was always something in Bergman's morose or mystifying films to catch the eye or think about. He was the only filmmaker who made me feel I wasn't wasting my time in a dark theater.

"This is more like it," I said to Gayle after I hung up the phone.

"So who's making this movie?"

"Peter Morganstein is the director."

"Who's he?"

"How would I know?"

"Don't you think you should find out? What's he done before this?"

I didn't want to think about it. If Peter Morganstein was an acolyte of Bergman, it was good enough for me.

"You're raining on my parade here, baby."

"Just watching out for you... Is there pay involved?"

"I don't have the part yet. But something along the lines of Bergman I can sink my teeth into. If I have to build up my list of credits, that's how I want to do it. And even if this guy is a neophyte, it doesn't mean anything. Remember that Scorsese was nobody when he started working with De Niro."

"Max, what are the chances -- "

"I don't want to talk about it."

The truth was that I didn't want to look too closely because I was afraid of what I might see.

8

I stood in a rehearsal space on Theater Row while three hipsters in black turtlenecks studied me from behind a table. The next thing I knew, I was in a movie. It was called *Paul And Wallace*.

"Do you have a lot of dialogue?" asked Gayle after I received the official news.

"I don't know. It was weird. They didn't ask me to read anything."

"What is this, a silent picture?"

"Christ, I hope not."

"What did you make of the filmmakers?"

"Not much. They didn't say anything. I guess you'd say they were, like, inscrutable."

"Well, good luck, Max."

I knew that Gayle wanted it to turn out well for me, but I

could hear the skepticism in her voice. By now I was getting used to it.

———————

A script landed in my mailbox. Morganstein had basically ripped off the storyline of *From The Life Of The Marionettes*, one of my favorite Bergman flicks, and rewrote it as a kind of gay melodrama.

No problem -- in New York everyone was gay, or so the *New York Times* would have you believe. Gay was guaranteed to attract an audience. Maybe, for once in my life, I'd landed in the right place at the right time.

But after closing it I still couldn't figure out what part I was supposed to play. There were a pair of gay lovers, an ex-wife and a policeman. I didn't think I fit either homosexual role, and the cop was supposed to be in his late fifties. What was I missing? Maybe Morganstein and his team were going to age me with makeup for the cop.

But why hadn't they told me which lines to look at? Film directors all thought of themselves as geniuses, and geniuses worked in mysterious ways...

———————

This time Morganstein himself was on the line.

"Max, would you mind coming to my apartment?"

"Okay," I said. Was Monday evening good?

No doubt a meeting with the boss would clear everything up. Maybe Morganstein was going to put me through some special exercise designed to ease a thespian into the proper frame of mind to tackle a specific role. Maybe we were going to work on the dialogue together. Or maybe we were going to talk about costumes.

His apartment was a rat's nest on the fourth floor of a former tenement on Rivington Street.

"What's up," I said after he got through throwing back all six bolts on the door.

"There's a revised script. I wanted to give it to you personally."

I didn't ask why he didn't just drop it in the mail. He handed it over and I fingered it. No doubt there was some revelation in the new pages that would illuminate all.

"Please -- come in."

The director was as jittery as a squirrel. His eyes, a pair of black holes, kept darting around his hovel, like he was high on meth. I followed him into a closet that was supposed to be his office.

"So, who am I playing in your movie?"

"Ah! I'm not sure yet. I prefer to talk to my actors first, get to know them, before making a final decision."

"I see."

"Ah -- you like Mishima."

At the time I happened to be carrying around a copy of

Forbidden Colors, which I'd been wrestling with over the past couple of weeks and losing the battle. Trying to decipher each sentence of the lousy translation was like slogging through quicksand. On the walk over from the subway I'd decided to cut my losses and abandon it.

"I've read a few of his books. *The Temple Of The Golden Pavilion. Spring Snow. The Sailor Who Fell From Grace With The Sea. Confessions Of A Mask* was my favorite."

"*Forbidden Colors* is a beautiful book," Morganstein sighed.

The novel was a muddle of all kinds of disconnected themes, but the most prominent that ran through it was homosexuality. Morganstein stared at me, as if waiting for me to do something. Suddenly I had the feeling that I was supposed to make a move on him.

"I wouldn't go that far," I said. "I've liked some of his other books a lot more."

This seemed to deflate him. His eyeballs were still bouncing all over the place, but the air had drained out of the room.

"So, uh, *when* do I get to learn who I'm playing?"

"Basically...basically...I still don't know yet. Still sorting all of that out, basically."

He elongated the word "basically," stroked it, sucked on it. It made me want to punch him in the face.

Why the hell had I trekked all the way over here? Did Morganstein just want to look at me again? Was he judging my "quality?" Did he want to fuck me in the ass? And why would he tell me I had a part if he didn't know what it was?

"So basically we'll call you," he said finally, getting up

and showing me the door.

"Sure, man. I hope you get it all sorted out."

9

I told Gayle what happened. She couldn't make heads or tails of it either.

"The most likely explanation is that he wanted to have sex with you and you didn't respond. That's how the game works, Max."

A week and a half later I was ordered to report to the set of *Paul And Wallace* at ten in the morning, which meant I had to take a day off from work without pay. It was okay. I was sick to death of writing about the market for mobile telephones in Africa and welcomed any excuse not to be there.

Shooting was to commence on the eighteenth floor of a luxury apartment tower in the Theater District. Whenever I was in that neighborhood I spotted famous faces: Jack Warden. E.G. Marshall. Henry Winkler. They looked as miserable as the rest of us. The difference, of course, was that they had the money to live there.

When I arrived, a small crew was dragging cables and fiddling with lights.

"Hey, our corpse is here!" one of them shouted.

I looked over my shoulder. Were they talking about

someone else?

Morganstein popped his head out of a bedroom.

"Max! You need to get into makeup as soon as possible! You're going to be our dead body!"

"What?"

"You'll be the man who Wallace murdered," he explained breathlessly, his delicate hands fluttering like butterflies. "That's how the film is going to begin -- with a close-up of your bashed and bloody face. I'm so excited!"

"You mean that's all I do?"

"You're a really important character in the movie, Max, even if you don't have any lines and you're only onscreen for a few seconds!"

"We're going to shoot you from several different angles!" one of the crew chimed in, as if it would make me feel better.

Gayle had hit it squarely on the head: I could be back at home working on a novel right now. Or better yet, making money on my day job.

But I was already here. The part of a dead man -- so long as he had a name, even if I made it up -- was another credit for my résumé. As long as I wasn't insulted by what they asked me to do, something was better than nothing... right?

"And we're still writing a scene for the end of the film, where we show you being bludgeoned to death!"

I went off into another bedroom and leaned back in a chair while a makeup artist splashed fake blood all over my face and clothes. While sitting there, my eyes followed the lovely blond actress in the white summer dress who flitted in and out of the room.

Makeup had me ready, but for some reason nothing happened. Nobody explained why. Everyone, actors and crew, sat around waiting for something. I hated being trapped on the high floor of a building, it roused my claustrophobia. I tried to read Highsmith's *A Dog's Ransom*, which I'd brought with me, but I couldn't concentrate. Instead, I wandered from room to room looking out the windows, killing time.

After a couple hours of this, it was finally time for me to get down on the floor. Before the camera rolled, Morganstein and his crew argued back and forth over where and how I should be positioned.

"I don't want the sun on his face!"

"But it's a lovely effect!"

"Yes, but it's supposed to be night!"

"Do you think there's enough blood?"

Etc. Finally an agreement was reached.

"Quiet down, everybody!"

"QUIET!"

"And... *action!*"

I lay still while the camera whirred from several different perspectives, with the character of Wallace dancing over me in a panic, trying to figure out what to do now that he'd committed murder. Morganstein kept cutting to him and his reaction to his ghastly crime. I could have been anything on the floor -- a glove, a shoe, a pubic hair.

When it was over, the director ran around the apartment shouting "Congratulations everyone! You've just completed the first scene of *Paul and Wallace!*"

Everybody clapped. The "talent" -- as the actors were

called -- were told to take a break downstairs in the plaza, where some food had been laid out on a table. I found myself sitting next to the pretty blond in the white dress.

"I just got out of rehab," Maureen explained, glancing at me nervously. Up close she looked more than a little beaten down. "Hazelden. Have you been?"

"Not yet. So far I've been lucky. If you want to call it that."

Everyone I knew had been in rehab at least once. It felt like an insider's thing I wasn't part of.

"Thank God for my mother," she went on. "She made sure to get me in there when things were just starting to turn ugly."

Maureen proceeded to tell me her life story. For some reason this always happened with people I just met. They seemed to need to unburden themselves to me, revealing every last detail. I just sat there and listened. About how when she was a kid her mother had taken her to live in Israel for a couple of years -- even though they weren't Jews -- on account of her mystical beliefs. It was the Kabbalah that lured her -- in those days her mother lived by it.

She smiled. "It was all right, I guess. But it really started going downhill for me when I met Barry..."

Who the hell was Barry?

"He's a pro football player with the Green Bay Packers. I wish I knew at the time how terrible it was going to be."

"Really."

"Oh, you don't know. Barry Jamerson was my boyfriend at the University of Wisconsin."

"Uh-huh."

"At the time we were heavily into coke. Barry had a violent temper. And then there was the fact that he was a big football star, a campus hero."

"So what happened?"

"The low point was when he threw me out of his apartment into the freezing Wisconsin night. Naked."

I looked at her and tried to picture the scene. If you had a sense of humor, it was funny.

"From there my addiction spiraled out of control... You know, I had hopes this movie would launch my career," she sighed. "The part of Paul's sister is decent enough, but..."

"What?"

Maureen's voice dropped into a whisper. "I heard something about the budget being less than firm, and -- "

Just then the actors playing Paul and Wallace emerged from the tower doors.

Maureen laid her finger across her lips.

Paul and Wallace jerked out chairs and plunked themselves down.

"I told Peter half a dozen times that we should shoot that scene *against* the window," Wallace complained bitchily. "And he won't *listen*! He insists on doing it *his* way."

"Well," whined Paul, "when you have a degree in painting from *Bennington* and a degree in filmmaking from the *Tisch School*, you are going to think you know everything there is to know about directing a movie, right?"

"Oh, pooh! He doesn't know *anything*! He's not even sure which team he's playing for!"

Paul looked at me. "As you've probably figured out, we're talking about our *director*. He's still trying to decide whether he's straight, or one of us."

"It's tough, being stranded between a rock and a hard place."

"How about you, Max? Hetero or bent?"

"Oh, he likes girls," said Wallace. He dismissed me with a wave of his fingers. "You can see that a mile away."

The boys quickly lost interest in me. What was worse than not being gay was the fact that I was only playing a dead body -- in other words, I wasn't important enough to talk to.

After a while everyone except for me was summoned back to the set. I slouched at the table, waiting, watching the flow of humanity over the sidewalk. I was bored shitless. Like a flash of lightning in a black sky, I had an epiphany: the only way to work on a movie is as star or director, when you get to call all the shots and everyone does your bidding. Gayle was right about the rest of us -- we were nothing but mannequins.

Two hours later I was still sitting there. Finally one of the crew members was sent down to tell me that I was no longer needed, and that I could go home whenever I wanted.

10

I waited and waited for the phone to ring, then waited some more. There was still the flashback scene to be shot for *Paul And Wallace*. They'd have to call me because they wouldn't have a finished product without that scene.

But the phone never rang. Finally, after a month had passed, I put in a call to Morganstein.

"Peter... it's Max Zajack."

Silence. Either the director didn't want to talk to me or he didn't remember who I was.

"Max...?"

"Yes, I was in your film, *Paul And Wallace*."

"Yes?"

"Yes. Remember I played the murder victim? The corpse on the floor?"

"Oh... sure."

It was like trying to pry the molars out of his skull.

"I was lounging on my terrace, admiring the daffodils and crocuses when I wondered whether you were ever going to shoot the ending of your movie."

"Yes, we were supposed to do that, weren't we...

Sorry, but there was a problem."

"Really."

"Yes. The plug has been pulled on *Paul And Wallace*."

"Why?"

Morganstein cleared his throat. "Creative differences

between some of the talent and myself, for one thing. For another, the producers decided that they didn't want to go forward with the project."

"So that's the end of it?"

"Sadly, this appears to be the case."

As a great songwriter once said, I was just a pawn in somebody else's game. If someone -- someone holding the purse strings -- decided to put the kibosh on a project,there was nothing, not a fucking thing that I could do about it. Working for nothing made it even more of a waste.

When I climbed into bed that night I told Gayle what had gone down.

"Had enough, Max?"

"No. And whatever you do, don't say you told me so."

11

The Woodmill Playhouse was one of the oldest and most prestigious regional theaters in America. Their upcoming production of *Sunrise At Campobello* was supposed to include a handful of non-union jobbers who just might get into Actors' Equity. I wasn't a fan of toothless chestnuts, but the Woodmill paid *money*. I could use some. Earning money as an actor would prove something -- at least to me.

After submitting my photo I got called in for a closer look. When I arrived at the studio on Eighth Avenue, I was asked to deliver a monologue.

"That night, I left my father's house forever. I took the first left and the second right and I didn't stop until I made it to California..."

There was something about that bit from *I Never Sang For My Father* that got to me. It turned my voice husky and made my eyes brim with fake tears.

"Very nice, Max. Very nice," said the young man seated across the room. He tweaked the gold studs in his right ear. "Thank you for coming in. We'll be in touch."

By now I'd gotten used to hearing those words. They meant nothing more than dog shit to a tree. But a week later, there was a message on my answering machine asking me to report to a rehearsal hall in Times Square at such and such a time -- I was in.

"You're the policeman and one of the stretcher-bearers," said Rendaldo Nobles, the assistant director, handing me a script. This fellow liked gold earrings. Today several dangled from each ear.

A double role? Not bad -- not bad at all. While waiting for rehearsal to begin I sat and read the play. Both characters were non-speaking roles and appeared on stage for all of five minutes. In other words, I was going to be a theater extra in *Sunrise At Campobello*. My soaring spirits crashed straight into the earth.

I was still light on credits, however. And I was actually going to be paid every Friday for a six-week run. It wouldn't allow me to purchase one of the Florida Keys, but it wasn't an insult, either. It was well known that the Playhouse treated its actors like royalty. For a few weeks I could live with that...

The star of the production, the actor who'd be playing Franklin Delano Roosevelt, was Robert Vaughn, a big name back in the Sixties for TV fluff like *The Man From U.N.C.L.E.* I was far from a celebrity hound, but being on stage with a renowned actor might be an experience worth hanging around for. Maybe I'd make a connection. Maybe I'd learn something. And maybe I wouldn't.

As the scenes were being blocked out, it dawned on me that I'd only been cast in *Sunrise At Campobello* because I was big enough to look like a cop, and strong enough to carry a stretcher. Acting talent -- if there is such a thing -- had nothing to do with it whatsoever.

Yeah, I was figuring out how things worked all the time... Something else I learned was that everybody -- and his brother, sister, mother and father -- were actors. It was a disease, like the chicken pox or flu. Once you were infected with the bug, the idea of becoming a STAR spread like a virus through the bloodstream. That was because from a distance everyone worshipped FAME. The easiest way to procure it was by becoming an actor. If you were an actor, you might even get yourself elected to high public office. And it was an easy life: you didn't have to apply paint to canvas, you didn't have to master a musical instrument, you didn't have to spend years laboring over a novel. All you had to do was stand there, spout the lines someone else had written if you could remember them, and hope that the world thought you were worth looking at.

Whenever we had a break, I'd hang outside and watch all the performers -- actors, dancers, singers -- scatter like insects into their various studios. I'd hear them warbling and shouting, declaiming and emoting, venting their spleens, spilling their guts in the frantic hope of being seen and heard by an invisible audience that doesn't know its ass from a hole in the ground, yet will sit in judgment of them. What sense did it make? Were we all so desperately needy?

And there were so *many* of us! We flocked here from all over the world. Every man, woman and child walking the streets of New York was awash in silly hopes and dreams. And if they weren't actors or singers or dancers, they'd written a screenplay, or a stage play or the story of their lives. What happened to these people when they got old and it all fizzled out, or worse, never happened?

It wasn't until you floated in the river with the shit that you realized how much shit there was...

12

Robert Vaughn bailed out of the production. In fact, he'd never even shown up. Another actor, an accomplished New York stage thespian with a much less recognizable name, had to be rushed in to take over as Franklin D. For a day or two there was confusion in the rehearsal space, but order was quickly restored.

Finally we put in at the theater, which was located in one of the wealthier Jersey suburbs and was a stunning piece of work. I'd never been in a place so sumptuous, even in New York. It was astonishing -- there wasn't money for the hungry and the homeless in the streets, but there was more than enough to mount and re-mount plays that had no relevance to real life.

The rest of the cast was a curious mix. Aside from the few like me, they were all accomplished, heavy hitters, at least once upon a time. The actress playing FDR's mother had been a star in British films like *Bunny Lake Is Missing*. One of FDR's kids had just finished shooting a major role in a film about the serial killer Hannibal Lecter. The woman cast as Roosevelt's wife was one of Broadway's most celebrated actresses. And so on.

Before long I came to detest the play, a sentimental, sugar-coated view of the long-dead president, as well as Bobby Norelini, who, like me, had multiple roles. It wasn't that I was jealous because he got to speak a few lines -- no, he was a loudmouth who wouldn't stop talking about himself. He was everything I loathed in a certain type ofactor, the kind of asshole who insisted that Sinatra with brass was better than Sinatra with strings, and when confronted with powerful evidence -- like *Point Of No Return* -- refused to give ground.

When I couldn't stand listening to him anymore, I'd drift down the hall to the dressing room of Lambert Wilkerson, who'd likewise been hot shit on Broadway in years gone by, originating a role in one of Peter Shaffer's most celebrated plays. Lambert was a very quiet gay black man who yearned for the good old days on the Great White Way.

"Everybody had style then," he would sigh. "The world wasn't like it is now."

Lambert always came across as very sad. Maybe he was depressed at having to play kowtow as FDR's butler after having been the Sun God on Broadway.

But I couldn't complain -- I was collecting a paycheck for standing around doing nothing. One day after I'd cleaned up in a backstage poker game, I noticed that Jon Denis was cradling a copy of *Big Sur And The Oranges Of Hieronymous Bosch*.

"Henry Miller, huh? He's my idol. The greatest American writer who ever lived. Well, I used to think so. I don't know what I'd think now."

Up to that point, Jon and I hadn't said boo to each other. He was another older guy, in his sixties or seventies, and tended to hang out with the other seasoned pros.

"People tell me that I look like good old Henry. I've been thinking about trying to play him onstage. I've not decided how yet, but..."

I took a step back and studied Jon Denis's features. Much of it was there: the baldness, the spectacles, the blue eyes, the slenderness. It just might work.

"See," said Denis, "my problem is that I don't write. You don't happen to write, do you?"

"That's what I'm supposed to be, a writer," I mumbled. "Acting is something I do on the side."

Denis rubbed his hands together. "Now that's interesting... Have you ever thought about writing a play about your idol?"

"I haven't. But that doesn't mean I wouldn't."

"I used to travel around the country doing a one-man show about Sherlock Holmes. I need something fresh."

How did you pull off a one-man show about Sherlock Holmes, I wondered. Wasn't Watson the really important one?

"What I've got in mind is something where Henry walks around in a bathrobe, and packages arrive at the door."

He seemed very excited about his idea.

"Packages...?"

"Yes! For instance, he would answer a knock, and there'd be a delivery for him. And he'd open the package and then he'd talk about what was on the inside..."

A one-man show. Miller in a bathrobe. Mysterious packages arriving at the door. It didn't add up.

"Maybe that would work," I lied. Perhaps, if I could pull it off, I'd break out as a playwright, then divert attention to my novels and stories.

We agreed to continue the discussion later. Denis went back to his cot and lay down. He was always lying down between scenes. A few times I caught him snoring. I'd never seen an actor prepare that way before.

"Places!"

I was already in my farmer's costume -- flannel shirt, jeans with suspenders, flea-bitten hat. I went over to wait stage right with the other jackasses who were supposed to lug the president down the stairs on his stretcher after he'd been stricken with polio.

The run of *Sunrise At Campobello* ended with a fancy dinner at an upscale restaurant. The producers delivered speeches about how great the cast was and how the production would live on in the minds of whoever had been lucky enough to see it. Then we all got up and went our separate ways. It was like *Sunrise At Campobello* had never even happened.

I didn't feel sentimental. I was happy it was over. Now I could spend my time writing. A strange life.

13

"Max -- let's work on Henry Miller."

Jon Denis was on the phone. We made an appointment to meet at his apartment near Lincoln Center. I rode the elevator to the eighth floor. When he opened up, he was wrapped in a flannel bathrobe and brandished an unlit cigarette.

"Well, it's Max Zajack, dontcha know..."

The bathrobe and cigarette. The nasal Brooklyn accent. He was already trying to do Miller. He wasn't bad, I had to admit. He could do more, but that would come with time.

"Have a seat, my friend... Now, like I was saying earlier, I really want to work in a scene or two where Henry opens a package that shows up at his door..."

"But I haven't started the play yet."

The more I'd thought about it, I really wasn't hot on

the idea of writing a one-man piece. The notion of a guy wandering around the stage talking to himself seemed hokey to me. Maybe I just didn't see its commercial possibilities -- I was good for that. I never seemed to understand what sold or why.

Pretty soon Jon seemed to forget about Miller. He started talking about himself. How he'd hitchhiked to New York from California when he was a young dude, and you could still do those things. How disappointed he was that he hadn't turned out to be a movie star. How now that he was getting older, he no longer enjoyed New York the way he once did. How he'd bought a spread of land in North Carolina and lived there with his wife and kids most of the time...

Then he started talking about "Gracia." She was the Puerto Rican lady who came around once a week to clean the apartment. They had a relationship, he confided -- a sexual relationship. This had complicated his life. Of course his wife and kids didn't know a thing about Gracia. They lived down South and he lived in New York most of the time, trying to find work.

I glanced at the clock on the wall. I'd been there a half-hour and we hadn't done a thing except talk about him and Gracia. Then he worked his way around to the subject of his father, who he detested. By now Miller had been completely lost. I started to feel trapped.

"Mind if I use the bathroom?"

"Down the hall and to the left."

When I opened the door, the stench was worse than the men's jake in the filthiest dive. The rim of the toilet was caked with dried urine, shit, hair and flecks of other unidentified matter. I could see that Gracia wasn't doing much cleaning when she came around. My gag reflex kicked in. I pissed and got the hell out of there.

I sat down again and listened to Jon Denis ramble. If we drifted back to the subject of the play, we never seemed to progress beyond his initial brainstorm of Miller padding around his Pacific Palisades mansion and answering the door to arriving gifts from fans. It was incredible, how people loved to waste time on bullshit. No wonder nothing of any worth was ever produced, and if it was, it was done by someone sitting by himself in a room, undisturbed by collaborators, directors, or producers.

"I'm going to have to think about how to set it up," I told him finally. It was the same exact thing I'd said when I walked in a couple of hours earlier.

"I'm sure you'll come up with something," Jon said as I backed out of the door.

14

I sat at the kitchen table and wrote thirty pages of the untitled Miller play before pulling the plug. Something wasn't right. Henry Miller shuffling around his house in slippers and muttering about the minutiae of his daily life didn't work. It was dead -- there was no spark, no fire, no reason to give a damn. When I tried it another way, forcing more weighty, philosophical observations into the character's mouth, it was even worse. Writing about Henry Miller, once my great literary hero, had turned into a deadly chore.

Maybe I wasn't meant to write a play about the "Brooklyn boy." But since not quitting easily was one of my vices and the project stayed stuck in my brain, occasionally I went back and gave it another shot, hoping that this time around it would erupt into life. But whenever I did, I encountered a strange and powerful resistance to working on it. I felt like a schoolkid with an overdue assignment who keeps putting it off. In the end, he knows it's never going to get done.

15

Club Venet down in Sayreville was a grubby roadhouse more famous for its musical and comedy acts than its dinner theater, but something had to be done to fill the space on the nights when no big names, like Leon Russell or Howard Stern, were on the marquis.

There wasn't the usual swarm of hopefuls at the open call for *Play It Again, Sam*. A long time ago I'd seen the movie -- funny as hell, maybe Woody Allen's best. I was handed a script and told to go up on stage and read the part of Dick. I wasn't half-bad. Some days that's how it was -- you nailed it or came pretty close.

While waiting to read a second time, I ducked into the men's room to take a leak.

"Hey, you were good up there."

The fellow with the whiny voice stood with his cock hanging a few urinals down. His eyes were bugging out behind the thick glasses.

"Oh, yeah?"

"You're right for that part."

"Think so?"

"I'm going to have a word with the director," he said, zipping up. "I'm Ira Gloss. I'm playing Allen Felix."

Gloss had the properly nebbishy look. He wasn't the spitting image of Woody Allen, but he gave off the same vibe.

The next day I got a call that the part was mine. Salary, one-fifty a week before taxes. That was decent. Six shows per week, with matinées on Wednesday and Saturday.

Going from the Woodmill to Club Benet was like making the proverbial trip from the penthouse to the outhouse. The dressing rooms were funky. The restrooms and shower were moldy. Even the stage and curtain smelled bad. The joint, for all its renown, was a real shit hole.

The director was a nervous little man by the name of Kenny Milkowski. After nearly every performance he rushed backstage waving his arms and shouting "Notes! Notes!" It meant he didn't like what he'd seen and he was out to fix it. We all had to gather onstage and listen to him harangue us.

"Gloss, you have to ease up on the self-pity! Allen sounds like a little girl instead of a grown man! Entirely too much whining and moaning...!"

"Linda -- not enough preoccupation! When you're with your husband, you're thinking about Allen. I'm not getting that at all!"

"Max... Tony needs to be even more distracted by his business..."

No matter what we did, Milkowski was never satisfied.

Unlike the Woodmill, you could never predict what kind of house you were going to draw. Sometimes the theater was packed with bodies that howled at every joke. Other times they bussed in seniors who talked through the action or snored and laughed at nothing. Some nights there was hardly anyone in the place. One evening we were forced to do a performance in front of a couple who happened to drift in for dinner.

———————

Before long boredom set in. I started bringing in my stories and working on them backstage when I should have been running lines or polishing my performance.

After one matinée, as I was changing out of my stage uniform, Ira ducked his head in and informed me that somebody out in the house wanted to talk to me.

What the fuck. Milkowski again. Who else would want to talk to me after a show? I must have exited stage left when I should have exited stage right or something like that.

I walked into the darkened house in my tee shirt and jeans. Instead of Milkowski, an elderly gent with fuzzy white hair was standing in the center aisle, hands in his pockets, contemplating the empty stage. He looked a little familiar. Then I remembered him from his photo in the theater vestibule: it was the owner of Club Venet himself, Joe Venotti.

"Max, right?"

"That's me."

He took a leisurely drag of his fat, putrid cigar. "You know, I've seen lots of actors -- some great ones -- on this stage over the years. Travolta... Vincent Gardenia... Lorna Luft, to name just a few. And I just wanted to tell you, kid, you got something up there."

I looked over my shoulder. Was he talking to me?

"Uh... thanks."

I didn't know what else to say. I wasn't really an actor. I couldn't take credit for anything other than trying not to make an ass of myself onstage.

The big boss and I stood there for a few more awkward seconds. Then he took another puff of his cigar and slowly faded into the darkness.

16

"Max, it's all about one thing -- the big time! You gotta keep moving in that direction -- to the big time!"

I'd gotten to be buddies with Dax Trummell, the guy playing Bogart's ghost in *Play It Again, Sam*. He was a lousy actor, getting regularly chewed out by Milkowski, but he was a hustler, always looking for ways to make a few bucks or move up the show business food chain. He crowed that he'd once played Jamie Gillis's chauffeur in a porn flick and been a stand-in for Charlie Sheen in another movie. He had no qualms whatsoever about running out for coffee or standing for hours in a snowstorm guarding equipment or helping a crew run cable -- anything, so long as he was near the action.

"I know all about moving in that direction, Dax, but how do you move in that direction?"

"You gotta be hungry, Max! You gotta jump on any and every opportunity that presents itself! You have to work for nothing when they want you to work for nothing! When they call and tell you to jump, you ask 'how high' and then you jump! *Because you never know what might happen!*"

It was an opportunistic philosophy, for sure, but it didn't seem to have occurred to Dax that he was being used. And Jesus, it sounded like a hell of a lot of work. Wasn't anything ever easy?

"Listen, Max... my buddy Joe Worthington was doing

extra work on *The King of Comedy*, and he got upgraded to day player! He was part of the crowd standing outside of Jerry Lewis's dressing room and Scorsese's AD singled him out to move closer to the camera and say a word!"

"Is that good, saying one word?"

"Are you fucking *kidding* me? It's GREAT! You get paid a hell of a lot more, and you can get into SAG if you're not already a member!"

Dax was pretty worked up over my naiveté. Well, he seemed to know what he wanted and what he was after, I had to give him that. He was also always trying to get laid, and he never let the existence of a wife stop him.

"Hey, Max, I'm an actor. It comes with the territory, know what I mean? That's what we're doing it for, right, to score pussy?"

I couldn't deny that he had a damned good point.

Near the end of the run of *Play It Again, Sam*, he cornered me. "How'd you like to be in *Wall Street*, the new Oliver Stone movie?"

"Sure, why not. Except for my job I got nothing else to do next week."

"Fuck your job! Think about it: Michael Douglas. Charlie Sheen. Sean Young. You'll be breathing the same air as they breathe. And you'll get paid for it, too!"

Dax's agency had asked him to round up some people who would look presentable in a suit and tie. On Tuesday we were on a midtown Manhattan set watching Douglas, as Gordon Gekko, harangue a room full of stockholders on how "greed is good." As the cameras circled, he must have delivered the speech twenty, twenty-five times. Between takes, a beautiful blonde production assistant lovingly stroked his hair with a brush, retouched his makeup, and dabbed his forehead and cheeks with a towel as if he were a crown prince. Later, no doubt, she would mount and ride him silly. For all of this torture, he would earn millions. And he hadn't even had to pay any dues, since his father was a legendary Hollywood star. Some guys truly did have all the luck.

Every time I dozed off in my chair, Dax nudged me.

"You don't want the camera to catch you sleeping, man!"

Right. Whenever the big star took a breather after a take, another assistant director walked around and reminded us to look alive, and as if we were really paying rapt attention to his speech, or else we'd have to do it again.

"How come those other people get to sit near the front?" I elbowed Dax, figuring if I were closer to the action, I wouldn't doze off.

"They're union," he sniffed.

"You mean all you get out of belonging to SAG is being an extra who sits closer?"

"If you're lucky. Ninety-nine percent of the union doesn't work."

"And for that privilege you get to pay dues? So how do you get into the fucking union?"

"It's complicated. You have to be a young star who is ushered straight in or be related to someone important. That's the way it usually works."

"Shit."

As usual, I wasn't a fit. The next morning I filled Gayle in on how it was working for 20th Century Fox.

"...and Oliver Stone swung around on a crane all day, doing take after take..."

She shook her head. "You and all these other idiots are being exploited, Max. What's wrong with you?"

When Dax called again with another offer of extra work, I didn't refuse. This time I stood for fourteen hours on a godforsaken Queens street while Robin Williams made himself a star in *Cadillac Man*.

I kept hearing from Dax how it was possible for an extra to get an upgrade, but it never happened. Nobody noticed that I was different or special. Was I? I thought so. But then every other extra felt that way too. In the end, all I did was wilt for hours in the heat while some kind of action happened out of my range of sight. Once in a while we were ordered through a bullhorn to turn this way or that, to take three steps to the left or the right, to pretend that we were watching some crisis unfolding in front of our eyes, to look up into the sky. Somewhere we couldn't see, Robin Williams was having a good time.

The pay for non-union extras -- like me -- was a total of sixty bucks before taxes.

17

The boss summoned me into his office one afternoon and told me to have a seat.

"I'm afraid that things are changing around here, Max, and we won't need you any longer."

My department at NT&T International was being phased out, and with it, me. They always tell you you're finished on Friday afternoon so you don't hang around all day moping, or worse, growing angry over the injustice perpetrated on you. The weekend gives you a couple of days to get it out of your system.

I'd had the feeling for some time that it was coming, but I'd been looking forward to it because I needed a change. But instead of going out and hustling another job when I saw the red flags flapping in the wind, I'd done nothing. The truth was that I really didn't want a survival job. I was always looking for some way to get out of having to work. The would-be artist only has one interest: his art. But after my unemployment benefits ran out, then what?

———————

For the first time in years there was nowhere I had to be, no superior to report to, no deadline to meet. I was ecstatic. Hey, I could get used to doing nothing but whatever

I wanted. Maybe losing my day gig was some kind of omen. Maybe now my novels and stories would finally start to sell. Maybe I'd land peach roles and make some money.

But I got no calls to audition, not even to work as an extra. Months passed. I wrote and revised stories, but they were always rejected. In an attempt to find something that might work, I aped some of my favorite authors. One day I was Tennessee Williams, the next, Chekhov, the next, Paul Bowles. Once in a great while I placed something in an obscure literary journal, but there was no money, not so much as a red penny, in it. *How the hell was a writer supposed to make a living?*

Whenever I walked into a bookstore and gazed at the crowded stacks and tables, I was immediately plunged into despair. *How could a writer ever make his work stand out in this ocean of vomit?* And how was it that everyone except for me was able to get published? What did they have that I didn't?

There were no answers.

18

"Max, you're going to have to do *something*. I can't take care of all of the bills myself anymore."

This was highly unusual. Gayle never got on my case about money. But my unemployment benefits had run out months ago. I'd burned through all of my meager savings.

Whenever I lost a job I nursed the fantasy that somehow a miracle would occur and I'd be discovered, or there'd be a windfall and I'd be saved, but of course it was nothing but a pipe dream...

It had already been a year since I'd worked for NT&T.

I'd produced more stories and a new novel that didn't find a publisher, and from time to time went back to the play about Henry Miller, but I still couldn't finish it. Gayle was right -- I was going to have to figure something out...

Down the street from our apartment they were opening a new branch of a nationwide department store chain. I walked in and asked if they needed help. Yes, they said, they could use someone to sweep the floors, haul out trash, and hang merchandise on hooks. The pay was eight bucks an hour. All I had to do was fill out an application. It would help if I didn't have a criminal record...

Two days later I reported. After first spending hours sweeping caked mud off the floors, I was ordered to hang merchandise. First it was toys. Then hardware, then dental floss and razor blades.

My supervisor was an obese man in a stained white shirt by the name of Raymond.

"Hey Zajack, think you can you get here earlier tomorrow?"

"Sure," I said.

It was one more mind-numbing gig, but at least I didn't have to interact with any humans. It's always best if you can operate alone, because when you're left to your own devices, no one knows what you're really up to...

After a few days I'd already had enough.

"I gotta get out of there," I told Gayle, "before I go insane."

"I don't know what to tell you, Max. All I know is that if we don't bring in more money, we're going to have to move out."

Pressure was something I detested. In America there's always pressure to come up with money, more money.

The next morning before I left for the store, the phone rang.

"Max -- want to be in a cable commercial?"

"When?"

"Right now."

It was Dax Trummell. He was working for a rinky-dink TV station in central Jersey and they were shooting a spot for a local gym. It would certainly beat stocking condoms and tampons. What was it Gore Vidal once said? "Never miss an opportunity to have sex or be on television." Something along those lines.

I phoned in a message to Raymond that I was sick and wouldn't be able to make it in that day. I donned my one jacket and tie and drove down to the studio, where I found myself in a scene with someone named Derek. Derek was one of those blandly handsome types I'd always despised, but by now I'd learned to shove my animosities aside since the industry was full of blandly handsome types. The action of the commercial consisted of my character struggling to do push-ups on a carpeted office floor. Derek bursts in and cries, "Bill -- what are you doing?" And Bill -- me -- answers, "Gotta get in shape!" The rest of the spot was a voiceover imploring the viewer to join a certain health club at a reasonable rate and do it the right way, rather than like the dumb white guy breaking his ass on the floor of his office...

So, I was wrong -- shooting a commercial was as dumb as sweeping the floor or hanging rubbers, but at least I was going to be on television.

Within a couple of hours it was all over. The check would arrive in the mail in a month or two.

"Great stuff -- right, Max?" said Dax afterwards.

"Incredible."

"Hey man, it's work. Don't knock it."

A couple months later I was sent a tape of the commercial along with my check. Gayle and I sat in front of the television and popped it into the VCR. My red, dripping, breathless mug filled the screen.

"*Bill -- what are you doing?*"

"*Gotta get in shape...*"

And so on.

"Well -- what do you think?"

Gayle shrugged. "You gave them what they wanted, right?"

She got up and walked away. I watched the spot again. It was embarrassing, all right, but that was acting -- embarrassing yourself in front of an audience. It was none other than Brando himself who said that the stuff you were given to say was "dreamed up in the bathtub," and that he didn't have the "moral courage" to walk away from the money that he earned as a trained monkey.

If anyone knew what he was talking about, it was Brando.

19

The store was all set up. I collected my last paycheck and was officially out of work again. One afternoon after I'd finished combing through all the help wanteds and was staring at a talk show featuring angry lesbians, I got another call from Dax Trummell. I hadn't heard from him in a while.

"Max, baby…"

Dax just happened to have landed in the business office of a movie shooting in Asbury Park. He was also doing a bit of stand-in work and production assistance. If I was hard up -- and he knew I was -- he could offer me a few days' work around the set.

"With a little luck, you might just get yourself cast as a day player. Like I always say, you never know."

"At this point I'll do anything, pal."

In the movie business things happen fast. One minute you're doing nothing, the next you're in the eye of the hurricane. After weeks of unemployment, I was up and out the next morning before the crack of dawn, rolling east on the highway toward Manhattan. I made a pit stop at Dunkin' Donuts, where I picked up a super-sized coffee, a pair of vanilla cream donuts, and a newspaper from the machine in the parking lot. Polishing off the junk food as I drove, I made it across the river before the rush hour. My orders were to first pick up a member of the production team in the Village and drop him off at another location, then re-cross the river to Jersey and commandeer the vehicle I was assigned to drive to the set.

That day I was in trouble right from the get-go. Either I'd been given the wrong information or 451 Bank Street didn't exist. I circled the blocks between Hudson and Washington Streets a few times before finally deciding to park and check whether "Jonathan" wasn't actually waiting for me at 541 or 514 or 415.

The sign at the curb read "No Standing Tuesdays 6 A.M. until 9 A.M. -- Street Cleaning." It was six-thirty, and it was Tuesday, but I didn't see any street sweepers or parking violation units, so I decided to take my chances.

I hopped out and dashed across the street, scanning the numbers on the brownstones. Sure enough, my man was waiting with folded arms inside the vestibule at 514. When he saw me, he frowned. "I was starting to think you'd never show up."

"Yeah, well, looks like someone gave me a bum address."

Jonathan was much younger than me. This came as a surprise. The word producer always conjured the image of a geezer with silver hair chomping on a cigar. Jonathan was soft and doughy and sported one of those ridiculous Banana Republic safari hats at a rakish angle. I didn't yield to the temptation to ask why the fuck he couldn't have stepped outside and kept his eyes peeled for me. *That paycheck*, I reminded myself. *Do nothing to jeopardize that paycheck.*

When we went out to the street, a uniform was filling out a citation, using the rust-pocked hood of my heap as his desk.

"Hey! *HEY!* I'm not really parked here! Can't you tear that thing up?"

The meter cop shook his head. "Already started. Can't cancel it once I'm started."

I had no choice but to throw myself on his mercy.

"Listen, *sir*. I really can't afford this ticket," I begged, with all the false humility I could muster.

Since he was black, I decided he had to be sympathetic to the plight of the underdog. But he didn't flinch.

"Look, bro... I been out of work going on two years now. I don't have a pot to piss in or a window to throw it out, know what I'm saying? You can dig that, can't you?"

"Ain't *my* problem."

"You gotta cut me a break, here. *Please*."

"Just doin' my job," he sniffed.

That's what they all say. He tore off the citation and handed it over.

"Gee, thanks, pal. You have yourself a real nice day."

He shrugged. "They all the same to me."

The problem with the world today is that no one has a beating heart.

"Tough break, huh?" Jonathan chuckled as I chauffeured him downtown.

"A seventy-five smacker ticket? I'd call that a very poor start to the day, yeah."

Soon Jonathan was on his mobile, dropping names like Penn and Hanks and Roberts. He was personally acquainted with them all, he wanted the party on the other end to know.

Everything about this guy -- from his baby fat to that

asinine hat -- irked me. As we rumbled over the cobblestones of lower Greenwich Street I heard him sigh in the back seat. "Too bad this dreamboat of yours isn't a company car."

"Why's that?"

"Because then we would have paid for the ticket."

"Yeah -- too bad for me."

"You can say that again. It's just your lousy luck that Dad needs to cut costs to the bone on *Rock And Roll Heaven*. No fucking around this time. No freebies. We gotta watch every penny. Which is why you're giving me this ride."

"Who's Dad?"

"Dad is Sol Blomberg."

"Should I know him?"

"Couldn't hurt. He's paying your salary on this shoot -- whatever it is you're doing."

"Sol Blomberg, you don't say..."

"*Pray For Death* Parts One, Two and Three? That's Dad -- executive producer. He's giving me a unit producer credit on this one."

Now I knew for sure why I loathed Jonathan. What I didn't understand was why, if his Daddy was so goddamned fixed, they had to make me part of the cost-cutting process. I realized that the subway was beneath someone like him, but couldn't junior just have grabbed a cab this morning?

I let him off in front of a warehouse near the Seaport. "Be careful where you park from now on," was his parting shot. The bastard didn't even thank me for the ride.

I watched him waddle away. Jonathan Blomberg looked so *sure* of himself. Maybe that was my problem: I lacked an air of self-confidence.

"Go fuck yourself," I said to his back. Then I gave it the gas.

———————

Back in Jersey I exchanged my car for a truck. I'd never driven a real truck in my life, certainly not one the size of a school bus. Wasn't a driver supposed to have special training to operate something as massive as a dinosaur?

Rumbling down the insane Turnpike at the height of the morning rush I was a nervous wreck. All of my anxieties and phobias had been jolted into life. My knuckles were white. My palms were wet. Sweat trickled down my spine. The mere sight of the Pulaski Skyway turned my stomach upside down. I hoped to Christ Gayle was happy I was working again...

Outside the window, horns blared. They were for me -- I was the offender. I got the finger for driving too slow. Some asshole shook his fist at me.

An hour and a half later I managed to maneuver the monster -- in one piece -- into production headquarters, which was a tall beachfront hotel.

A teenage boy I'd never seen in my life ran shouting up to my window. "Unload on the double! People are waiting on this stuff! *What the hell took you so long?*"

The kid walked off, leaving a hand truck on the curb for me.

Fine, I thought to myself, I'm getting paid -- minus the

cost of that parking summons -- so don't make a stink, just do what the young punk says.

It took me over an hour to haul every last case of Coca-Cola Classic, Diet Coke, Caffeine-Free Coke, and cartons of Doritos and Hershey's chocolate bars seven flights up to Control Central.

My pal Trummell was nowhere to be seen. Another kid informed me that he was my boss.

"What's your name?"

I told him. Call him Jason, he said. He was the line producer for *Rock And Roll Heaven*.

Another producer. Everybody was a producer. I wondered who he was related to.

It took another half-hour to stack the cases and cartons in a corner of the big suite, which was swarming with frenetic activity. Everyone around me was jabbering about what a handsome, talented hunk the star of *Rock And Roll Heaven* was. When this film hit the silver screen, Michael Sandstone would be an even bigger star than he was already.

I wasn't paying attention to where I was walking, and tripped over a cable.

"Jesus -- can't you be careful?"

The boy who gave me hell looked all of nineteen years old. *Shove it, motherfucker*, I thought before reminding myself again of that paycheck.

When I was finally finished with the crates, I stood in a corner, popped a Coke and took a swig. Before I could even swallow, Jason was at my side.

"Your buddy Dax tells me you're an actor."

"Let's put it this way: I'll do anything for money. But I'm a writer, actually."

"So, what have I read that you've written?"

It was a question I hated because I didn't have a good answer to it. In fact, I had no answer of any kind.

"Nothing, probably, unless you subscribe to unknown literary journals." I reeled off a couple of titles. He shook his head. Then he nodded at my drink. "By the way, that stuff isn't for the gofers. It's only for the cast, crew and production team. When it's time for your break, there's a 7-Eleven up the street. And you'll have to use your own money."

"Sorry I stepped out of line."

"Forget it... Listen, there's something else I need you to do."

"All right..."

"I'd like you to drive down to Philly and pick up a property for one of our actresses."

"You're the boss." Suddenly I was petrified that I'd have to get behind the wheel of that infernal truck again. "What is it you need?"

"A wig."

"A wig?"

"That's right. Tiffany Silva –- you know her from *The Bold And The Beautiful* -- wears a customized wig in the scene scheduled for late tonight. You can take one of the cars in the pool."

No, I'd never heard of Tiffany Silva, but this was more like it. I began to daydream about sitting in an air-conditioned vehicle for a couple of hours and listening to the radio. Maybe I'd take my sweet time coming back, tell Jason I got stuck in a traffic jam or something.

"All I need is directions."

"And I want you step on it, hear? Things are really going to be crazy around here later."

"Whatever you say."

"Oh -- and one more thing. I got a call from Jonathan Blomberg. He mentioned something about you getting a parking summons when you picked him up this morning?"

"I won't deny it."

"He said to remind you to be more careful when operating our vehicle today." Jason nodded to himself sagely. "I say that's good advice."

Who was I to argue? He wrote out the address and I headed for the elevator.

I drew the runt of the Goldmine Pictures fleet -- a sad-looking, stripped-down, dented Plymouth K, with not even an AM radio to keep me company. No air conditioner either, and the late June Jersey heat already had teeth.

My destination was a millinery shop in North Philly. Some people referred to Philadelphia as "Filthydelphia," which I found funny. After meandering through the maze of unfamiliar, litter-strewn streets, I finally managed to locate the address, a hole in the wall called "FAZAKAS' HATS AND WIGS."

No wonder they'd assigned me this job, I thought. Nobody else would do it.

I flopped on a sagging couch and waited while the hag who ran the place applied the finishing touches to the hairpiece in the back room. Except for Hungarian newspapers there was nothing to read. Not being fluent in Hungarian, I sat there staring into space. The shop wasn't air-conditioned either. The heaviness of the atmosphere made me drowsy, and soon I was lost in a dream...

I was about to seduce a dancer named Mariska I'd once met in a strip joint. She was topless, her globes were enormous and bouncing, and she wanted me to do the honor of removing her bottoms. I was reaching out to pull the string when I felt a tap on my shoulder...

The old lady was pushing a circular box at me.

"She veel be veddy hoppy vid dees veeg."

I signed for it and hopped into the Plymouth. Another hour and a half back to the set. The intense summer heat kept trying to coax me to sleep at the wheel.

The second I walked through the door Jason charged me, waving a piece of paper.

"What are you doing? I thought you'd never get back!"

I tried to explain that his directions were a little off and that the wigmaker hadn't been through with the fake hair when I arrived at the shop, but he was too distracted to pay attention.

"Well, never mind that now. Just take care of this stuff ASAP."

He handed over the paper. I was to run out for three

cartons of cigarettes. Then move some boxes around. Get rid of all the empty soda cases. Haul the trash to the dumpsters at the back of the hotel. Go down to the second floor and gather up the loose electrical cords. When I was through with all that, I was to head over to the hardware store and pick up some gaffer tape and two-inch nails...

———————

Word got back from the set: Sandstone had pronounced himself satisfied with the day's takes. The message sent the production staff into ecstasy, complete with applause. By now it was more than clear to me that I wasn't getting anywhere *near* that set -- so much for being hired as a day player. Like extra work, it's nothing but a shiny carrot dangled in front of your nose to keep you doing the dirty work.

Around midnight, while running the vacuum over the carpet, I was informed by one of Jason's flunkeys -- who also happened to be a smoking hot little brunette with a killer body -- that I could go home as soon as I *cleaned the bathrooms*.

Now I wasn't just a gofer, but a janitor, too.

"What did you say?"

"Jason said for you to do it. Then he'll sign your time sheet."

"I wasn't hired to clean shithouses."

The little hottie pretended not to hear. "Everything you'll need is in there, Jason said. Brush, cleanser, you name it. This place has to be kept spick and span! It's like our home for the next couple of weeks, right? We can't have a filthy bathroom at home, can we?"

I stared at her. Someone of my formidable talents should not be swabbing a john for the likes of her and Sandstone and Blomberg and Jason. But if I argued, if I refused -- no paycheck.

What the hell. I'd done worse. I rolled up my sleeves and attacked the pubic hairs and the piss stains and the shit-spattered toilet seat. At the same time I tried to forget exactly what I was doing. I wanted to go on working for the next couple of days. Dax had promised me that.

Just as I was wiping down the base of the commode with a filthy towel, Jason popped his head in.

"Hey writer, I hate to be the bearer of bad news, but it looks like you won't be needed anymore after today. Jonathan just informed me that we're already in danger of going over budget. Soon as you're finished, I'll sign your time sheet. Your check will arrive from California within ninety days."

"Ninety days? Can't anything be done to speed up the process?"

The line producer swallowed a mouthful of his broccoli pizza.

"Not a chance. Goldmine's parent company issues those checks, and there's always lag time. You'll just have to suck it up until then."

The night had turned as scorching as a furnace. I was assigned an empty van to drive back to the depot where I'd picked up the truck that morning. First thing tomorrow I'd have to mount a new attack on the help wanteds. To hell with my latest novel. It wasn't going anywhere anyway...

After docking the van and depositing the keys in the drop, I circled the building to the visitors' parking area. It was pitch black back there. I blinked. Then I blinked again. When my vision adjusted, my wreck was nowhere to be seen.

I marched back and forth. "Son of a bitch," I cursed. Maybe I was in the wrong place? I retraced my steps and searched again. It was gone, all right. My old station wagon was history, stolen right off the lot.

Why would anyone want that hunk of shit? Now I was going to have to shell out seventy-five bucks on a citation for a car *I no longer had*. It was so funny I had to laugh.

When I stopped laughing, I checked my watch: two-thirty in the morning. I'd have to call the cops. Then I'd have to wake up Gayle to come and pick me up, unless I wanted to spend the night trying to sleep on the asphalt.

I dropped my ass on the curb and watched the lights of the planes circling one of the metropolitan airports. And I thought about how Sandstone was probably screwing that lovely production assistant right about now...

I got up and went looking for a phone booth. I felt in my pockets for change, and realized that I didn't have a fucking dime.

20

Not long afterwards, Dax showed up at my door. He had to talk to me. After the fiasco on the set of *Rock And Roll Heaven* I had no real desire to see him.

"What's it about?"

"Come on outside, man -- please."

"Ah, shit..."

Gayle was in the kitchen. We'd been rustling up dinner together. Tonight it was fish and corn on the cob chased by French Gewurztraminer.

I shut the glass door behind me. Our place had a two by four patio with a couple of chairs. Dax pulled his up close to mine.

"I did it again, Max."

I already knew what he was whispering about.

He folded his hands and leaned towards me confidentially, as if he were about to confess to a priest. It was bizarre.

"I can't help it. When an opportunity comes up, I... I'm weak. She was one of those production assistants on the movie. We got into my car and the next thing I knew..."

Suddenly I was green. "Was it that hot little brunette?"

He shook his head. "No. A blonde by the name of Alexandra."

The same old problem -- Dax couldn't stop cheating on his wife. It was a compulsion with him.

"So what happened?"

"We did it. Right there in the car."

"Maybe you shouldn't be married," I said.

"You're probably right. But I can't leave my wife. I've told you before, Max, her sick mother lives with us. She needs me. She wouldn't know what to do without me."

"Then maybe you shouldn't let it bother you, have you thought of that? Just put it out of your mind and keep doing what you're doing."

Dax nodded sadly. He looked defeated and ashamed.

"I love my wife, Max. I feel sorry for her. If only she wouldn't donate all of our money to those fake TV preachers..."

"Huh?"

"That's what she does -- she gives all our dough away to those phonies. She believes in them. She believes they're going to send her to heaven someday."

"Maybe she's right."

Dax scoffed. "Still, I shouldn't be doing what I'm doing..."

"Does she know what you're up to? If she doesn't know, then it's not happening, right?"

I knew it was bullshit, but I had nothing better to tell him. Dax wasn't really interested in analyzing the situation anyway. He only wanted to get something off his chest. He went on to tell me about the girl he screwed at the movie theater where he sometimes ushered, and all the extras he'd nailed because they thought he was someone important.

"Maybe you need a real priest."

"They don't understand, Max. They just tell you that

you're committing a sin. But you understand, I know you do..."

"I have to go inside. Gayle is waiting for me to bread the flounder. I wish there was something I could say to help you out."

"Thanks for listening."

"No problem. You know, Dax, if your wife is throwing away all your money, you'll have to get rid of her."

"I'll keep it in mind, Max."

21

"Max Zajack?"

"Yes?"

"Jay Zinicock for Loma Films. We'd like to see you for Fenton Levitzky's new film."

Fenton Levitzky was a name. He was the founder of Loma Films, a producer of some of the most popular cult movies of the past two decades. Everybody had heard of *The Radioactive Vindicator*, even if they hadn't seen it. It was, of course, nothing but a steaming pile of offal, eighty minutes of junk for glue-sniffing teenagers, but in America that's what grabs attention. It's a strange country, America. It claims to be the world's arbiter of taste and culture, but it mostly sells horse manure. Occasionally a great artist or a masterpiece somehow slips into view, but like a blue moon, they are few and far between.

The following afternoon I made my way through the hordes in Times Square, past a wax museum... chain restaurants... camera outlets... toy stores... theaters featuring musical tripe... hucksters of everything from peanuts to hats to tee shirts... and a muscle-headed cowboy in his underwear strumming a guitar. Tourists from the world over scrambled to get here, convinced it was the center of the universe, the source of all energy, but Times Square always made me feel like nothing but a husk, a Kafkaesque insect, a non-being. "Depersonalized," the shrinks would call it.

I arrived at the studio early. There were no other actors around, and no sides to look at. The guy at the table was twisting a pencil in his fingers and looking very bored. No doubt he hadn't gotten what he was after so far, and I was the answer to all of his prayers.

"Name."

"Zajack. Max."

He checked his pad and made a mark.

"Okay."

"There weren't any sides out there."

"You don't need sides."

Okay, I told myself, sometimes good parts don't have many lines.

The guy sat there staring at me. He must be evaluating me, I reasoned, making sure I was a physical match for what he needed.

"Right," he nodded finally, "drop your pants."

Hm. Maybe I was really auditioning for a porn flick.

Maybe Loma was nothing but a front. Or maybe the guy wanted to suck me off.

I wasn't about to let this dude blow me, but I was curious about what might happen. I yanked on the tongue of my belt. Then I undid the button of my trousers and let them fall to the floor. The guy's eyes were riveted to my crotch.

"Now the underwear."

"Mind if I ask you what -- "

"You want to be considered for this film or not?"

Well, I was here, wasn't I? I bent forward and worked the jockeys down. My dick was mashed into something unrecognizable. If this fellow was after length, I was going to come up small.

After getting an eyeful, he said, "Thanks. We'll call you if we need you."

"You mean that's it?"

"That's it."

I hiked up my drawers and pants, turned around and walked out.

What the fuck was that all about, I wondered as I plunged into the stinking river on Broadway. Did that guy want to see how far I would go? Did he want to see if I took direction without protesting? Being an actor means that you have no choice but to humiliate yourself on a regular basis.

When I told her what happened, Gayle couldn't stop laughing. "So, what did he want you to do once your pants were down?"

"Like I said -- nothing."

"Nothing at all?"

"What did I just tell you?"

"He just wanted to look?"

"Your guess is as good as mine."

She shook her head. She was still cracking up over the image of me with my pants around my ankles.

"Did you get hard?"

"Over what?"

"I don't know, Max. Do you still not think this whole thing is a big fool's errand?"

Of course it was, but if I didn't go out there and try, I'd think I was missing something. At first I'd attempted to convince myself that I was after parts because I was desperate for my writing to be noticed, but by this time I didn't know whether I even believed that anymore...

22

Loma Films never called. That casting director must not have liked what he saw when my pants were down. It didn't make a whole lot of difference. By now I was spending every free moment running all over the city hopingto nail anything I could -- whether or not it paid. I went on scores, maybe even hundreds of auditions, and one day I got a call from a suburban cable TV station...

"I never knew that Union, New Jersey even had a TV station," I said to Gayle after hanging up.

"What do they want you for?"

"A commercial. That's all they told me. And it pays -- green money."

The very next day I was down there. Two guys, Dean and Robert, were producing the spot. Nice boys, not much younger than me. What was unusual was that they seemed to have already decided on me.

"So, Max, this commercial is for a local hot dog vendor. What we need you to do is put on this outfit. The dressing room is right over there."

The costume consisted of a full Indian headdress and serape. When I walked out in that getup, I felt like a goddamned buffoon. And I couldn't figure out what it had to do with hot dogs.

"You look great!" cried Dean.

His partner sat there laughing his ass off.

I was handed a script. The scene involved two Native Americans arguing over who made the better frankfurter.

"You're 'The Chief,'" said Robert.

I read the words. This was a new depth of mindlessness, but funny in a politically incorrect way. If the Native Americans had a sense of humor, there wouldn't be a problem.

"Memorize those lines," said Dean, sending me into another room. After a half-hour, I was summoned back to the studio.

"We're going to shoot right now," announced Robert.

They made me sign a few release forms first. The other actor was decked out to look like Tonto, from the original

Lone Ranger TV series. We looked at each other and shook our heads. There was nothing else to do.

A makeup girl lathered war paint on our faces. Then we were shuttled to another, larger studio, where we took our places on a fake log, just two injuns on their asses, a scene straight out of an old-time Hollywood Western.

"And... action!"

The camera rolled.

"Me hungry for hot dog!"

"You want best hot dog, Chief Yellow Mustard? Try this!"

I took a bite of a Sal's hot dog.

"Mm! This *good*!"

"Good? Sal's hot dog is *great*! Best hot dog in whole world!"

I took another bite. I swallowed. I nodded in agreement.

"Sal's hot dogs best in whole universe!"

Tonto grunted, then I grunted. We both grunted like apes. The camera slowly panned to the "Sal's Hot Dogs" cart.

The makeup girl ran in with fresh weenies.

"Okay! One more time! Take two! Slate it! Quiet on the set! And...*action!*"

We went through it a few more times. No matter how we did it, the pair of us still sounded ridiculous. We'd given the redskins all of our diseases, taken all of their land, herded them onto reservations, and now we were poking fun at them. And what the hell would a pair of Native Americans want with Sal's hot dogs?

I was embarrassed, but too much of a whore to walk out, even when we were ordered to make "woo-woo" whoops like Indians on the warpath.

When the spot aired, there wasn't a single complaint...

23

That week a production company named Z-Cinema posted a call in *Backstage* for a micro-budget indie based on the life of the daughter of the infamous mass murderer John List. A nerdy accountant and Sunday school teacher, he'd offed his entire family in a wealthy New Jersey suburb after he ran into financial problems and got sick and tired of supporting them.

"All types and ages needed, both men and women..."

Mass murderers and serial killers fascinated me. To make an impression, I showed up for the audition in jacket and tie. All the other hopefuls were swarming around like bugs. Before the kid at the desk could sign me in, someone grabbed my arm.

"Would you come with me, please?" The guy hustled me towards a back room. "What's your name?"

I told him.

"Max! I'm glad you came in. I'd like you to meet someone."

He knocked on a door, then turned the handle and

went in without waiting for an answer. Two serious-looking figures were stationed at opposite ends of a long folding table, stacks of headshots in front of them.

"You wanted me to find you a new William Shatner -- well, here he is!"

The two guys looked up at me and squinted.

"Give him something to read," said one of them, a pudgy, bald fellow in a white golf shirt.

I was handed a few sheets of paper. I quickly skimmed the scene then did it, using the dude who escorted me in as a partner. It was unremarkable, a situation in which a distressed high school teacher arrives at a police station worried about one of his students, a girl who hasn't shown up to school for a few days. I was reading the part of a police lieutenant who's heard the man's complaints before and demands some kind of evidence that anything out of the ordinary has actually happened.

"That's our lieutenant," said the fat, bald guy when we were finished.

On my way out I was handed an envelope containing the script.

"What's the pay?" I asked.

"No pay up front. You get paid when the movie gets distribution. But don't worry, it's going to be great."

24

In the envelope there was also a synopsis with a special note. Apparently the author of the script, Walter Wallace -- the blubbery man in the golf shirt -- had been Patricia List's real-life high school dramatics coach twenty years earlier. He also claimed that they'd been having a sexual affair at the time, which accounted for his extreme concern when she didn't show up to school. (Why a high school teacher was screwing a sixteen-year-old girl wasn't explained.) Now, decades after the murders, Walter Wallace decided that he had a story to tell and, further, that he was a writer and an actor who could carry an entire film. Despite my skepticism, the project had possibilities -- "legs" as everyone liked to say. *The Patricia List Story* was something that would automatically find an audience.

I sat down with the script and let my head fall back. I could already hear the interview being conducted by the attractive TV journalist...

"Max, you were terrific as the reluctant police lieutenant in The Patricia List Story. *Can you tell us what you have in store for the future?"*

"If I continue to get good scripts, I'll do more acting, at least here and there. Otherwise, I'll spend my time writing, which is what I do every single day, no matter what..."

"When do we get to read what you've written?"

"It's out there for anyone willing to dig."

"So, are you what we might call a multi-faceted creative monster -- a renaissance man?"

"That's an interesting way of putting it. And without intending to sound full of myself, it's probably true."

"Do you think that the success of The Patricia List Story *is going to raise your profile as a writer?"*

"We'll see, won't we? It wouldn't be off the mark to say that my work is overdue for some kind of recognition..."

It was going to be beautiful, all right. *The Patricia List Story* might just be my ticket.

I flipped the script open and began to read. I didn't have to get more than a few pages in to figure out that *The Patricia List Story* was bad. It wasn't just bad, it was ghastly bad. It was in fact ridiculously awful.

The problem was that Walter Wallace couldn't write -- at all. He didn't know how. He didn't know grammar. He didn't understand punctuation. He had no idea how to spell.

But none of that truly mattered when it came to a screenplay. Some very good screenplays had those problems. The real issue was that he couldn't tell a story. Every scene was flabby and overwritten. The dialogue was dull and uninteresting. Even the stage directions were a mess.

I jumped ahead several pages. It was even worse further along. A seven-year-old could have done a better job on *The Patricia List Story*. And Walter Wallace had been a teacher? How had he made it through grammar school himself? It never ceased to amaze me that people who were devoid of talent with words insisted on calling themselves writers. The arrogance! The delusion! It was the equivalent of saying that you could be a brain surgeon when you'd flunked sixth-grade science. And yet the world was full of writers.

How the hell had Walter Wallace persuaded a film company to put up money for this trash? No wonder it was called Z-Cinema.

In a matter of minutes I'd gone from high to crestfallen. I threw the script down in disgust.

"I don't get it," I said after showing it to Gayle. "How did this shit get a green light?"

"Max, don't you understand how things work? None of this has anything to do with talent. It has to do with names, and who knows who, and who can generate the most publicity. And this story will generate publicity."

I'd heard it all before, but I was naïve and seemed to always forget just how the game was played. For some reason I wanted to believe that quality rose to the top, like the cream in a milk bottle. But no one cared about quality -- whatever it was. Maybe nobody knew. In the end it was really always about dollars and cents.

Well... maybe it wouldn't end up quite as horrible as I thought, though I failed to understand how a poor screenplay could be made into a decent movie. On the other hand, perhaps someone was going to rewrite it, edit it, tighten it, before the cameras rolled. Surely I couldn't be the only one who thought it was so shitty -- right?

Of course, that had to be the case... and if it wasn't repaired on the page, then maybe everything would be made right in the editing phase. "Fixing it in post" was something that always happened. Hell, there was no need for me to get all bent out of shape before a single take was in the can...

By the time I reported to the set in a suburban police station, not a single word in the script had been changed. The director, a greasy, mustachioed guy named Allen Stonicker, seemed confused about what he wanted. When it came time to shoot, he didn't give me a single suggestion for how he'd like the scene played. Walter Wallace, the only other actor in the scene, wouldn't be mistaken for Olivier. He was stiff and unpolished, and since he looked old and grizzled enough to be my father, I had trouble picturing him in a love scene with a sixteen-year-old girl. Maybe they were going to apply enough makeup to transform him into a younger version of himself? Maybe they had another actor to portray him at a different age? Maybe lots of things...

25

A few months later I received an invitation in the mail to attend a screening of *The Patricia List Story* in the lounge of a hotel out in Rockaway. According to the accompanying note, it had been masterfully edited and the sound had been fixed. Now it was time for audience reaction. The producers firmly believed they had a winner on their hands...

Gayle and I arrived on the early side. The place was packed with bodies. Friends, relatives, actors, producers, crew personnel -- they all wanted to be near the spotlight, even if it was second-rate. Everybody was excited. Those of us who had parts in the film were already fantasizing about cashing in. Gayle and I made straight for the bar and ordered drinks. It was a good sign that we didn't have to pay.

When everyone was settled in, the executive producer, a man with the last name of Mamoukas, got up and made an introductory speech thanking the cast and crew for all of their hard work. Then Walter Wallace got up and talked about how he had fulfiled his vision at long last, and how this movie, *The Patricia List Story*, was the pinnacle of his life.

Gayle elbowed me.

"Who's that supposed to be?" she whispered.

"Walter Wallace. He's the writer and star of the movie. Remember I told you about him?"

"Ugh -- he's repulsive!"

"Think so? There's a scene where his character is in bed with a sixteen-year-old girl. But they must be using a younger actor for that. Or they've cut it altogether."

"That's crazy. He's seventy if he's a day. If he climbs into bed with an underage girl, someone will have to notify the authorities."

"Ssh!"

"*Sssshhhh!*"

Now we'd pissed off everyone around us.

"Okay, okay, sorry!"

Finally Wallace shut up, sat down, and the room went dark. The opening credits rolled. They were eerie and quite riveting, the names of the performers, producers, and writer-director intercut with fuzzy shots of a child's hand in the lazy process of drawing a crude picture. So far, I liked what I was seeing.

Then the action kicked in. There I was, behind my desk at the police station, when Walter Wallace bursts in and begins voicing his concerns about his missing student. The police lieutenant -- me -- is utterly exasperated that Wallace has shown up and is bugging him yet again about the same damned thing.

It was a bad moment. My overacting was painful to watch. My eyes kept rolling back in my head, as if I'd been socked in the jaw. I'd telegraphed every emotion. The camera had been positioned so low that it made me look like some kind of hammy weirdo instead of an indifferent cop.

Even I had to admit that I sucked. On top of everything, the quality of the film was grainy and blurry, it was poorly lit, and the frames shook as if the cinematographer was a rank amateur, had never handled a camera before and didn't know the difference between one lens and another. At best the production values were cheesy. Jesus Christ -- did anyone involved in this thing know what the hell they were doing?

Enduring the crappy scene was torture. It skidded to a halt with a bumpy cut, before the movie lurched into another sequence.

I leaned over to Gayle.

"What do you think?"

"I'll tell you later."

"Ssh!"

The Patricia List Story deteriorated from terrible to

atrocious. The dialogue was stilted and laughable. The camera work regressed to abysmal from merely lousy. The sets hadn't been well thought out and were third-rate at best. There was no evidence whatsoever of a director's hand. None of the actors, including me, knew how to act.

The audience began to groan.

"This is *bad*," whispered Gayle. "Very, very bad."

"I know. I got eyes."

I began to zone out. When that happened I tended to be out on the basketball court, playing games in my mind, shooting from long range... until suddenly, a half-hour in, the flabby, middle-aged, hairy-backed Walter Wallace was in bed, naked, with a clearly underage girl -- the Patricia List character. As the scene opened they rolled away from one another, and it was obvious that they'd just finished having sex. The image conjured up pedophilia, even incest.

The Patricia List Story was no longer just crappy -- it was downright creepy.

The flick ran only around eighty minutes, but it felt like an eternity of torture. Any thought of it doing good things for my career was dead and buried before the final credits rolled.

When the lights came up, there was a smattering of weak applause. Everyone there knew beyond a doubt that Z-Cinema had a big, fat turkey on its hands, and that there wasn't a snowball's chance in hell that the damned thing would ever be released. Hadn't anyone seen what was happening? Why hadn't they pulled the plug after the first day?

We all shuffled out in silence, nobody daring to even look at Walter Wallace, who was at the other end of the bar staring at the drink in front of him, waiting for someone to tell him how great he was. I only hoped he wasn't thinking about making another movie...

———————

The experience of endless disappointment does something to you. You begin to expect things to never change. You expect your life to continue moving south, as if it's normal. You get used to feeling beaten down. Slowly you find yourself no longer giving a damn.

From time to time I wondered what had happened to *The Patricia List Story*. One day I rummaged for the Z-Cinema phone number, dialed it, and got a taped message:

"This number is no longer in service. There is no forwarding number..."

I knew what it meant: the company had folded its tent and retreated under a rock, never to be heard from again.

How the fuck did I keep finding the losers? Maybe I was one of them too?

26

There I was, back at square one, exactly where I'd started. I'd long known that nothing mattered in life, but a man needed at least an illusion in order to get out of bed in the morning...

Every New York actor takes classes. It's one of the slickest rackets in the world. All the wannabes who can't get arrested flock to the gurus who tell them what they're doing wrong and promise to set them moving in the right direction. But the gurus are mostly egomaniacs who've missed the boat themselves, or whose time has come and gone. Rejection and failure twist their heads until they fancy themselves coaches and teachers, and they take out all of their frustrations on the fools paying their fees -- and go on paying their fees despite the abuse they're taking.

The teachers who attract the most rabid following are the famous actors, the celebrities, who happen to be out of work at the moment or on their way to the far side of the hill. The aspiring thespian will shell out a small fortune to sit at their feet and be regaled with their tales of working with other stars. What was it like being on the set with Brando in *The Godfather*? Or Pacino in *Cruising*? Or Hackman on *The French Connection*?

Meanwhile, all of the hot young actresses and handsome young studs are actually working in the soaps and TV series and movies -- they're not sitting in classes with the losers. The gurus assure you that you'll get there someday too, if you just keep working hard and shelling out for their guidance...

I laid down my forty bucks for a seat in the class of the renowned actress Mandy Bennis. She'd won all kinds of prizes for her theater work, and even an Academy Award for supporting actress in *Who's Afraid Of Oscar Wilde?* I'd seen a couple of her flicks, but I couldn't say that I could ever figure out what she was doing. She wasn't especially good-looking, which is everything for an actress, and she was a mess of neurotic tics, constantly licking her lips, or delivering lines in a quirky, halting manner, or fluttering her fingers like an asylum inmate. Whatever she did was distracting as hell and not particularly interesting, but for some reason she'd been very successful and worked all the time, until the past few years. She was getting old.

We were all breathlessly impressed at being in the great lady's presence. Our fantasy was that after watching a scene, she would anoint someone a great actor or actress. Then she might pick up the phone and call one of her powerful director or producer friends and tell them, "You have to see this girl I've got in my class. When you're casting your next project, make sure she's at the front of the line..."

Of course that shit never happened.

"It's got be *natural*, like you really mean it! You can't look like you're trying...!"

Mandy Bennis loved to pontificate from her desk at the front of the room. Of course it had to be natural, everybody knew that. But if there was some great secret to acting, none of us ever got it. And if someone thought they got it, they were only kidding themselves.

"Oh, hell. Sometimes I don't even know if I know what good acting is anymore," she admitted, pushing her gray hair back and running her purple tongue over her buck teeth. She was bored watching us. She didn't want to be there, really. She was doing us a favor by showing up at all. She didn't come out and say it, but I could tell she hoped we realized it...

Afterwards most of the class would retire to the White Horse Tavern, where Dylan Thomas had legendarily drunk himself to death. The place smelled like a giant piss-hole and the beer was flat and warm, but by crossing the threshold alone you were supposed to feel that you'd entered the sacred realm of the Bohemians.

One afternoon I found myself at the same table as Andrea Pappas, who was always hanging around Mandy Bennis and liked to give the impression of being her right-hand girl.

"I spend nearly every weekend up at Mandy's place in Connecticut..."

This was supposed to be a confidential revelation, but Andrea purposely let it slip. Everybody looked at her with a bit of envy and awe.

"What do you do up there?" someone asked.

"Her laundry. Cook dinner. And I help with her cats..."

Mandy Bennis was one of those freaky cat people. She had three dozen of the creatures living at her mansion.

Once she got started divulging her so-called secrets, Andrea wouldn't shut up. Actors love talking about themselves, especially the ones who have very little to talk about. The famous variety, on the other hand, are aloof and disdainful, as if they're above it all.

For an actress, Andrea was already long in the tooth, and she wasn't particularly attractive, but she seemed very sure of herself.

"My psychic told me that when I hit the age of thirty-three, my career is going to take off," she stated matter-of-factly. "That's in only another year! And she's never been wrong yet..."

"Remember the peasants when you get rich and famous," I joked. But if she got lucky I had the feeling that she wasn't going to remember anyone but herself and Mandy Bennis.

27

One day I found myself sitting next to a stunning blonde, the type of goddess so beautiful she makes you feel uncomfortable. I didn't recall seeing her in class before, and I would have remembered. At the time Mandy happened to be into one of her stream of consciousness critiques.

"Any idea what she's talking about?" I whispered to the blonde.

"Not a clue."

"Have you done a scene yet?" she asked after class.

"No. But I guess I should."

"Do you have a partner?"

"Uh-uh."

"Would you like to do something together?"

"What do you have in mind?"

"I've been thinking about this scene between a psychiatrist and his patient..."

I'd certainly had enough experience with shrinks, so for me it would hardly be acting. And it would be something different from the creaky stuff -- Williams, O'Neill, Chekhov, Shakespeare -- everybody else was doing. She mentioned the name of the play, but I didn't recognize it.

"Next class I'll give you the sides."

Her name, she said as we walked towards Hudson Street, was Scarlett Sarkis. It didn't ring a bell. "I was a child actress," she added.

She must have done very well. She was decked out like a fashion model.

"Then I took some time off, went to boarding school, and earned a degree in art history."

Scarlett was a different cut of actress from most others I'd encountered. She was well-spoken, discreet, intelligent.

"So what are you doing in this filthy racket?"

"It's in my blood. After being cast in *A Melody In The Mountains* when I was five years old, I was hooked."

A Melody In The Mountains. I hadn't seen it. Musicals weren't my thing. But everybody in the world knew it was probably the most popular and successful one of all time.

That Wednesday we took the scene into class, me playing a Freud type to her disturbed patient. I thought we executed it pretty damned well, considering that it was a static, talky scene devoid of physical action or humor and we'd only rehearsed it for a half-hour at a coffee shop.

When we were through, Mandy Bennis sat there and stared at us. Then she shook her head.

"I don't know... I didn't like it. It was just... like I didn't feel *anything* watching it. I mean I *hate* that scene. I JUST HATE THAT FUCKING SCENE!"

Wow. I'd never seen her so outraged before. She'd never attacked any of the other students, even when they were awful, and this felt like some kind of assault.

"And I don't know what you can do to fix it. You *can't* fix it. I mean, it was just... it just wasn't any good."

Scarlett and I sat there like a couple of dunces being berated by a sadistic schoolteacher. Neither of us said anything. We got up and shuffled back to our seats in the peanut gallery.

"What was that all about?" she whispered. She looked quite shaken up.

I shrugged. "I don't think she digs that scene."

We'd just wasted our forty dollars. Mandy Bennis wasn't about to recommend either of us for *anything*.

What really happened, I figured out later, was that Mandy Bennis was *jealous* of Scarlett Sarkis. Jealous of her youth. Jealous of her beauty. Jealous of her intelligence. Jealous that she'd been in the cast of *A Melody In The Fucking Mountains*. Everybody in show business is jealous, even if they swear the opposite on the Bible itself.

We were finished, Scarlett and I. We certainly weren't going to be doing any more scenes together.

"Didn't you mention that you were a writer?" she asked on the street afterwards.

"I don't know. I might have."

"What have you written?"

"Novels, plays, stories, poems, music -- whatever you can think of. I used to work for newspapers and magazines too."

"So you're a professional!"

"Well, I've made money as a writer, but it was nothing I really wanted to do."

"Have you ever written a screenplay?"

"Those too."

"Produced?

"Afraid not."

"Listen, Max... I've been thinking about writing a screen adaptation of *The Moonstone*, by Wilkie Collins. Do you know it?"

I did. "But I haven't actually read it."

"Maybe you'd like to read it and collaborate with me on the screenplay."

She launched into an enthusiastic explanation of how *The Moonstone* would work on the big silver. There was, naturally, a major part in the film for her.

"Let me think about it, okay?"

"Give me a call, and we can discuss it. I've got connections in the film world, Max."

"I'm sure you do." No surprise there. Anyone who looked

like Scarlett Sarkis was going to have connections wherever and whenever she wanted them.

"I look forward to talking to you, Max. *The Moonstone*. Keep it in mind." She took off north on Hudson Street.

I went to the library, picked up a copy of the novel and started to read. You have to be in the right head to read a certain book at a certain time. After a few pages, I realized that mine wasn't into *The Moonstone*. Maybe at another time I'd be able to get into it, but...

What the hell was wrong with me? I'd been handed a golden opportunity, hadn't I? Yet I kept thinking of reasons I couldn't go through with it. I wasn't a natural collaborator -- I preferred working alone. I'd lie in bed at night and turn it this way and that in my mind, imagine myself tearing *The Moonstone* apart and distilling it to its essence for the screen, but I couldn't get excited at all over the prospect. I told myself that maybe I'd change my mind, that soon I'd work up a head of steam and want to attack the project, but it was the Henry Miller play all over again...

28

"Max, *really* -- you're going to have to bring some money in. I know I've said it before, but..."

The funds were dwindling. Gayle wasn't the materialistic type, but after a few years of living under the same roof, she had to be wondering what she'd gotten herself into. When we'd started, I'd at least been able to shoulder my share of the expenses. Now where was I? I was a writer who couldn't move his work, I was an actor who never got paid, and I didn't even have a real job anymore. On top of it all, I was broke. Whenever Gayle wanted to take a vacation or go out to eat, I was forced to beg off. Maybe she and I weren't going to make it after all -- not that I ever thought we would.

"Don't pressure me, baby."

"I'm just saying, Max..."

"I know what you're saying."

"I need you to know that my funds have a limit, and --"

"I'm on it, okay? Haven't I always coughed up my nut?"

She couldn't deny it, and I couldn't deny that things were growing more and more tense between us. What the hell was I going to do? The last thing I wanted was another stultifying gig, but how else was I going to make a living? I'd done the attics and basements for many years while trying to write, and didn't want to do them again if I could avoid it. But I might not have a choice.

Back to the wanteds. It seemed like I never stopped searching them. When I came up empty, I called people I hadn't talked to in months and begged for work. I knocked on doors and filled out applications for any kind of job I could think of, from postman to short order cook. No matter what I did, the phone refused to ring. Max Zajack was as cold as the Arctic on New Year's Day.

When it finally did make a sound, the person on the other end was someone named Lynette Blane. Her name didn't set off any chimes. She would like to see me in her office.

What was it all about, I asked. I'd sent her a headshot and résumé. Was I interested in becoming part of her troupe? There was money to be made doing psychodrama improvisational programs for the big corporations.

The next day I was in Lynette's sterile office over in Summit. She was a thin, intense, tight woman who sat back in her chair, looked me over, then recited a job description.

"Think you could handle that?" She fixed me with her large, sober blue eyes.

"No question," I answered, even though I didn't know what she was talking about.

"Have you had any of the following diseases?"

She reeled off a long list. I answered no to every one, even though I lied about depression and anxiety.

"Any problems with alcohol or drugs?"

"Not today," I laughed.

She didn't. The lack of a sense of humor is always a bad sign.

"You might have to travel," she warned me. "We do business all over the country. Chicago. Atlanta. Houston. Miami."

I liked the idea of Miami. Turquoise water. Heat. Party girls in bikinis.

"Are you free to travel?"

"Sure..."

I had no desire to travel. The idea of traveling for a job I didn't want had never interested me.

"Well, Max, we can use your type. As soon as there's an assignment, we'll contact you."

29

My first performance was scheduled for the following week at a communications company in central Jersey, where we'd be conning a group of corporate drones on a range of social issues. The actors were supposed to sit in front of an audience of employees and pretend to argue over subjects like racial and gender bias, salary inequities, and other hot-button issues. It sounded easy enough, and the pay was respectable.

My partners on the gig were Donna Crews and William Tingleman. Tingleman was a tall, black, genteel fellow with the mellifluous basso of a trained opera singer. Donna was a tough but attractive blond. She had a lethal body, including big, firm breasts that she thrust forward like weapons whenever she moved. There was something about this bitch, something smoldering and sexy. But something a little off too, something I couldn't quite put my finger on.

We were outside taking a break after one of the sessions when we found ourselves sitting next to each other.

"So, how long have you been an actor?" she said between drags of her cigarette.

"Too long."

She shot me a look. "Really? That's what I want to do when I quit my full-time job -- act."

"You must have a really lousy full-time job."

"I'm a police officer."

She mentioned the town on the Jersey Shore where she worked.

"Good luck," I told her.

She fired me another look.

I shrugged. "Well, you know, unless you're a star, it's just another job."

All the while I was checking her out, subtle-like. That dense, curvy body of hers made my mouth water. Donna Crews needed to be fucked. I didn't know who she was banging, but it should have been me. A fantasy bloomed like a flower in my brain: Donna and I were together in a motel room somewhere when she pressed herself up against me, then stripped off her police uniform and gun, and before I knew it I had it buried deep inside her. One of her naked thighs was high up on my hip while I pounded her and came in huge, powerful thrusts.

"Again," she begged.

"*Why? Why should I?*"

"*Because I'm the law, and I'm giving you an order!*"

Without taking it out, I started ramming until I worked up enough juice to *boom boom boom* inside her pussy again...

"Any tips for making it in the business?"

"Not really. I can't figure out how to do it myself."

Suddenly Donna seemed to think that I was funny. People always think you're funny when you're doing nothing but telling the truth. The truth is usually a sad thing, but it's often very, very funny too.

Where did I live? I told her, but nothing about Gayle. I never liked giving up too much information. Where did she live?

"In Aberdeen -- *with my girlfriend.*"

"I see..."

But I hadn't really seen at all. Donna Crews was a lesbian: that was the vibe I'd picked up but couldn't identify.

"We've been lovers for three years now. I met Sasha when I was having an affair with another officer on the force -- a married man."

Okay, so she *wasn't* exactly a lesbian. Donna Crews apparently licked both sides of the stamp. She ground her cigarette out on the pavement and went back inside. A few minutes later Tingleman opened the door and sat where she'd been sitting.

"Interesting work, wouldn't you say?" he asked in his very refined, slightly effeminate voice.

"If you like seeing the ruck stirred up." I was thinking of the argument that broke out that morning among a roomful of men when we announced that women employees were going to be paid more than their male counterparts. It had all been just a ploy, of course, to stimulate a discussion.

"Good point." He too wanted to know what kind of acting work I got. Actors are always into each other's business, hoping to steal a lead.

"Next summer I'm going to tour with 'Up With People,'" he announced proudly.

"'Up With People'? What's that?"

He proceeded to explain that it was an organization of actors that travelled around the world singing and dancing for world peace. I could easily picture William Tingleman singing and dancing. He would make, I thought, a perfect

Broadway hoofer. The Great White Way needed men who were light on their feet.

"That's a rather lofty goal."

He beamed. "I think so. Hey, what do you think of Donna?"

"Interesting," I said. "As far as I can tell."

"Yes, she is." But we had to be thinking of Donna in very different ways, didn't we?

William was a very nice boy. His father was a doctor and his mother was a professor of science at an Ivy League university. No wonder he sounded whiter than most white people. There wasn't a black bone in the kid's body.

30

After the gig in Jersey, we got booked to take the act to Chicago. Except for William Tingleman, all of the performers assembled at the airport bar and immediately started drinking. On the plane, Donna and I were seated next to each other. As soon as we took off, we ordered drinks from the stewardess. Beer, margaritas, wine.

Anything and everything.

"I hate flying," said Donna.

"So do I. Let's have another drink." I let my leg graze hers.

"Great idea!"

William was seated on the other side of the aisle, watching us with envy.

We got along famously, Donna and I. I couldn't help but think about what might happen when we reached Chicago. I never had any intention of cheating on Gayle, but when it came to women, I was weak. The drunker Donna got, the friendlier she became, and she kept leaning over and touching my arm or my leg. I did nothing, said nothing in response. Even though I was feeling the booze, it wasn't quite enough for me to make a fool of myself -- not yet at least...

That afternoon and evening we did our schtick in front of a few roomfuls of pharmaceuticals geeks, then retired to the hotel. Whoever made the arrangements had booked me into a double with William. The ladies all got single rooms.

I undid my tie, unbuttoned my shirt, and flopped on the bed. For some reason William couldn't stop pacing. He seemed agitated about something.

"Aren't you tired?" I said to him, wondering what Donna was up to next door.

"No."

"Why don't you have a drink or something? That will make you drowsy, take the edge off. It always works for me."

"I'm not allowed to drink. I'm a Jehovah's Witness."

Oh, *shit*, I thought. Two of my father's brothers and their families had turned that way. They were strict oddballs, the Witnesses, forbidding everything from card playing to music to birthday parties, and always predicting the end of the world, which never happened. Jehovah's Witnesses were the ones who had you running and hiding on Saturday mornings when they rang your doorbell, looking to convert you to the cause.

"Listen, William, I won't tell Jehovah if you have a couple of shots tonight, okay?"

I didn't give a shit if William drank or not. I just wanted him to quit circling the carpet. He was making me nervous.

A knock at the door. I rolled off the bed and answered it. There stood Donna, holding a half-empty glass. She was still in her blue business suit and pumps.

"Come on in..."

I could tell from her eyes that she'd been drinking again. She might even have a bit of a problem. We all sat around for a few minutes looking at one another, until I began to feel a weird vibe -- that Donna and William were somehow interested in one another, and that I was in the way.

"Well, good night, boys."

She disappeared, and I got undressed and into bed with my travel-sized Dewar's bottle.

William was in front of the full-length mirror, preening, turning his head this way and that. "Max, do you think that Donna is interested in me?"

"Huh?"

"Do you think Donna is, you know, *attracted* to me?"

"How the hell would I know?"

"But if you had to give your opinion."

"Can't say I've thought much about it."

"But if you were *forced* to say yes or no?"

"What are we, in high school or something?"

He laughed sheepishly. "You're right, Max."

He opened the door and went out. I took another hit of Dewar's, then switched off the light and fell asleep with the TV chirping in the background...

———————

"I think Willie has the hots for you."

We were on the plane home the next evening. I was curious to see Donna's reaction.

"He has a very nice body."

How did she know he had a nice body? Now that I thought of it, I didn't remember William coming back into the room last night, though he was there when I woke up.

"But isn't he... gay?"

"He's quite good-looking," she sighed. She sounded a little lovesick -- or disappointed.

"Yeah?"

"Oh, yes -- he's *very* handsome."

"Then he'll stand out in 'Up With People.'"

"I suppose..."

She gazed out the window at the glowing clouds. It was obvious she was struggling with something. Donna was a woman who ate pussy, and now she was interested in a guy who came across as a homosexual. For a few seconds I tried to make sense of it, but couldn't. But I knew where it left me.

What little interest I'd had in Donna Crews was dead and gone. The flight attendant stopped by with her cart, but neither of us wanted a drink.

31

On Tuesday Lynette Blane phoned and asked if I wanted to travel to Atlanta in two weeks to do the program again.

The money wasn't good enough to kill a few days -- I needed to find a better job, and quickly. But the real truth was that I was already bored.

"I can't make it, Lynette. Maybe next time."

She quickly hung up.

The next week I got a call from her secretary informing me that I was fired.

Among many others, I applied for a job as a writer at a sweatshop over in Edison. White-collar salt-mines were no different from the blue-collar variety -- I knew it from experience. In some ways they were worse, because you wouldn't get paid as much as a plumber and you actually had to *think*, sometimes hard, in order to do your job.

"I see you've worked at lots of different places," said the man who interviewed me. He had a mop of black hair slashed with a pure white streak, as if someone had dumped a can of paint over his head. "Why don't you ever stay?"

"It keeps me fresh," I lied.

I don't think he bought it. Nevertheless, he agreed to

hire me at twenty an hour, but he didn't seem all that jazzed about it.

"A lot of work needs to be done around here," he grumbled, looking at me over his crowded desk.

They were, of course, the last words I wanted to hear. What I really desired was a gig where I didn't have to do much of anything, where I could waltz in whenever I wanted and work on my own stuff. But those jobs were impossible to come by.

"Start Monday?"

"Sure."

"Nine o'clock. When you report, ask for Jean. She'll tell you what to do. And make sure you're on time."

My first assignment was to compose the operating manual of a new model of copy machine. Since I have no head whatever for technology, I couldn't make heads or tails of the damned thing. What made it all worse was that I was supposed to write it on a Mac, but I'd never used one before, and couldn't figure out the first fucking thing about it.

Within a couple of hours I was defeated. I sat there wondering how I managed to get caught in the same trap over and over again, and how it was likely I was never going to escape. That was the most horrible thought of all -- *that nothing was ever going to change*. And that thought is inevitable when effort after effort fails, when dream after dream is crushed, when idea after idea is stolen. It's a dangerous place to find yourself, the intersection at which hope and dreams die, because it means that life itself is meaningless, even more meaningless than it usually is, and from that point on, just getting out of bed in the morning is an ugly battle. If you don't overdose or hang yourself, you try to keep flailing through, and at the end of every afternoon you feel a little more like a zombie. And there you are... with all the other mediocrities and never-weres... with nothing to look forward to but another day at the office or the factory, and, if you're lucky, two weeks' vacation next August...

I kept barging into his office and asking questions until the supervisor finally figured out that his operating manual was never going to be finished by yours truly. He switched me onto the main floor, where I was added to the pool of proofreaders. To the normal person it would have been humiliating, but it wasn't to me. I was beyond humiliation. And anyway, proofreading was much easier work than writing...

You know you're in trouble when you begin to devise ways of staying away from your desk: you concoct fraudulent errands, you tell yourself you need to breathe the air outside the building for a few minutes to keep from falling asleep, you decide you have to see what's happening on the other floors...

I was only a couple of weeks in when I was already pulling my hair out from tedium. You're supposed to take an interest in your work, you're supposed to be grateful you had a job and could pay your way through life, but I could never seem to muster it. My favorite escape at Fairmount Solutions was ducking into the men's room one floor up in the company of the exotic Paul Bowles, who I was obsessed with at the time. I was deep into *The Delicate Prey* after dropping a few turds one morning when out of habit I reached behind myself and flushed. Before I could lift my ass off the seat, a tsunami surged up from the depths. Some genius had left the toilet clogged and walked away.

I scrambled off the throne and looked down. The seat of my khakis all the way to the knees had gotten soaked with sewer water, complete with piss and dung. Now what the hell was I going to do? There was a stack of work waiting on my desk, and most of it had an early afternoon deadline.

This was my punishment for ducking out on the man.

I couldn't go back to my station in my underwear, so I didn't have much choice but to hike 'em up. The sensation of cold water on my buttocks and balls was awful enough, and now I had to worry about the stench of human waste. Home was nearly an hour away. Driving all the way back there for a dry pair of trousers would kill half the day and get me fired. It was impossible, impossible...

When I went back downstairs, I could feel all eyes on me.

"Hey, Zajack, what'd you do, piss yourself?"

I dropped into the chair in my wet pants and tried to concentrate. It was going to be a very long day. body.

32

For a while I managed to hang on by my fingernails at Fairmount Solutions. Gayle and I hung on too...

Every day, every single day, I somehow managed to write. Three, maybe four times a year one of my stories would appear in the little magazines or literary journals, publications no one had ever heard of, sometimes after damned near a hundred submissions. I don't believe anyone ever actually read what I wrote, but having my words appear *somewhere* kept me going. I would have kept going anyway, but being published out there in the world, even Arkansas and Oklahoma, held back the specters of despair and madness and suicide. Writing was my dope. It had been from the beginning. It obliterated the need to drink or use drugs -- or kill myself or someone else.

But there were new problems on the horizon: the era of the great white male writer was over. Last time I checked, I was white and a man. No one wanted *new* white male writers. No, there was a need for "fresh, diverse voices." More writers of color. African and Asian writers. The marginalized and victimized, the oppressed and displaced. A straight white man could never understand what it meant to be on the outside looking in. He could never understand *suffering*. Worse, the white man was the cause of every evil known to the world, and he had it too easy. Above all, we needed more *women*. As one very successful female screenwriter of the moment told an interviewer, "I'm tired of hearing that white, male voice." To question the talent of any female or person of color meant that you were the worst type of reactionary, someone who didn't get it at all. In fact, you were practically a *criminal*, a murderer.

But in order to keep forging ahead, you had to push all the doubt and jealousy and resentment out of your mind. Hatred, on the other hand, well, that was something else. Hatred could always be used on the page...

33

Somehow I managed to land a leading role in a new play. It was to debut at a roach-infested third-floor space on the fringe of the Theater District. The first read-through took place on a Tuesday night. I looked around at the cast. Five guys about my age. Five guys who looked a lot like me, none of us particularly happy to be there. We were all sitting on that sad borderline between has-been and never-was. None of us was going anywhere anytime soon.

The play left so little impression that as soon as we finished reading it I'd already forgotten what it was about. "I love you all so much," exclaimed the playwright, a mousy woman named Carole Jones. "You are the colors of my rainbow, the light of my life! You are my perfect dream!"

"She'd better hope we don't turn into her nightmare," I laughed to the guy sitting next to me. Biff Mandolfino was a balding, stout, taciturn fellow with a bulbous nose who looked as if he could explode into a blimp after just a few more pizzas topped with pepperoni and sausage.

Like a cow he nodded slowly, but he didn't crack a smile. There was a dull but steely look in his eyes. Was he dumb or full of himself -- or both? Well, he *was* an actor... but I'm always wary when the guy next to me in the foxhole doesn't know how to laugh.

———

A week into rehearsals for *The Ugly Warriors* I got a call from a director who'd seen my headshot and wanted to know whether I was interested in doing a short film based on a Raymond Carver story.

Now this was more like it: something with a little meat on the bone. I admired Carver as a writer; even though he was a Pacific Northwest guy, his experience was close to mine. I liked that his writing was devoid of frills and bullshit. It might be interesting as hell to play one of his characters.

I went over to a space on Forty-second Street and read for the director, Gil Moss. He wanted me in his film, he said afterwards. He was one of those boys who'd come out of a prestigious cinema program that everybody in New York was talking about. Maybe he'd end up the next Altman and take me with him on his journey into immortality...

But there was a problem. It was either the play or the film; I couldn't do both because the schedules conflicted. And there was my job of course. Jobs complicated everything. I thought it over. Either way I wasn't going to make money. *The Ugly Warriors* wasn't very good, and in that dump of a theater it wasn't likely to attract any movers and shakers. I'd come to realize that if a theater wasn't right down there on street level, it was highly unlikely that anyone of importance -- a producer, an agent, a casting director -- would show up. To boot, the play was going to take up a lot of time, as all plays do. The film, on the other hand, would only require a few days of shooting. In and out, and for better or worse the performance is preserved forever.

I picked up the phone and called Moss. "Okay, I'm in."

It was only after I bailed on the play and had been replaced by another actor that Moss divulged that he hadn't cleared the rights to the Carver story.

"What?"

"I wrote Carver's agent, Sandy Urvan, and she said no way I could have the film rights to *The Student's Wife* without paying her fifteen grand. *Fuck you*, I thought to myself. That's more than my shooting budget."

"But Carver's dead."

"Doesn't matter to her. So at this point *The Student's Wife* is going to be for my reel only."

In other words, I was going to have to work for nothing so that Gil Moss could procure paying work as a director. And if

I was lucky, very, very lucky, he'd remember me and hire me when he became a big shot -- if he became a big shot...

Motherfucker. What sense did any of it make?

34

When I rang Moss's buzzer way out in Brooklyn, he opened up sporting a black eye that on the edges was turning the green hue of rotting meat.

"That doesn't look too good on you," I said.

"Got mugged again."

"Maybe you need a gun."

He shrugged -- he was getting used to it. We went up to the bedroom, where I said hello to his producer, Geoff Hillsick. And hello to the actress he'd picked to play my wife. Athena Church wasn't the girl I'd liked best during the auditions. She was southern and one of those lost hippie-waifs, her brain in another zone. She wasn't really a Carver female. But the money for the film was coming out of Moss's pocket. My opinion didn't count for shit.

The action wasn't much. In fact, there wasn't any. The story was one of Carver's quieter numbers, mostly internal and suggestive, and called for the two blue-collar characters to do nothing more than lie on a bed. The exhausted husband tries to ignore his wife and go to sleep, but she won't stop rambling, about everything she wants out of life but won't ever have. It wasn't my favorite Carver story, and certainly not one I'd ever pick to film, but maybe it made sense as a low-budget project since there was only one set.

I stripped down to my underwear. Athena and I got into position and began running the scene. The further into it we got, I noticed Moss just sitting there, his jaw unhinged, a confounded look on his face. He picked up the camera, but stared at it as if he'd never seen one before. Hillsick yanked it out of his hands.

"Watch -- here's how you do it!"

The producer took over and proceeded to give Moss an impromptu lesson on camera angles as well as everything else about the craft of moviemaking. So what the hell had Moss learned at the big-time film school? And I was about to waste my valuable time working for this chump?

And why wasn't I doing the directing? When you threw out the technical part of it -- lighting, lenses, sound, etc. -- all it took was a little imagination to figure out how to bring scenes to life and string them together.

In the end, directing was just one more rich man's hobby. The ocean of terrible movies attested to the fact that money and privilege will triumph over talent every day of the week...

"Okay. Let's run it again!"

35

Before climbing the long flight of ancient marble steps to the third floor loft, I cracked, bought a pack of cigarettes, and smoked a couple while waiting on the sidewalk in the twilight. I'd quit -- again -- tomorrow.

It was a little embarrassing to show up to a party when there wasn't even any music playing yet. The occasion was the premiere of *The Student's Wife*. I'd arrived on the early side, even though I'd mistakenly boarded the wrong subway and was forced to retrace my route...

Tonight was a big deal for Gil Moss. Producers had been invited. Even though he really didn't know how to wield a camera, a William Morris agent was supposedly courting him, and she might be on hand too. Rumor was that the director Bart Barlow, who'd become a sensation on the indie scene, would also be in attendance. Maybe my performance would get noticed by one of these big shots and I'd get some work out of it, the kind that paid money. That was how you were supposed to think about these stupid gatherings.

The loft was as huge as the floor of a department store. An old refrigerator stood alone at one end of the vast room and a few movie posters, featuring the images of De Niro and Scorsese and Woody Allen, hung on the otherwise naked walls. Moss had recently broken up with his girlfriend, and now lived here with three or four other dudes, all of whom were up-and-coming filmmakers or fashion photographers, in perfect bohemian style.

I grabbed a Heineken out of a cooler, and with Moss as my guide, took a tour. His bedroom contained only a cot, some clothes tossed into a corner, a few empty wine bottles, and a shelf with some books. He was living like a young bachelor on the make, and according to him, going through women like they were water. Sure, it made sense -- every woman wants a shot at getting in front of the camera.

I looked at the book titles: Stephen King (everybody except for me seemed to read him). The latest Raymond Carver collection. Something by a Spaniard on the art of cinematography. *The Notebook of Anton Chekhov*.

"Ah, the Russians," I said, fingering the volume.

"That book is crap. I got gypped."

"How's that?"

"Carver loved Chekhov, and as you know, I love Carver. I thought maybe I'd find some interesting ideas for future projects in *The Notebook*, stuff I wouldn't have to option since Chekhov's in the public domain. But no dice. Nothing in there worth looking at twice."

I was just about to tell him I'd dug the book when the other guests began arriving. They were mostly downtown types, twenty-somethings decked out in black from head to toe, with pierced noses and eyebrows and lips, all trying to appear cool and unaffected and stoned. The pretty girls looked at me without a shred of interest.

Moss tried to appear nonchalant too. He lit a cigarette, sipped his brew, and made the rounds, schmoozing with everyone. He'd forgotten about me, so I drifted like a ghost, waiting for something to happen.

Finally it was time to watch *The Student's Wife*. Bodies flopped on the floor around a big screen, which had been set up against one of the walls. Just before the lights went down, the great Bart Barlow himself made his grand entrance. It was like he'd been cued in, as if the whole thing had been planned beforehand. He was accompanied by a sleek, exotic Asian beauty with long black hair and outsized breasts who clung desperately to his arm. I looked him over: the celebrated *auteur* was one of the goofiest-looking humans I'd ever seen, with his idiot's blank eyes, dyed ebony hair, Ichabod Crane body, and long buck teeth that protruded over a nonexistent lower jaw. It was astonishing that he was viewed as a genius, a savant, or even remotely attractive. For the life of me I couldn't understand what any woman would see in him. Yet there he was, with a drop-dead knockout vixen draped all over him, commanding the attention of everyone in the room.

A buzz trembled the crowd. The sea of guests parted to allow the fashionable latecomers to sit directly in front of the screen.

The Student's Wife had a running time of only 16 minutes, but when the final credits rolled, it felt like a solid achievement. For a change, I didn't dislike my own performance, maybe because I identified so closely with the character I played.

"Nice job, Moss..."

"Hey, you did it, man...!"

A few other polite comments were tossed off, but they

sounded perfunctory and phony. Nobody said a thing to me about the film or my performance. Maybe no one recognized me.

"Hey, why don't we watch *All The Incredible Lies*?"

That was the title of Bart Barlow's indie hit, the one that had launched his career, made him a Gotham star, collected rave reviews in the likes of the *New York Times* and *Village Voice*, and snagged him an Oriental beauty.

Barlow's agent, who was on the premises, just happened to have a dub with him.

"Yeah!" someone else shouted, "let's see it again!"

Maybe Bart Barlow was someone to know after all. And he was sitting only a few feet away. If this was how the business worked, maybe I was going to have to learn to play the game.

I grabbed another beer, then settled in for the show.

After only a few minutes, I was pulverized by boredom. *All the Incredible Lies* was nothing but one more case of overrated pretentiousness. The laid-back, deadpan, sardonic humor wasn't funny at all, even for the most rarefied types. I tried, but couldn't figure out what the hell the movie was supposed to be about, and I'd bet that no one else -- including Bart Barlow -- could, either. The geek had pulled one over on everybody.

Still, there's no accounting for taste. Many people in the audience -- the females, mostly -- actually seemed tuned into the action (or lack of it) on the screen, which had vaguely to do with a suburban adolescent girl and her callous family who failed to understand her hypersensitive soul.

I quickly lost track of what was going on in *All The Incredible Lies* and didn't care. I closed my eyes and tried to doze through the rest of the flick, hoping I didn't snore or topple over. When the lights finally came up an hour or so later, Barlow was surrounded again, mostly by women, but also a few ultra-hip, frail-looking, fey young men.

"Brilliant!"

"You're going to be around for a long, long time, Bart!"

"Nothing short of genius!"

"Can't wait to see the next one!"

"Bravo!"

"You're the greatest filmmaker working in America today! Better than Scorsese! Better than Allen! Even better than Welles!"

That guy was dead, but everyone got the point. I waded through the bodies. The only topic of conversation was *All The Incredible Lies* -- *The Student's Wife* had already been completely forgotten, if it had made any impression at all. There was some kind of crazed light in the eyes of the fawners and sycophants as they danced around Bart Barlow, happy merely to be basking in the young prodigy's reflected glory.

My mood grew more and more surly. But instead of leaving, I kept drinking. I downed two more, fast, then stumbled into Moss, who was perched on a windowsill with a cigarette.

"So, what did you think of Bart's film?"

"Well," I said, "to be a hundred percent honest with you, I thought it sucked."

Moss pursed his lips and nodded. "Interesting."

The booze had loosened my tongue. "I don't think he's got much talent, frankly. At least not as a filmmaker. Maybe in some other line of work."

Moss nodded again. "You might think that, Max, but Bart's fielded calls from the Hollywood suits begging him to direct new projects. Major projects. He's being inundated with offers and scripts. Demi Moore wants to work with him. So does Jennifer Jason Leigh."

"Doesn't surprise me. Doesn't surprise me in the least. But it doesn't mean he's got any talent."

I didn't see any reason to not voice my opinion. Moss smirked. What I said seemed to rub him the wrong way. "But that's exactly the point! Hollywood sees real talent there -- right there!" He pointed at Barlow across the room.

All of a sudden I felt like I was under attack. I'd thought that Moss and I were cool with each other. I thought we could talk. He'd always been as vocal as me about who and what he didn't like -- like Chekhov. What the hell had happened between then and now?

There was poison in the air. If I didn't shut up, an argument was going to break out. Moss slid off the sill without another word, and went back to mingling with the other guests.

I stood there with my thumb up my ass. Barlow was still in front of the movie screen, surrounded by a fresh set of young foxes, leeches and groupies. The great young artist sucked it all in like an enormous vacuum cleaner.

Without saying a word to anyone, I slipped down the

stairs to the street. Outside, the humid late summer night had turned nearly bearable. Even though I was drunk, I made sure this time to get on the right subway.

36

Days passed. Weeks passed. Then months. Moss had promised that he'd call me in to read for a new film project. I was still waiting.

More time went by. I left a couple of messages on his machine but they were ignored. The third time I called the number was disconnected.

Walking by a movie theater on the Upper West Side one afternoon I noticed Moss's name in the production credits of a just-released feature. He'd been busy, all right -- just not with *The Student's Wife*.

I had the phone number of one of the crew members -- his nickname was Nutsy -- from the shoot. I called and coaxed Moss's latest number out of the him.

"Just don't tell him it was me who gave it to you, Max."

It was a frigid afternoon in late winter when I finally got Moss on the line.

"It's Max Zajack..."

"Who?"

"Zajack. From *The Student's Wife?*"

Why did these jerk-offs always pretend not to know you?

There was a long silence. "Oh. Oh, yeah, Max Zajack."

"I'll cut through the bullshit. I thought I'd give you a ring and see if you could use me in anything. I've noticed you've been working. Congratulations."

"Right now I don't think so. *Bart and I have decided to go in another direction.*"

"You and Barlow are working together?"

"Yeah, didn't you know? I'm producing one of his new films, *The Neophyte*. Isabelle Huppert is going to star. In fact, I'm dating one of the other actresses in the movie... Anyway, Bart realizes that since he's got major studio backing now, he can afford to use more high-profile talent. No more unknowns. No more B-list talent. We're looking at Sean Penn and Dylan McDermott for the male leads in this thing. That's the business. You know how it is -- nothing personal."

"Yeah, I know how it is... Well, how about something small, a supporting role or something like that?"

"Everything's already been cast."

"*Everything*? Even the stand-ins?"

"Yup."

"So what gives, man? You promised to get me in to read for something legit as payment for working on *The Student's Wife*."

Silence again.

"I'm gonna level with you, Max. You and I have a serious difference of opinion. I, for one, happen to think that Bart Barlow's a *genius*. Let's face it -- the money people in this industry don't make too many mistakes. Stars go hot and cold, but genius is genius no matter what."

"I respect your opinion," I said, even though I didn't. You can't argue with people over every single thing. If you did, life would be nothing but one long war.

"Hey, I've always loved Bart," Moss went on. "After all, *he's my half-brother*."

Uh-oh. Right there was my problem. I'd insulted Moss's own flesh and blood.

"Well, that explains the resemblance," I said lamely.

There was yet another long silence. I began to wonder whether Moss had hung up on me.

"Hello?"

"Yeah, I'm here."

"So, uh, if you change your mind..." Now I was groveling, and I hated myself for it.

"Sure," said Moss. He sounded like he was already very far away. "Sure I will, Max..."

———————

The way things were shaking out, the road wasn't about to get any smoother for me. Whenever I succeeded in forging some sort of connection or opening a door, I proceeded to somehow fuck up the opportunity. I was awful at networking and ass-licking. Maybe I wasn't cut out to be an actor, where you had to be good at all of it. And maybe New York was the problem. I belonged in Los Angeles -- maybe my luck would be better out there...

After hanging up, I was at a loss for what to do. Gayle was

at her job and I had the place to myself. I thought about calling one of my buddies and telling him what had happened, then realized I didn't feel like talking at all...

I sat in front of the patio door with a cup of coffee. An enormous rat had taken up residence in the drainpipe between our place and the next-door neighbor. Occasionally I saw its black head sticking out, nostrils twitching at the air, and at night I heard it scratching and gnawing on the pipes in the wall. I kept watching for it, but today it didn't show itself...

Eleven in the morning and not a speck of action on the horizon. As usual, the phone wasn't ringing. It was going to be another long day.

37

I'd hit another dry spell. Whenever the phone rang, it was a solicitor wanting to sell me something -- a magazine subscription, life insurance, a cruise through the Panama Canal. There were no calls to audition, no offers of work of any kind. Suddenly Fairmount Solutions had no more hours for me. I got up every morning and attacked something: a story, a novel, a song, a play. I'd send the work out faithfully, relentlessly, but with very rare exceptions, it came back rejected. Sometimes I'd lie on the bed, stare at the ceiling and fear that I was losing my mind again, because I'd lost it a couple of times before. I told myself that I couldn't go on doing the same things again and again and again and getting the same result. But that's exactly what I did, because I didn't know what else to do.

"I don't know what to tell you, Max," said Gayle. She'd always thought I had something, some kind of talent, but she was getting sick of all the failure too, though she never came out and said it. "You have to realize that you're in it for the long haul."

"Yeah, the long haul... but at what point does the long haul become sheer insanity?"

38

It was incredible. To a man, the critics were all beside themselves over a new TV show about the North Jersey arm of the mob. Anything having to do with organized crime was fatally tired, played out, done to death by the likes of Coppola and Scorsese. What more was there to do with it?

I kept reading the latest article in the *Times*. The star of the series, which was called *The Altos*, was someone named Biff Mandolfino, who played the head of the crime family. According to everyone who'd seen the first few episodes, he was magnificent, smoking with charisma, a heavyweight performer in the old tradition. Just wait until everyone saw *this* actor do his stuff...

The name faintly rang a bell. I wracked my brain.

Mandolfino... Mandolfino... Mandolfino.

I phoned my friend Bentt Larsen, who had a flawless, photographic memory for the most obscure writers and actors. He'd been in one of my plays and we'd stayed in touch.

"You ever hear me mention an actor by the name of Biff Mandolfino?"

"Nah, Max. Can't say that I do."

So this time I was wrong. Maybe I'd only imagined that the name was familiar.

"If it comes to you, let me know."

I hung up, and that's when it hit me.

"*You are the colors of my rainbow...*"

The Ugly Warriors. The fat, balding, humorless lump who refused to talk to anyone. The one who thought his shit didn't stink. *That* fucking asshole.

When I hadn't noticed, Mandolfino had landed a couple of supporting roles on Broadway, as well as a few small movie parts. Now he was carrying an entire TV series. Many, many people, people all over the world, would notice him. He'd make truckloads of money. He'd have women busting down his door. It wasn't all that long ago that we were sitting next to each other in the same smelly theater on Eighth Avenue, about to work for nothing.

———————

This is how it happens sometimes. Once in a lifetime if you're really, really lucky.

Overnight, *The Altos* turned into the runaway hit of the season. Viewers by the millions tuned in every week to catch the latest antics of the fairytale crime family. You couldn't turn on the TV set or radio, or open any New York newspaper without hearing or reading about how unbelievably brilliant everything about the show was. And the cast was the real deal -- ex-jailbirds, the lead guitarist for a major rock band, a handful of seasoned pros. The single figure who stood out above everyone, however, was Biff Mandolfino. The show's creator even referred to him as a "Mozart of actors."

It was nauseating -- and it was only the beginning. In what seemed a matter of minutes, Mandolfino became the biggest star in America. His picture was everywhere. The entertainment shows covered his every move. The fact that he refused to speak to the media was regarded as a sign of his super coolness.

I couldn't afford to pay for the cable station that broadcast the show, so I didn't get to see it. Besides, hadn't we had enough of the *Cosa Nostra*? Artists were always counseled to give the world something fresh and new, but when it came down to it, we only wanted the same old shit.

One evening after another futile audition I stumbled into a bar where *The Altos* was playing on the big TV screen. Every set of eyes in the place was riveted to it.

"Can I get some service here?"

The bartender seemed annoyed that I'd interrupted his viewing.

"What's on tap?"

"Carlsberg, Heineken, Bass."

"I'll go with the first."

I took a stool and watched. This was my chance, finally, to figure out why *The Altos* had gotten such a vice-grip on America.

The mobsters, all dressed in black suits, were gathered in a funeral parlor. They sat around in a circle, glowering at each other. The camera swept the room, closing in on the actors' faces, one by one. There were a few primitive grunts, but no one said a word. This went on for a couple of minutes.

"Another beer?"

"No thanks," I said.

I left my money on the bar and headed into the night.

———————

I was walking through Times Square when I glanced up and caught Biff Mandolfino's gigantic mug on a massive, flashing billboard. *The Altos* had now been certified the most watched cable TV presentation in American history.

That son of a bitch had done it, all right. He'd gone from a mouse-infested, third floor, Off-Off Broadway closet to a penthouse in Tribeca, leaving all of us losers in the dust.

I shuffled along, dejected and dispirited. What the hell was wrong with me? Why was I jealous and full of resentment? I didn't give a damn about being a TV star. I wanted something more. I wanted to be Knut Hamsun, Dostoyevsky, Henry Miller. Or Camus or Simenon or Sartre -- someone with real substance, soul, genius. How had I allowed myself to get caught up in this head game that I couldn't win?

It was America's fault, America, that fucking whore, who made you feel like you were nothing if you weren't a cheap celebrity on the cover of *People*, that's who was to blame...

I might think I had something unique, but the world didn't want what I had, whatever it was. The world didn't know I was alive, and it wouldn't give a fuck if I didn't exist. That was my reality. I had to face it. I kept walking, the enormous, pig-like, contemptuous eyes of Biff Mandolfino looking down on me...

39

Herbie Ziegler was on the phone. Herbie was an agent who sometimes got me out to read for commercials, which I never booked. I couldn't figure out why he still bothered to call.

"Zajack, I got something for you."

"Something good, I hope."

"Hell, yes! Would I send you out for something that wasn't good? Want to play a mafioso on the "Mob Week" promo for A&E?"

On account of the unprecedented and overwhelming success of *The Altos*, anything having to do with the mafia was suddenly all the rage again. Because I had dark hair and eyes, people sometimes mistook me for a *paisan*.

"You don't even have to audition, Zajack. They gave me a quota of five men to send over to the set, so you're already in."

Goddamn it. Extra work again. That was bad. Once you got typecast as an extra, it was impossible to break out of the mold.

"Yeah, I suppose..."

"Hey man, I can get someone else if you don't want to do it. There are thousands of actors in New York who would kill to have the chance."

"Okay," I agreed, remembering that no matter what, the money was what really mattered, and as usual, I was in need.

"Face time on camera, Zajack, remember that. It could happen -- you never know."

"What's the pay?"

"For non-SAG, one hundred dollars."

"What's the address?"

He told me and I wrote it down.

"And make sure you're on time."

"What do you think of this outfit," I asked Gayle.

I'd pulled on an out-of-date navy blue, double-breasted blazer and a pair of gray slacks. I was supposed to wear a black or gray suit, which I didn't own. Most of my duds I'd had to throw out because they were riddled with holes from cigarette ashes, and I was down to only a few pieces. I'd never had an interest in clothes, but a would-be actor needed some kind of wardrobe, some kind of style. No wonder I didn't win roles.

"Well, I've seen better. But maybe if you have your shirt laundered and find a nice tie..."

"Mind pressing the shirt?"

She rolled her big green eyes.

"Hey, do I ask you for much?"

The set was a shuttered nightclub on East Houston Street. They'd brought in damned near every goombah in the city to stand around while Mike Moon, who'd had a bit part in *Goodfellas*, marched up and down the staircase a hundred times doing his intro and assorted other bits.

That day I was feeling more than a little humiliated. After a few years I was still nothing but a prop for guys I thought were no better than me. But fool that I was, I kept getting suckered.

By now I was beginning to run into the same faces again and again.

"Hey Max, did you book that toy store commercial?"

"Not me."

"Didn't I see you at the open call for that lumberyard industrial?"

"Yeah, that was me, all right..."

"Any luck?"

"Fuck, no! I got called back, but never heard anything. The director's son probably booked it!"

"You know, sometimes those things never even get shot..."

There was always some good reason why it didn't work out. We had every rationalization down... That's how it is with all the bottom feeders...

40

"Max, we need to talk."

Whenever a woman says she needs to talk, it's never a good thing. In fact, it nearly always means trouble.

Since I'd poisoned the rat, we could sit out on the patio again. Gayle liked her wine, so we grabbed a bottle and went out there.

"Max... we're not making it anymore. You know that. There has to be a change."

"You met somebody else, right?"

"No, that's not what I'm talking about. I need to do something to increase my earning power."

Gayle had recently left the company she'd been working for and was living off her savings. She took another gulp of wine.

"I keep applying for new jobs, and all I hear is that I'm not in the running unless I have an advanced degree. So I have to go back to school. I need to become competitive again."

"Okay..."

"I'm just warning you in advance."

"Right..."

"Once I'm admitted somewhere, I won't be able to maintain this place any longer. I'm going to have to take out loans and find an affordable place to live wherever I land."

"Uh-huh..."

"I wish you could come with me, but I need to concentrate on my work. And you'd need to find a job..."

I was beginning to see the picture very, very clearly, and it wasn't pretty: Gayle was splitting, and I was going to have to vacate the place we'd been living in for the past seven years. It was the longest I'd lived in one place since I was a kid. And it meant I was going to have to scrape up a very reliable job in order to keep a roof over, my head.

Gayle got up and went inside. Even though it was obvious that things hadn't been working out between us for a long time, I found myself suddenly mired inside a black cloud.

The sun was dropping into the west, leaving the western sky a stunning wash of blue and orange. I was forty. I'd gotten exactly nowhere with anything I'd ever attempted in my life. I wasn't an artist, and I couldn't make myself fit into the normal, workaday world. Worse, I didn't want to be in that world, which made me something less than a normal human being. Apparently I couldn't hold a woman, either. Ever since the age of twelve, damned near thirty years, they'd given me nothing but trouble, and my troubles were about to start all over again...

I reached out, filled my glass with what was left in the bottle and slammed it down. Obliteration was what I was after, but instead my brain automatically fixed on what had to be done tomorrow. There were the help wanteds. Finding a place to live. And by the way, there wasn't much in the fridge...

That night it all felt so tiresome and futile. Life wore you down, and when you were down, it wouldn't stop beating on you. But I had to remind myself that this was America, the land of big chances and golden opportunities, and that I was white, which supposedly gave me a leg up on everybody else, so there was no reason to be depressed -- none whatsoever. I had it better than practically everyone else walking around.

I swept up the empty bottle and glasses and brought them inside. Then I went upstairs and crawled into bed next to Gayle, who was already sawing wood.

41

This audition felt different from the others. The black eyes of the guy sitting behind the table shone with a little more intelligence. When he opened his mouth, he was soft-spoken and articulate. With a sexy, tattooed, Goth-type girl sporting a safety pin in her lower lip as my partner, I read from sides that for a change weren't riddled with grammatical errors, misspellings, and punctuation gaffes.

When I was through and the Goth babe had disappeared, the guy asked, "Who are your favorite directors?"

"The Europeans. Bergman, Bertolucci, Polanski, for starters."

"Oh, yes, *The Fearless Vampire Killers* was a great one!"

"That's not the one I had in mind, actually, but it was funny as hell."

Ray Bint sat there nodding. I kept wondering where that sexy bitch had gotten to, and if by any chance she was going to be part of the film I'd just read for.

Bint explained that his movie had to do with vampires. *Lesbian* vampires, specifically. But he intended to give the genre a completely different spin. I didn't even realize it was a genre.

"Is this your first feature?"

"No, I made one other -- *Sangre Songet*. It was released on video. Have you seen it?"

The title meant nothing to me. "No, but I don't get to see everything that comes out..."

"Too bad. Because I'm one of the most interesting filmmakers working in the business today."

"Is that so?" Ray Bint certainly didn't lack for confidence, I had to give him that.

"Without a doubt. When I got back from *Operation Urgent Fury* -- the invasion of Grenada -- with a Purple Heart for bravery a few years back, I decided that it was up to me to inject American filmmaking with some much-needed fire, and that's exactly what I'm doing."

"Congratulations."

"It takes a member of MENSA," he added smugly.

"Impressive. We need more Einsteins in the world."

"Thank you. So listen... I want you for the part of the father in my picture. You will be paid at the rate of five hundred dollars per week when we shoot."

Now that was decent. Maybe Ray Bint's movie would be good enough to get picked up in a distribution deal, shown in select movie theaters, and I'd finally earn my SAG card.

"Sick Vampire Productions will cover all of your transportation to and from rehearsals and the set, as well as hotel accommodation and meals."

It was sounding better and better. I could hardly believe my ears.

"There are a few more parts to cast. The read-through is next Monday. We begin rehearsals in June and shoot in July. On your way out, Tara will give you the script."

Max, I told myself on the elevator down to Forty-second Street, your luck has finally changed.

42

The read-through of *Amelia* went down in a cavern-like space on West Forty-fifth Street. The actresses were all sleazy "10s" and dressed like high-priced streetwalkers. I thought I recognized a couple of them from the pages of Guccione's magazine. The redhead with her ass cheeks hanging out of her Daisy Dukes had been a "Pet Of The Month." The brunette with the forty-inch tits was the one featured urinating on guys wearing dog collars. This Ray Bint certainly had it going on. Maybe MENSA really did count for something after all.

"Okay, let's get started, shall we...?"

We breezed through the script. It turned out to be one more piece of trash, but unlike most of the so-called writer/directors I'd rubbed up against, Bint was actually capable of laying down a cogent sentence and okay dialogue.

Young dudes with bulging muscles, splashy tats and no-bullshit expressions leaned against the walls of the big room, watching and listening. It was obvious that they were the boyfriends and husbands of Bint's sex kittens. When you owned hot property, you had to keep an eye on it, you had to prevent the other wolves from getting too close. They were the steroided goons who followed their girls to the strip clubs where they moonlighted and made sure they didn't fuck someone else -- unless of course they were pimping them out. What an exhausting job it had to be. And when the lights were out and they screwed, it was the same as fucking an ugly grandmom. It seemed like a hell of a lot of effort to end up in the exact same place...

———————

I rode the train all the way out to the peak of Long Island, where my scenes were going to be rehearsed over the weekend at the Holiday Inn. It took forever to get out there, but Bint sent someone to pick me up at the station and I was given my own room at the hotel. For a change we were off to a fine start...

In Bint's suite we read through a few scenes of the movie again. None of the Penthouse Pets were around -- they were going to figure in the soft-core sequences, licking and sucking on each other's bodies. Then we started blocking the action that involved me and the characters of my wife and daughter. The plotline was that I was a vampire who molests my own child, thereby turning her into another vampire. At the same time, I'm having wild, ferocious sex with my wife. If it didn't quite add up for me, it made sense to Bint, which was all that mattered.

He sat on one of the beds and took it all in through his tortoise-shell glasses. After we ran through every scene a second time, he settled back into the pillow.

"It works," he sighed with deep satisfaction, a dreamy, triumphant look in his eyes. "It really works..."

The director was supremely pleased with himself. I wasn't exactly unhappy, since my action was groping and pawing Alison Sanders, the actress portraying my wife, then, later, pretending to screw Lena Manukas, the actress playing my daughter. Alison had a succulent body, at that perfect age between young and ripe. Lena was sleek and tight, like most twenty-year-olds. Making it with either of them would be very nice, even if I was only pretending.

"So, what do you think?" Alison asked me after the rehearsal and we were on our way back to our rooms.

"He seems organized, I have to say."

"Thank God he hasn't made a move on me."

"Ray? He looks like the timid type despite the alleged military background."

"I don't know about that. Rumor is that all of his actresses have to sleep with him," said Alison.

"All I care about is that he finishes *Amelia* and it's good," I said. "Did you happen to see the other movie he made?"

"No. I didn't know there was one."

She unlocked the door to her room, and I continued down the hall to mine.

I ate dinner by myself in the hotel dining room. Everything was soggy -- the fried flounder, the carrots, the green beans. The bread tasted stale. The waitress, an older woman with snow-white hair, seemed a bit surprised and even irritated at having to serve a customer. I was instructed that whenever I ordered anything at the hotel to bill it to Sick Vampire Productions. For a change it was nice to not have to open my wallet...

I was lying on my bed with a Simenon when there was a soft knock at the door. It was Bint and his leading lady, Lena, who was playing my incest-traumatized daughter and vampire in the making.

"Great day of rehearsals, Max!"

"I'd say so."

"Everything okay?"

"Fine, just fine."

"Dinner was good?"

"It did the job."

"Wonderful! And you charged it to the production company?"

"I followed your orders."

Lena stood there smiling. She didn't look well. Her complexion was very pale. As we talked, I had the growing impression that she might be a little interested in me.

And I could see why. Bint wasn't much to look at. He was gawky. He wore those thick lenses. He had a weird mop of straight black hair that looked like it had been dyed. In other words, he was out of the same closet as a nerd like Bart Barlow.

Beyond that, I really didn't know what to make of him. The theatrical arts are filled with such charlatans and con-men that you can never figure out whether you're dealing with a genuine human being or one more phony wannabe...

The longer I studied Ray Bint, the more I was assailed by doubts. I was just about to ask him where his production money was coming from when he said, "Well, it's time to get Lena back into the darkness! I have to keep her skin as white as milk -- she's a vampire, you know!"

And with that they were gone. Come to think of it, I didn't know what to make of either of them.

The next morning we ran through the scenes again, then Bint drove me back to the train station. He was very excited about *Amelia*.

"It's going to be a *classic*, Max." There was an ecstatic look in his eyes, but for some reason I had a strangely uneasy feeling.

In the distance I could make out the harsh eye of the train that would transport me back to the city.

"Ray, let me ask you something... is there a firm date for shooting to commence?"

"Working on it. You'll be informed of everything that happens as it happens, don't worry. I don't like to keep anyone, including the actors, in the dark. And I predict you're going to be an award-winner in this film, Max. If I do say so myself, I think I did an awesome job of casting!"

"No question," I said, thinking of the women. But I still needed more information. "So what's the format?"

Just then the train rolled in with a blast of thunder, the doors flew open and the passengers emptied out.

The last words I heard from Ray Bint were that his producers, whoever they were, had filled a warehouse with super 16 film stock for his exclusive use...

43

I made my way through the crowds and up the grimy, sweating stairs of Penn Station into the Manhattan afternoon. The weather was just like it was out on Long Island, except worse: smoggy, humid, not a cloud in the mid-June sky.

I was antsy, even a little manic, and drenched in erotic fantasies from rubbing up against Alison and Lena for the past couple of days. I decided to walk for a while, try to work off some of that energy. The minute Gayle got in from her job, I'd try to coax her into bed, but I wasn't optimistic. Ever since she'd announced that she was leaving for graduate school, we hadn't exactly been burning up the sheets.

"Interested in a blowjob?"

Without noticing, I'd made it all the way over to Tenth Avenue, a no-man's land where the High Line now stands. She was tall, maybe five-ten, with long, shiny black hair that might have been a wig. She was dressed in a halter, her full breasts spilling out, knee-high plastic boots and black panties. I could see everything through her clothes. Some tunnel bunnies are actually men, or used to be once upon a time, but there was no chance whatsoever with this one, not with that body. She was with another hooker, a peroxide blonde, who barely registered.

"No," I fired back automatically. The thought of having my cock sucked made me hard as stone, but I never touched street trade. The girls were too sad, nothing but human slaves, too obviously drugged out and disease-ridden, and besides, I didn't want to find a pimp's blade at my throat when my pants were down.

"Only twenty-five bucks," she pleaded, looking me up and down. "Come *on*, honey!"

"I only have fifteen," I lied.

"I don't believe you!"

She grinned. There was a black hole where an incisor should have been. The rest of her teeth weren't too great either.

I kept walking. I couldn't help turning for another gander as the pair of them swung their asses around the corner. Their haunches moved in perfect time, like a set of pistons. My mouth began to water.

"Wait! Let's talk..."

That stopped them.

"No -- just her," I nodded.

Peroxide caught on quickly. "Bye, honey! Have a good ti-ime!" She went strutting down Tenth Avenue.

The dark-haired whore came straight towards me. "Change your mind?"

"Look, I only have a few minutes..."

Suddenly I was nervous. I didn't know what I wanted. Where the hell was I supposed to go with a hooker in broad daylight?

On her face was a demented smile, which flashed the gap where that tooth should have grown. "No worries, baby."

She led me around the corner, into the shade of the railroad trestle. Just below one of the rusted pillars was a door, which probably opened at one time into an area where equipment was stored, or something like that. The space was just big enough for two bodies.

"In here," she said. Right off I knew she'd worked the spot before.

I followed her in.

"Money first," she insisted, pawing at my pockets.

I hesitated, arguing with myself whether or not I should go through with it. Then I reached around for my wallet. I jimmied my shoulder so she couldn't see what was in there, then pulled out two tens and a five.

She looked at the bills. "I thought you were short."

"Yeah, well, there was more than I remembered."

She slipped them into her boot. Then she proceeded to undo my belt. There was nobody around, but I was jittery. My only hope at that moment was that I could keep it up. Getting it on practically in the open with a streetwalker is not exactly a relaxing proposition.

She dropped to her knees and peeled my tool out of my

shorts. Popping it into her mouth, she began to suck with long, deft strokes.

It was incredible. I quickly forgot all about the world around me.

"Good, baby, *good*. Just keep doing what you're doing..."

She worked faster. The thought of contracting a deadly disease shot into my cortex, but I didn't give a damn. If she gave me chlamydia or gonorrhea I'd just go to the doctor and have it taken care of, and make sure to stay away from Gayle. I could only hope she wouldn't expose me to HIV or something worse -- if there was anything worse.

I reached down and cupped those oversized tits. Whether they were real or fake, I had no way of knowing. I began to work them, caressing and squeezing, until I heard her -- whatever her name was -- begin to whinny and moan.

Instead of asking for more money -- which is what normally happens if you overstep the boundary with a professional -- she seemed to have gotten lost in the moment too. My cock was like a steel rod. Her tongue was doing something to the crown, gently massaging it in perfect circles. The difference between her and any another woman was that she really knew what she was doing. If she had to, she could have you off and out of there in a matter of three minutes flat...

I decided that I had to have her properly. I pulled her up, inserted my thumbs into her panties and worked them down. Instead of resisting, she helped me. I ran my hand over her cunt. To my delight, she was waxed clean. I'd always wanted to penetrate a hairless pussy and right there in the dark doorway I was going to have my shot.

When the underwear had dropped past her boots, I hoisted her up. She was warm and wet and surprisingly tight. I cradled each perfect buttock, worked it in and rammed like a goat.

My brains were in a scramble. What if someone -— her pimp or a cop -- surprised us? There would be consequences, ugly consequences I didn't need...

But she pushed against me, harder. I came in huge liquid blasts, like a gun pumping out caulking. I imagined my juices shooting straight up her tubes, swimming frantically for their lives in the darkness, trying to get somewhere before they died, knowing that all along they were condemned to do exactly that. Men can conjure up some really inane crap when they're in the saddle...

Rocking back and forth, I stayed inside her until every last drop oozed out. She didn't move either, except to dig her nails into my deltoids and lick the sweat off my neck. Whores are supposed to be cold and unfeeling cash registers, but this one seemed anything but. Finally I began to collapse under her weight, thinking on the way to the ground about how I was going to hide the lapse from Gayle, since she always maintained that I was a lousy liar.

"Gotta go," she announced when I slid out. She drew her panties up. "Fast but fun."

"Yeah," I said, watching her flounce around the corner. No doubt her mack was nearby, waiting for his cut. If it wasn't for that missing tooth, I thought, my streetwalker would have been quite exquisite. And we'd had a genuine connection there, hadn't we? How the hell had she fallen so low? Surely, despite her teeth, she could have come up with a better way to make a living? Those drugs she was addicted to were very powerful agents of evil, positively demonic...

A kid with curly red hair and a knapsack on his back glanced in as I sat crumpled in the doorway. He hesitated and moved on quickly, thinking no doubt that I was a dope fiend or a nut case and he should stay away from people like me. That's New York.

I tried to untangle my jeans and hike them up. In a post-coital daze I shouldered my bag and began to trudge up Tenth Avenue again.

After crossing the bridge that spanned the train yard I noticed that something about me was... *different*. I felt lighter somehow, as if one of my limbs was missing. Like a hiker attacked by a plague of insects, I started patting myself all over.

My wallet. My fucking wallet...!

It was gone. That bitch was a pro all right, as much as I wanted to believe differently for a stray, stupid moment. When I wasn't watching, she'd somehow managed to relieve me of everything -- fifty in cash, my cards, my driver's license.

I turned and bolted down the avenue, but she'd pulled a neat disappearing act. Since the city is the perfect place to vanish into thin air, the chances that I'd ever see her again were slim to none -- at best...

44

At worst, I figured, *Amelia* would give me something to occupy myself with while Gayle was in the process of moving out. She'd been accepted at a graduate program -- which she'd have to finance with a slew of loans -- up in Boston and would be decamping near the end of August.

"I hope you find yourself a place to live soon, Max. September first this place gets rented out and I don't think you can afford it on your own."

"What gives you that idea, honey?"

"I'm just saying you'd better do something."

"I'm working on it, I'm working on it..."

It was a bitter moment. After seven years of living under the same roof, the longest I'd ever cohabited with a woman, even longer than a psycho case named Olivia, it was about to end the same way that all the others had. The difference was that this time I wasn't even sure what had gone wrong.

I landed a job working at a place in Roseland where payroll was processed. I sat trapped in a cubicle for eight hours, sometimes more, dabbing red ink on paper. What was I reading? I didn't know -- it was all in a code I couldn't understand, and didn't have to in order to carry out the function. I'd wanted the life of a writer, but now I'd turned into a robot.

When I wrapped it up every evening I scanned the listings for rooms and drove all over creation looking for a new crib.

The first place I checked out was a chicken coop that had been converted into an apartment of some sort on a farm in a town called Lamington. The landlord showed me inside.

"Not exactly the lap of luxury," he sniffed, "but it's functional."

It was an unholy mess. Between the stray shoots of straw on the wooden planks and the wire mesh over the windows, it looked like the kind of dead end where a registered sex offender might find himself after being released from the joint. Except for a moldy shower stall and a table that could hold a hot plate, there was nothing in it. It reeked of chicken shit and fertilizer. That day the mercury must have hit ninety-eight degrees, which made the stench vomitous.

"Air conditioning?" I asked. It was supposed to be a joke.

"You'd have to install it yourself. Though where you'd fit a unit, I don't know."

"What's the rent?"

"Two-fifty a month."

"I'll think about it," I said. But I didn't, not for even two seconds.

The next place I looked at was over a garage on the main street in Peapack. It stank of gasoline. There were long yellow weeds growing through the cracks in the windows. *Jesus Christ*, I thought, another latrine.

"How much?"

"Three hundred a month."

"For this?"

"Listen," said the realtor, a middle-aged bleached blond who glared at me disdainfully. "In the range you're asking, it's not going to be easy to find something that's even half-decent. Maybe you should be looking elsewhere."

I could have been offended, but the snooty bitch was speaking the truth.

The last thing I wanted was to draw out the process. All I was after was a place to stash my belongings and get back to writing. I'd recently begun a long blackly comical novel based on my childhood years that for the time being I was calling *This Bourgeois World*. And I was putting the finishing touches on another. I was working on stories and plays, too, in addition to running around to auditions. There wasn't time to waste looking for a tidy place to live.

Morristown was not my style, but I found a basement apartment up there on Searing Avenue, not far from the courthouse. At one-fifty a month, it was the best deal I could dig up. The joint even had a stove. I hated having to live in yet another basement where there was no natural light, but I was weary, so I signed the lease. They told me I could move in on the Labor Day weekend...

45

I kept waiting to hear when *Amelia* was going to shoot, but the phone didn't ring. I dialed the number for Sick Vampire Productions, but it was out of service. I checked the Manhattan directory. No listing for Ray Bint either. What the fuck?

I'd been through all of this shit a dozen times before, it seemed. I dug around for the number of my movie wife, Alison, and found it in a suitcase full of manuscripts and notebooks.

"Remember me? Max Zajack."

"Hey there, Max."

"You heard anything from Ray Bint?"

"No -- have you?"

"That's why I'm calling."

"We were supposed to start shooting about now, weren't we?"

"That's what they told me."

"Maybe they're just behind schedule. It always happens with low-budget films."

"True -- but there's a problem."

"Which is?"

"There's no way to get in touch with his company."

"What do you mean?"

"Sick Vampire has been disconnected and there isn't a new listing."

"Oh, no."

"Exactly."

"Max, I'll be honest with you. I thought Ray Bint was a bit of a flake."

"What did I tell you? It comes with the territory, right?"

"I guess. But the thought of all that preparation and rehearsal for nothing..."

"I think we've been had, Alison."

"I think maybe you're right, Max."

"Well, good luck to you."
"You, too..."
"If I hear anything..."
"Yeah."

———————

I turned around and Gayle was gone too. I reported to the office every day, hunched in my cage, and worked over fat, nonsensical payroll manuals, then came home and banged on the typewriter until I pulled out my sofa bed and collapsed at around midnight. On the floor above was a gang of frat boys who liked to party on the weekends. There's no worse torture than listening to someone else's music pouring through your ceiling...

The days had already become a burden and a bore, the eternal curse of the drone worker, with no hope ahead and nothing but confusion and regret and defeat in the past.

Most days I felt like a rat -- or a mouse. How does a mouse get off a treadmill? How does a man break out of the straitjacket and still manage to eat? I asked myself the same questions every night when I went to bed, and then again when my eyes opened in the morning...

46

The blinking light on the answering machine was a message inviting me to read for a role in a dinner theater production of something called *Boudoirs*, a fluffy farce whipped up by a married Broadway couple who'd turned to writing when their acting careers fizzled.

"Where is David's Country Theater?" I said when I returned the call. I had no recollection of sending a headshot to anyone there -- wherever the hell it was.

"Hackettstown."

Mother of Christ, I thought. *That's at least an hour away -- in the middle of nowhere.*

"Seven-thirty Wednesday evening? Can I pencil you in for an audition?"

Where else did I have to be? I needed to get out of the basement -- I was beginning to talk to the walls. If nothing else, it was an opportunity to take a drive through the woods, breathe some fresh air.

"I'll see you then."

David's Country Theater was a dinosaur of an old hotel that took up an entire city block. It was painted a gaudy shade of yellow, and over the second floor railing hung a banner advertising the dinner theater.

It was all very quaint, but... what was I doing here? The entirely insane idea of becoming an actor had only one point from the beginning: to somehow find an audience for my writing. Now here I was, trying out for a part in a third-rate dinner theater production where I'd be lucky if the mice noticed.

Since David's Country Theater was at such a distance from civilization, there weren't all that many actors, maybe seven or eight, waiting to read. I wasn't about to complain. I could use a little less competition for a change.

Hannah Smith was a chunky, middle-aged blond and the director. At one time, before she packed on all that weight, she would have been pretty fine in the looks department. But now... well, she was out here in the sticks, wasn't she? She handed me sides and asked me to go up on stage, where I read with a couple of different actresses. I was unimpressed with both the play and them. But the third performer to make her way up to the boards was a stunner: coal black hair, midnight blue eyes, and a face that would turn the young Ava Gardner green with envy.

"Hi. I'm Cordelia..."

Suddenly I had an altogether different feeling about *Boudoirs* and David's Country Theater. If Cordelia scored a part, I wanted one too.

We went through everything again. But my concentration was shot. I didn't even know what I was reading anymore.

"You will get a call," the director said to us when we were through.

The next night the phone rang. It was Hannah Smith.

"The part in *Boudoirs* is yours if you want it," she said. "Cordelia Cabrino -- the actress you read with -- will be doing the other lead."

"Yes," I said. I didn't even bother to inquire about the pay.

47

I was a free man. Gayle was history. Ever since she left town the blue devils had dogged me, and now a sliver of light shone into my otherwise dismal existence. After a long day in that miserable, soul-sucking office, I looked forward to rehearsals for *Boudoirs*, even though I had no interest in the play itself. Since I was getting paid a small salary, I forced myself to learn my lines, but all I really wanted was to see Cordelia again.

When rehearsal was over I'd try to lure her into a conversation without being obvious about it. But the conversations never seemed to go anywhere.

"So, where do you live?"

"On the West Side, in Hell's Kitchen. I've been there for six months now, trying to make it as an actress."

"Finding work? Aside from this, I mean?"

"No. It's very difficult to crack into the soap operas."

It made sense. Cordelia Cabrino certainly had one of those faces, the angelic sort you could gaze at all day long and never get tired. It was just a matter of time, I told her, before she hit something. But I didn't fawn over her. Beautiful women think it's their birthright to hear how beautiful they are. They lap up the attention like starving cats. What's the point of telling them what they already know? Once you start down that road, they know they've got you by the agates. What was it Stanley said in *A Streetcar Named Desire*? "I don't go in for that stuff... compliments to women about their looks."

"The problem is that I'm not landing many auditions," she went on. "And I'm getting tired of sweating it out as a telephone solicitor."

"Yeah, that's a tough one. What do you sell?"

"Theater subscriptions." She frowned. "I'll give it six more months. If nothing happens, I'll start looking for a real job. Begging people to buy tickets is not what I expected to do with my drama degree."

The universities spewed out hundreds of thousands of fresh aspirants every year. The vast majority weren't going anywhere and never would. It wasn't always a matter of talent, of course; luck and who you fucked had much more to do with it. Cordelia was most likely just one of the many girls who believed that there was hope when there was really none.

"My boyfriend is an actor too. And a dancer."

This was no surprise. I knew the boyfriend would have to make an appearance at some point.

"Is he working?" I really didn't give a damn, but I was a little curious about the competition.

"He's on a national tour right now -- dancing."

Well, I thought, if this boy is *dancing*, he shouldn't pose much of a threat.

"He's going to try and catch one of our shows. It's very hard, though, keeping a relationship alive when you're always apart..."

"I know what you mean," I said, thinking of Gayle. We talked once in a while by telephone, but it wasn't the same anymore.

The best part of every rehearsal was laying a kiss on Cordelia, which was how the play ended. I always had the crazy urge to push her down on the boards and part her legs, but sinking my ass into boiling water over something like *Boudoirs* was no way worth it.

It might have been boredom. It might have been the blues. Whatever -- Cordelia got under my skin. I'm twice her age, I thought -- what the hell am I doing?

"Want to go out sometime, get a drink or something? I know I'm a little older than you, but..."

Shit. There it was, I'd done it, after the Thursday rehearsal. Even to myself I sounded like some kind of desperado.

"It's okay. I used to go out with one of my bosses. He was in his forties too."

Great. So I was an old geezer.

"I stay with my parents on weekends. You can call me at their house. The number is in the directory."

She walked off and left me there to think about it. Jesus Christ. There I was, forty years old, and about to move on a babe who lived *with her parents*?

The run was over, and I hadn't done a thing with Cordelia. Her entire family was in the audience for the last show and afterwards there was a little party out in the lobby.

"Max, this is my father..."

I shook hands with all of them, said hello, nice to meet you.

"Nice performance," somebody said.

"Thanks..."

The praise was lukewarm, but I couldn't care less.

"And this is Kevin," Cordelia announced when I retreated to the drinks table.

I took him in at a glance. This boy was very clean. He sported a spiffy haircut. I suppose the ladies would think he was handsome. He looked as if he'd never suffered even a single day in his life. Maybe he hadn't.

He stuck out his hand. We shook.

"I really enjoyed the play," he lied. How could he really enjoy the sight of another man kissing his woman, squeezing and kneading her?

We exchanged some meaningless words. The gathering began to break up. One of Cordelia's clan mentioned something about retiring to a nearby restaurant. I wasn't invited. *Boudoirs* -- the evening -- everything -- was over, and I was half in the bag with nowhere to go.

———————

A couple days later I looked up the number of Cordelia's parents in the phone book. Then I sat down and stared at the receiver and began to imagine the various possibilities if I made the call.

"Cordelia, please?"

"And who is this?"

"It's Max Zajack."

"Who?"

"I did a play with her. I believe you saw it."

"Hm...no, she's not here. Can I take a message?"

"No thanks, I'll try another time..."

It was nothing more than a queasy feeling in the gut, but I knew which way this thing would go. The last thing I wanted was to be made a fool of, like Professor Unrat in *The Blue Angel*. I'd had enough of being a fool at the hands of women, enough to last me several lifetimes. If I could help it, I wasn't going through it again, not ever.

I kept staring at the telephone, trying to decide something, but I never reached out to pick it up.

48

Gayle drove down from Boston and spent the weekend. The time apart had rejuvenated our sex life. We used every square inch of the basement as a bordello.

"So what are you going to do when it's over?" I asked when

we were lying on the sofa bed, my cock still glistening and hard and twitching in the air.

"I'm going to have to get a job to pay off all the loans…You don't happen to have any extra money, do you, Max?"

That was funny, all right, and I laughed. "Are you kidding me? I can hardly make the rent on this dump. Listen, I wish I could help you out, but it just isn't there." And it wasn't.

"It's all right, Max. I never thought I could rely on you anyway."

"That would be very smart thinking on your part."

———————

Gayle got her degree, which was supposed to land her a better job, but she was still hanging around Boston, in hopes that something would come off through her new connections.

"I like it up here, Max."

I did too. Aside from the natives' irksome accent, Boston was cool. I'd loved the Celtics from the days of Bill Russell and John Havlicek, and the Red Sox ever since Ted Williams roamed left field at Fenway Park. But it was a little too small time. Whenever I got too far away from New York, indifferent, bitchy mistress though she was, I began to get nervous.

"Would you ever consider moving up here, Max?"

I didn't get it. She hadn't wanted me in Boston in the first place, and now she'd changed her mind?

"What the hell am I going to do in Boston?"

"You could write. You can write anywhere, right?"

"And I love lobster, too. But it would be the same old shit, honey. I'd have to find a job, and there aren't as many up there as there are down here. And what kind of film and theater prospects would I dig up in Boston?"

"What are you digging up in New York?"

"Give me a break, baby."

"You might do better up here, Max -- you know, a bigger fish in a smaller pond."

"You know me, darling. I like to do things the hard way."

———————

A week later Gayle showed up at my door with her suitcases.

"The job never came through, so here I am... Jesus, Max, what's that smell? Did you hide a dead body in here or something?"

"A family of skunks took up residence in the garage."

"You're not serious."

"Would I make up something like that?"

"Ugh! It's *horrible*! Can't somebody around here do something?"

"I've called the landlord a few times. He seems to think it's funny."

"We've got to find a better place to live, Max. I can't deal with this."

She gave me a look. I hoisted her suitcases and we went inside.

———————

For a few months we lived in the basement. That's how it was when we met -- we lived in a basement. There was a certain romance in being squeezed into a tight spot: the nowhere artist and his muse. I went to work every day, and Gayle looked for a job. Eventually she found one, on a high floor of one of the World Trade Center towers, and we moved into another condo in another suburb without a name.

49

Then I lost my gig at the payroll company and found myself scrambling for money all over again.

After weeks of nothing, nothing, nothing, I read for a dinner theater production of *Crossing DeLancey*, a mushy confection that had already been made into a romcom for the big screen. The day after the audition I was offered a part. It paid a couple hundred bucks a week, and I jumped at it.

Part of the actors' job was to set the tables of the Theater Cafe before each performance and clean up afterwards. In other words, I was a combination actor-waiter-busboy. Maybe not such a great deal after all.

Even though I was playing the part of an arrogant, self-absorbed, egotistical writer, *Crossing DeLancey* did nothing for me. The task was to figure out how to keep my head engaged in the show for the duration of a six-week run. The actress playing the lead was perfectly nice but dull -- she wasn't going to be enough...

I couldn't do it. During the final matinée, in the closing scene of the play, I went blank -- utterly and completely blank -- just as I was about to deliver a lengthy monologue. Suddenly I had no idea what I was supposed to do... or that I was an actor in a play... or even where I was. I stared at my partner as if I'd never seen her before. I circled her, circled her again, but still couldn't remember the words that would bring me back into the action.

She looked at me and smiled. When second after second ticked away and I still couldn't think of the goddamned line, her smile slowly collapsed. I began to sweat. Bloody spots whirled and danced before my eyes...

After meandering the set a few more times in a panic, I walked off, straight down the steps to the rear exit, and into the night...

50

I began to have terrible nightmares about being late for a stage performance in which I didn't have my lines memorized.

It wasn't like I wasn't sure of a cue here and there -- I wasn't even close. In fact, it was insane that I would even consider performing and expect an audience to pay for it. But there was no way out -- the show had to go on. Just as I was about to take to the stage, I would wake up in a cold sweat...

———————

That Sunday there was an item in the *New York Times* for anything related to Henry Miller: letters, documents, photos, etc. The writer was preparing a biography and would appreciate any such materials.

It just so happened that I had some letters in my possession from a previous Miller biographer and America's premier writer -- Ira Sender -- on the subject. "I have correspondence you might be interested in," I wrote back. "Or maybe not."

Before long Linda Bullworth and I were talking on the phone. She suggested we meet for drinks.

"I think you should go," said Gayle. "You never know what it might lead to."

"Nothing ever leads to anything."

"You need connections, Max. You need to know other writers. Maybe she can hook you up with her agent, have you thought of that?"

Nothing I'd ever seen or heard would indicate that she was right. Then again, I didn't know many writers. In fact, I knew none at all.

We met at a Chinese restaurant in Chelsea. Linda

Bullworth was the ancient cliché of a female writer. Her hair was mousy, she wore glasses, and she dressed in baggy jeans, moth-eaten sweater, and moccasins. In other words, she didn't give a damn how she looked. Or maybe she preferred women to men. But she had all the right stuff. Degrees from all over the Ivy League -- Dartmouth, Penn, Princeton. She'd even taught at some of the same institutions. Her father was a prominent Yale-trained molecular biophysicist who'd established trust funds for her and her siblings. She'd received money from prestigious foundations for her research and grants to put food on her table even though she didn't need it. She told me all of this matter-of-factly. The problem with the privileged is that they assume everyone else is privileged. But it was all utterly bewildering to someone like me, who could never shake a penny out of anyone.

"How do you regard Miller," she asked as we waited for our drinks to arrive. I noticed that her hands were shaking.

"The greatest American writer. He came closest to capturing the whole man, from the ridiculous to the sublime. How I'll feel about him in another thirty years, I don't know."

"And he had to live on handouts."

"Well, that part bothers me. Especially since I've been working since the age of ten. Myself, I couldn't sponge off people."

The concept of having to work for a living seemed to baffle Linda Bullworth. "So tell me about yourself, Max."

It was impossible to explain, so I danced around the question. Something else occurred to me.

"You know, I tried a few times to write a one-man play

about Miller before throwing my hands up in defeat. But for some reason the idea keeps jabbing at me, like unfinished business. I'm stuck with a notion of him wandering around on stage by himself, and that doesn't do it for me..."

"Maybe you should write about when Henry lived with June and Jean in a *ménage à trois*, before he went off to Paris. It was the most critical time of his life. And you could have it all take place in a single room."

A light bulb went off in my brain. Hell, yes. What Linda Bullworth suggested was a neglected period of Henry's life that practically cried out for the stage. Why hadn't I thought of it myself?

"That's not bad -- not bad at all," I said.

After a third scotch, another topic found its way into Linda's conversation.

"I'm telling you, Max, just after I signed my book contract, I was on the verge of losing it."

"How do you mean?"

"Like I wanted to have sex with *everybody*!"

I reached out and rested my hand on the back of her chair. "No kidding -- everybody?" I was on my third drink too. Alcohol always made me do things I wouldn't normally do, or even think of doing.

"Yes! I even thought about screwing my butcher in Brooklyn!"

It was always promising when a woman started talking about her intimate past. I maneuvered my hand onto the back of Linda's neck. She didn't shake it off. "And did you?"

"No, I slept with one of my friends, a photographer,

instead. Thank God his wife never found out! I would have gone further, I know it, but I started to feel a little guilty about Philip..."

"Who's Philip?"

"The man I live with."

"I see."

She shook her head.

"I've been diagnosed as borderline schizophrenic, Max. I've been seeing a shrink for a very long time. Actually, a series of them. When I slip into a psychotic phase, or forget to take my meds, I go a little out of control..."

No wonder the poor girl had the shakes. My hand slid right off Linda Bullworth's neck. Just my luck. If at all possible, I'd learned, you had to stay away from the nuts. They might fascinate you, they might be incredible in bed, but they could also be dangerous and erratic and bring you all kinds of troubles you didn't need -- and I knew it from years of hard experience. Her name was Olivia, and we'd come very, very close to murdering each other. It was truly a miracle that I escaped from her with my life. Now all I wanted in a woman was *sane*. Sane was much easier, and it was trouble enough. And sex was sex. When the lights were out, it was pretty much all the same.

Besides, I liked to remind myself, I had a tough enough time dealing with myself. Adding another lunatic to the mix was not advisable.

———————

I thought over my conversation with Linda Bullworth for a few days, then began writing. To my surprise, after all the blockage and angst over how to execute a play about Henry Miller, the words flowed, as if I'd known all along what I was going to do and how I was going to do it. It helped of course that I knew my subject inside and out -- it was as if I were right inside the great writer's skin.

Maybe this was the one that would finally take me somewhere. I felt good about it -- damned good.

The problem was that whenever I felt good about something, it was the kiss of death...

51

Gayle was worn out from traveling back and forth to her job in the city. By Friday evening when she got off the train, there wasn't much left of her.

"Why don't we move closer," she suggested to me one day.

"What do you have in mind?"

"Hoboken. It's only six minutes to my office."

"Ah, shit, I don't know."

"It'll be easier for you too, Max. Look how much time you kill going back and forth to auditions."

She had a point. Sometimes just one appointment in Manhattan murdered an entire day.

"But it's going to cost more, right?"

"Everything costs, Max. Life is expensive."

Well, she wasn't wrong about that.

"But it shouldn't be all that awful. The rent is only fifteen hundred a month. And think about this: we won't have to use the car."

On paper it sounded good, but in life if you don't spend money in one place, you'll blow it in another.

And I was lazy. Once I was in a groove, even if it left much to be desired, I was reluctant to make a change. Though I detested the suburbs, there were few distractions writing in a place that was as clean and quiet as a graveyard. In Hoboken, I'd be surrounded by all the wannabes and pretenders and never-weres. Worst of all, there would be *writers*. And I knew that their presence would only bug me, that they would make me lie awake at night feeling more miserable than I already did.

On the other hand, maybe I needed a change. Change is good, we're always told. Whether it's true or not I don't know, but that's what they say.

"Come on, Max. You can always leave if you don't like it."

———————

Our new lease kicked in on New Year's Day. When Christmas was history for another year, we drove over to 205 Hudson Street to pick up our keys and sign some papers. Afterwards we stopped at a place that specialized in bagel sandwiches before heading back to the chore of packing. We hadn't even made it back to the condo before something hit me as hard as the heavy barrel of a baseball bat.

"I'm sick. Really sick."

I went inside, climbed straight into bed and lapsed into a delirium. My head was on fire. My hands and feet were freezing. My teeth began to chatter uncontrollably. My stomach was doing somersaults.

"Max... please! You can't just lie there like you're dead! We have to get out of here! The new tenants move in day after tomorrow. You've got to help me -- I can't possibly pack and move all this stuff myself!"

I groaned. Through half-shut eyelids I could see Gayle moving around the room, pulling clothes out of the closet, cramming boxes and suitcases. Then I began to see other things -- horses, boats, dinosaurs, ghosts. The fever was causing hallucinations.

"MAX! Please get off your ass and help me!"

I couldn't open my mouth... I began to fade... until I was carried away on a swift river and didn't hear another word...

———————

I was awake. My eyeballs ached. Where the hell was I? What day of the week was it? I struggled for my bearings. I felt like I'd fought a long, bloody battle against some dark entity and lost.

Somehow I mustered the strength to stagger into the bathroom, hold on to the wall for support, and let go a gusher.

I was on a carousel, the room swirling around me. I struggled to stay on my feet until the whirling motion stopped. Then I stumbled back to bed. Gayle rushed in with another suitcase, swung it up on the bed next to my legs,and began filling it with underwear and socks.

"Awake?"

"I think so..."

"You missed all the fun."

"Don't start, honey. Please. I'm in no mood for it this morning. Or whatever the fuck time it is."

"Well, all you have to do is put some clothes on and get into the car. I did pretty much everything else." She didn't sound ecstatic about it.

After a while I crawled out from under the covers and inched myself down the hallway. Gayle wasn't exaggerating. All of our worldly goods had been packed up. The walls werebare, and the cupboards were empty...

52

The new digs were ten flights up and featured a mind-blowing view of New York City from the George Washington Bridge all the way down to the Verrazano-Narrows, including the Statue of Liberty and Ellis Island along the way. At night the light show was spectacular, something out of a prize-winning photograph. When it snowed the world was magical.

My favorite pastime of all, though, was watching the ocean liners leaving New York Harbor for someplace I was never going...

But it doesn't matter where you pitch your tent -- life trails you like succubus... Whether you move to Montana or Mongolia, whatever haunts you stays fastened to your skin like a plague of leeches...

———————

One night Gayle and I were strolling along Greenwich Street when I spotted a notice outside an Indian restaurant where we sometimes ate.

TONIGHT ONLY AT SALAAM BOMBAY -- READINGS BY THE RENOWNED INDIAN ASTROLOGER AND PALMIST V. ASHOK SHANKER ONLY $15.

A long, pointing finger showed the way inside.

"Hey, let's stop in. I want to see this guy. I've never had my palm read."

"I thought you were tight," said Gayle.

"It's only fifteen bucks. Some things are more important than money."

"Didn't you tell me not long ago that all psychic claims were a load of bullshit?"

"A lot of it is. But this fellow is Indian."

"Which means?"

"The Hindus are the masters of Vedic astrology. They've been living by it for centuries. The Vedic method is allegedly more accurate than the western brand."

"How do you know?"

"I read it somewhere, maybe in Madame Blavatsky."

"What if he's a Muslim?"

"We can still eat."

"It sounds like a waste of time to me, Max. Why can't you just open your mind to whatever happens and quit trying to guess the future? What happened to your Zen outlook on life?"

"My Zen outlook on life is getting me nowhere. Just order a couple of drinks, shrimp nargisi, and a tandoori appetizer, okay?"

We were shown to a table, then I paid my fee and waited for the soothsayer to be finished with his current mark.

It was my turn. Shanker was a slender man with black hair, thick lenses and golden skin. He wasn't the healthiest looking specimen.

"Please. Your palm," he said in a reedy voice.

I extended my hand. Suddenly I felt like a bit of a douche, a dizzy teenaged girl who doesn't have anything better to do but consult the local old maid fortune-teller.

"No, the left one, if you please..."

He peered into it as if trying to read the depths of a dark pool.

"Ah! You are going to be a famous person!" He sounded surprised, as if it was the last thing he expected to see.

Damn, I thought, *what kind of crime am I going to commit? And will it be on such a grand scale that it will make the news?*

"Yes. Right here!" Shanker pointed. "The hand never lies. A man's entire destiny is right there, in the lines."

"No kidding..."

"But you'll have to wait several more years. Be patient!"

"Sure, sure, I'm nothing if not patient..."

"I don't know what it is you do," Shanker went on, "but you have a brilliant head line that indicates great originality of thought."

"I do?"

"Right here," he said, indicating a long, wavering canal that cut from the heel of my palm all the way to the index finger.

"I'm a writer," I said. "Well, that's what I'm trying to be." It felt weird to admit, embarrassing, almost, because I'd written nothing, not a single word, that anyone was familiar with.

"Ah -- an artist...!" He kept staring at my hand, turning it this way and that for a better look.

"You will be fifty-two years old..."

Fuck, I thought. That's still many years off. I might not make it that far. Besides, I'll be an old man...

"And something else."

"What?"

"From that time onwards, you will call two different countries home for the rest of your life."

This charlatan was making absolutely outrageous claims. Maybe he was clinically insane.

"You had a tough start in life... Your health wasn't so good and you had to struggle for everything. When you were young you didn't get much help, did you?"

Well, maybe he did know a little something.

"Until the age of thirty-three you were stranded in a black hole of despair. You felt as if you were living on the brink of madness."

True, but I didn't feel out of the woods, even now -- far from it. Maybe he didn't know what he was talking about after all.

"Your life line shows a span of more than ninety years..."

"Even after all the nicotine, booze and dope?"

Shanker smiled. He went on a bit longer, nailing past events and their dates with uncanny accuracy. By the time I went back to the table, my head was spinning.

"Shrimp nargisi, your favorite," Gayle said as I pulled out the chair. She'd also ordered me a Kingfisher beer, samosas and naan bread. A fine-looking dinner.

I dug in. The spices of southern India made my mouth water. Sometimes I wondered whether I'd lived at least one lifetime there.

When I looked up, Gayle was staring at me.

"So -- what happened? You look like you've seen a ghost."

"You were right," I said, "it was a waste of money."

53

205 Hudson Street was the eighteenth or nineteenth address I'd called home, but nothing much had changed.

"Max, according to my calculations, we don't have enough to cover all the bills next month..."

"Oh, fuck. Not again."

I'd recently landed a gig writing weekend features for the *Star-Ledger* of Newark, but it wasn't enough to meet even a quarter of my half of the expenses.

"You told me that living here would be cheaper!"

"Oh, stop it, Max! If you want cheap, you belong in Nebraska or Kansas. Don't you ever quit complaining?"

"It's my nature. You should know that by now."

"We'll talk about it later, Max. I have to go to work..."

———————

The first few months in Hoboken were a peculiar time. Despite the rosy prognostications of the Indian seer, things went sideways. Suddenly I was paralyzed. I couldn't write. For hours I sat staring at the Manhattan skyline. The only thing that lured me out of bed every day was the OJ Simpson trial. The circus opened on TV at about one in the afternoon and took me all the way through to dinner time...

Before long my newspaper assignments became more sporadic. After putting it off for as long as possible, I visited a downtown employment agency and submitted to a test that would qualify me as a proofreader of pharmaceutical ads. It seemed to be the only work around, unless I wanted to go back to sweeping floors or frying hamburgers. Soon I was on the circuit of ad agencies -- Manhattan, Secaucus, Fort Lee, Parsippany, Morristown -- for twenty-five an hour. For a while, at least, I'd be set: the entire world was on some kind of meds, and it wasn't about to change anytime soon...

But like all the others, they were soul-slaughtering assignments, vacuous and boring and often backbreaking. Some lasted two days, some lasted months. I never met a single interesting human being on any of them. The minute I walked in the door, all I wanted was to escape.

54

They wanted me for the role of a cop in an indie feature called *Faggots And Retards*.

"What a title," said Gayle. "Are you sure this thing is for real?"

"Herbie Ziegler's outfit booked it. He wouldn't waste the time if there wasn't at least some money involved. That's why agents are in business."

"How big of a role?"

"Fuck if I know."

"Don't you think you'd better find out?"

"And what will it change if I do?"

"Suit yourself, Max. I'm just trying to look out for you, though I don't know why since you never listen to me. *Faggots And Retards*. My God, can you sink any lower?"

The set was way out in West Caldwell. I was scheduled for a single night of shooting. When I arrived, there were hordes of people hustling back and forth. Thick electrical cables ran in and out of the big suburban mansion where my scene was to be shot. I checked in with one of the PAs and was told to report to wardrobe.

The mistress was a wholesome beauty by the name of Summer. It was love at first sight, at least for me. I told her who I was and she consulted her sheet. "Max Zajack...so you're going to play a patrol officer in *Faggots And Retards*."

She ducked into her tent and returned with a blue uniform on a hanger.

"What if it doesn't fit?"

"Don't worry, Max -- we'll get you into it."

There was something about Summer, her soft blue eyes and chestnut hair, her understated beauty, that none of the vainglorious actresses running around could hold a match to. She made me feel like taking her far, far away, to a ranch way out west or a deserted island. She had something that made me want to forget about being a writer, or an actor, or anything else for that matter...

"So what the hell are we doing here on a spectacular summer night?"

Summer looked up at me from under her long eyelashes. "A good question."

"And why aren't you in front of the camera?"

"Oh, no. Not me."

"You're a very smart girl."

"All right, Max, would you mind trying this shirt on?"

When it was on my back, Summer straightened the fabric. It felt good to be manipulated by those lovely hands.

"Okay, off with it. I have to let it out a little. You have big shoulders."

"Hey," I said confidentially, "should we take off for somewhere no one will ever find us, you and me?"

"Like where?"

"Oh, I don't know -- an atoll in the south Pacific... or a cabin in Wyoming."

She laughed. "Then what? Unless you're independently wealthy, what would we live on?"

"We'd figure something out."

"It's a very romantic thought, Max. But whatever troubles you're running from, and whatever issues I've got, they'd still be there, on a Pacific atoll or in Wyoming." No doubt Summer had an actor boyfriend or producer husband, one of those rich or pretty boys bound for glory in the business. Or maybe she had an actress or producer girlfriend, and I was nothing but a joke to her.

"Come back in twenty minutes and the outfit will be ready. Oh -- and don't forget to return it after your scene is wrapped!"

When I walked away, I spotted another guy dressed as a cop. He was watching a scene that was being filmed in the backyard.

"I'm Ira," he whispered when I drifted over.

His eyes were as wide as saucers. With the reverence of a nun at the Vatican, he started going on about how great it was to be on a movie set. "I can't believe I'm really here..."

"You're here, man," I assured him.

"You know," he confided, "I'm beginning to think I might be able to make it as an actor."

"What gives you that idea?"

He glanced at me. His brown irises were earnest, like a kid's.

"Well, I used to live in this building on Sixteenth Street, and every morning when I left my apartment, the guy leaving his place across the hall was... guess who?"

"The King of Norway."

Ira looked at me again.

"No-o..."

"Sir Laurence Olivier."

"No!"

"Okay, I give up."

He mentioned the name of a hot sitcom actor. He pronounced it as if it were sacred.

"You don't say... but I don't quite get the connection between --"

Ira's star-struck eyeballs were positively shining.

"Later, after I realized who he was, I started thinking that if *he'd* made it big, *this guy who'd lived on the same floor as me*, maybe I could too."

"Uh-huh..."

"I mean, he pulls his pants on one leg at a time, just like me, and if I gave it all I had..."

"Right..."

Ira's naïve confidence annoyed me. Then I felt sorry for him. He reminded me why I loathed movie sets -- it wasn't so much the filming process itself, which could be bad enough -- it was the goddamned actors. We were all such pathetically sad creatures, entertaining the fantasies of little girls, yearning for what we couldn't have, idolizing fools and mediocrities. Then I started to feel sorry for myself.

"Break a leg, Ira."

I wandered around the yard. For an independent film, there were more people than usual, both cast and crew, scurrying about. This told me that there was some real money behind *Faggots And Retards*. I grabbed a bottle of water from the craft service table and checked my watch. In a few minutes I'd have to go back and pick up my costume.

Suddenly there was a commotion. A flabby teenaged girl in a flowery dress came running out of the front door, while a small mob brought up the rear. The girl was waving her arms and screaming "No! No! Not another one! NOT ANOTHER TAKE!" at the top of her lungs.

"What's going on?" I asked a bearded guy in a soaked tee shirt who was dragging some cable around the lawn.

"That's Holly Mozzarella. She's the star of *Faggots And Retards*. Looks like she's throwing another diva fit."

"How often does that happen?"

"At least once a night."

"Jesus. Is it worth it?"

"You'd have to ask the director."

That was somebody named Rand Sudwitz. I fetched my costume, pulled it on, then went back to the yard to wait. The hysterical actress had disappeared.

I was leaning against the picket fence when a skinny nebbish in madras shirt and khaki pants stumbled out of the back door and dropped his bony ass on the steps. He ran his hands back and forth nervously over his thinning hair. Then he pulled off his tortoise-shell glasses and swabbed the lenses with his shirttail.

One of the crew members immediately ran up to him.

"Rand -- are we getting Holly back tonight?"

So, this was our director. He looked up and shook his head.

"No. The law says she can't work anymore today. We'll have to shoot around her."

Rand Sudwitz spoke with the delicate voice of a grammar school female. Ira drifted out of the shadows to get closer, and a little group began to coagulate as the director began to pontificate with great authority on this and that.

"In the old days, young gifted artists like Hemingway would go off to Paris to write their novels. Now young gifted artists go off to the suburbs and make independent films."

That was him, presumably. Rand Sudwitz seemed to have it all figured out. But didn't it cost a hell of a lot more to make a movie than to buy a typewriter?

I nudged Ira. "I wonder what universe he's living in."

Ira leaned towards me and whispered.

"Rand doesn't have to worry about money. His family gave him nearly a million to make *Faggots And Retards*. They have great faith in his talent."

Sudwitz had finally stopped talking. He went on massaging his head and emitting whinnies full of anguish after a long day of shooting and wrangling with the likes of Holly Mozzarella. What did he have to be unhappy about, I wondered. Finally he got up and went back into the house.

A few minutes later I was summoned to the set. My action was to walk in and out of the kitchen in the company of a police sergeant and Ira while the camera panned over us. Then Sudwitz shot it all from a different angle. Then a third angle. At a certain point in the action I was supposed to call out "What's going on here?"

A couple of hours later it was over. When I went to the wardrobe tent to return my costume, Summer was nowhere to be seen.

———————

To my astonishment, *Faggots And Retards* became the indie sensation of the season. The reviews were scintillating. It was, the critics decided, the greatest, most important movie ever made about adolescence and the middle school experience in America. A new voice had been discovered! Rand Sudwitz, the quintessential outcast -- despite the fact that he'd graduated from Brown and Yale and one of the most prestigious prep schools in the country according to his bio -- was lionized by everyone, starting with the *New York Times*. His sour, geeky countenance stared into the camera with defiance. He knew who he was, and all along he'd known he was a genius and so did his family. And now the world would know it too.

It seemed I'd finally lucked into the right project. When my copy of *Faggots And Retards* arrived in the mail, I tore it open and slipped it into the video player. I was stunned. I'd expected some kind of quirky masterpiece, but the acting was amateurish, grade C at best. The script was inane, a cartoon masquerading as a drama -- or a comedy, I couldn't tell which. When I was finished slogging through it, I was more baffled than ever about what constituted creative value, and what it took to become a so-called "artistic success."

Worst of all, my single line -- "What's going on here?" -- had been excised from the final cut. All the audience would ever see of my brief performance was the back of Summer's costume for a total of three seconds.

And when the final credits rolled, my name was nowhere to be seen...

55

The years were wasting away, but I never stopped writing. Twice I'd started a novel about the seriously deranged five years spent living with Olivia, but I couldn't get it to work either time. I'd been determined to lay down everything about that volatile, agonizing period -- every single thought, every single move, every single fuck and fight -- but when I started typing, the words were stillborn. On my first attempt I'd filled thirty pages, forty the second, but neither version had any life, any fire. I couldn't figure out what was wrong. Maybe, I concluded, even after so many years I was still too close to the source of pain to come to grips with it...

Then one night, up there on the tenth floor with the world asleep and the lights of Manhattan chirping across the river, I gave it another, final shot. This time, my third crack at it, something different happened. It started with a first line that had been niggling me until I sat down and banged it out.

"The war was over, but it didn't mean a thing."
Now that line crackled. It sizzled. Very simple words, but they set you up for something, something heavy. Something mysterious. And something funny, too. I liked it. I liked it a lot.

The rest of it came spewing out in a miraculous geyser. This time around, instead of getting mired in the significance of every single second of what had gone down, and what I'd been thinking, and what I'd been feeling, I simply recorded the events of those five whacked-out years as they unfolded. I didn't give a damn about who was right and who was wrong, or whether or not I portrayed Olivia -- or myself, for that matter -- fairly or humanely or sympathetically. All I cared about was that I got the story down and that it kept me interested -- and entertained.

The keys skipped easily from one line to the next, until I had one chapter, then two, then three. In a matter of a few weeks of stolen hours I was finished with the first draft. It was one of those solitary, quiet periods when the phone wasn't ringing and, aside from my job, distractions were few. I didn't know whether what I'd produced was any good, and I didn't care. But a voice inside told me that this time I was really onto something.

56

One evening I got home from the grind to find a fat letter from *Ellery Queen's Mystery Magazine* waiting for me. This was unusual -- I'd been sending them and their sister publication, *Alfred Hitchcock's Mystery Magazine*, stories for years, and their rejections always arrived in a thin envelope that I'd enclosed for a response: "Sorry, but it's not for us, we wish you the best of luck," etc. This time, for some reason, they'd apparently decided to send back my entire manuscript, and on their dime.

"Look at this," I called to Gayle, who was moving around the kitchen.

"I noticed, Max... What do you feel like eating?"

"I don't care. Whatever you're eating."

It was okay. I was used to, if never happy with, rejection by now. I knew I'd never get into the gaudy or big-name magazines -- like the *New Yorker*, or *Ellery Queen* -- that was for the chosen few. I'd do what I always did when turned down -- send the story out somewhere else. This time at least, the editors had saved me a trip to the Xerox machine. I ripped open the flap with my thumb and pulled out the folded up sheets.

Enclosed is the publication contract for your story "The Pursuit Of The Nonexistent"...

"Hey, listen to this!" I yelled to Gayle.
The best part was that the magazine paid three hundred

dollars for the tale I'd concocted about a biologist who wanders with his fiancé into a very dangerous place in the tropics on his quest to discover a new species of bird. It was written for no other reason than to make money, and it had worked. My name would now forever stand beside -- at least in one place -- the likes of Simenon and Faulkner and Highsmith and Chandler -- as well as lots of very bad writers, but what the hell.

I read the letter again. And again. And again. I could hardly believe it. After years of effort, I'd finally reached the pinnacle of *something*. The editors of *EQMM* -- long considered the best mystery/suspense journal in America, if not the entire world -- saw tens of thousands of manuscripts each year, and somehow, miraculously, mine stood out from the others. What made it even sweeter was that my name *wasn't* Hammett, or Borges, or Maugham. And that I had no other connections to speak of. It might have been tough, even brutal, but I'd done it *on my own*.

For a few days I walked around in ether. Maybe I wasn't hopeless after all. I might be getting old, but maybe, just maybe, if I never gave up, the game would turn in my favor...

57

The afterglow of a pleasant dream always fades, and in the morning another reality wins out. I realized soon enough that the appearance of a story in a national magazine wasn't going to change my life. As a matter of fact, when it hit the stands, no one even noticed. I went back to the job the next morning as if nothing whatsoever had happened...

Gayle had flown out to visit her family in California over the Christmas holidays. When she came back after the first of the year, she was green at the gills.

"I can't figure it out. I've been sick to my stomach every day. I can't stop throwing up."

"Stay away from me then, baby. You must have the flu, and I can't afford to come down with it."

"Don't worry -- I'll stay away. And you can sleep on the couch tonight."

"What? Wait a second. Why the hell am I the one who has to move?"

"But it's the strangest thing -- once I get through vomiting in the morning, I'm pretty much okay the rest of the day."

By midnight I'd forgotten all about it and hit the sack -- on the couch. When I walked into the bedroom the next morning, I noticed that Gayle's breasts, which were full jugs as it was, seemed to have grown even bigger. Just below the surface of the powder-white skin was a tangle of blue veins. I'd never noticed them before.

Just then she opened her eyes.

"What's wrong? What are you staring at?"

"Your tits."

"Why? I thought you liked them."

"I do. I love them."

"Then what's the problem?"

"No problem. It's just that... they blew up overnight."

"What are you talking about?"

"I'm telling you, honey -- they're twice the size they were before you left for L.A."

She jumped out of bed and confronted herself in the mirror.

"Oh, my God! I see what you mean...!"

"Wait a second, just wait a second here... Hey, you're not pregnant, are you?"

"*What*? No... at least I don't *think* so."

Suddenly there was doubt in her eyes. It was early January and freezing, and she was due at her job. She began to get dressed, but could barely harness those coconuts.

"I'm going to the pharmacy."

"What for?"

"To pick up a test."

Now it was me who was queasy. If Gayle was going to have a baby -- and I was forced to be part of it -- I was screwed. I wasn't cut out to be a parent. I wasn't made for the conventional, workaday world, supporting a family and all that. Christ, I'd spent the past twenty-five years trying to avoid it! And even though it had gotten me nowhere, I'd grown used to the way I was living. Now what?

I looked out the window. The hard and brittle winter sun was shining brightly. Manhattan was under a glaze of ice. I reached down and stroked my soft cock, but it refused to stir. I was supposed to be at my job within the hour. A fantasy suddenly bloomed in my brain: I'd quickly pack a bag, board a bus and ride for a long time before finding myself in Florida, or Arizona, or Mexico, maybe, and disappearing into the heat and sun. My memory would be wiped clean, and life would start all over again. No one would be able to find me. And I'd never come back. I'd never even think about coming back...

Instead of making my escape, I showered and was pulling my clothes on when Gayle walked into the bedroom.

"What's the verdict?"

"Positive. I'm pregnant."

"*What?* There has to be some mistake! I'm old. You're old. It's crazy."

"If it satisfies you, I'll take the test again, but it's telling me yes."

I shook my head and headed for the door. "I'll talk to you about it later," I said. Then I walked out.

58

I sat at my desk, thinking: I should have kept the fucking thing in my pants. But how do you keep the beast locked in its cage? I'd had dozens of women over the years and so far as I knew, hadn't knocked any of them up. But my luck had finally run out...

I was working at a measly eighteen an hour for a company out in the Meadowlands that specialized in the business of home heating. It was my responsibility to proofread a newsletter that went out to people all over the country who purchased fuel oil for their homes. At the bottom of the newsletter was a coupon for a cup of free coffee.

"Zajack!"

It was Blackford, my supervisor. He was a real pain in the ass who liked to sneak up on me to check whether I was actually working or goofing off.

"I'm here."

His mug appeared above the cubicle wall.

"You'd *better* be here. Today we have LaCrosse, Wisconsin and half of the state of Minnesota to turn around. I'll bring over the first stack of newsletters as soon as they come out of graphics."

"I'm not going anywhere."

"What's the matter, Zajack? You don't sound very happy. Don't forget, if you don't like it here, we can always get somebody to take your place. Ha-ha."

As always, Blackford was only half-joking. The other half was deadly serious.

"Not at eighteen bucks an hour, you couldn't."

My attempt at a comeback. Blackford didn't laugh.

I sat there cradling my head in my hands. I'd always had a horror of being trapped, it had plagued me all my life, and now my fear had truly come to pass. If I had to support a kid and a wife, I was going to be marooned in a place like this for the rest of my life...

A few minutes later Blackford came bouncing back with a tall stack of broadsides for the common man's comfort.

"Here they are, Zajack! Go to it! And remember, this is the height of the season, so move your ass!"

I picked up the red pen and hoisted it over the newsletter bound for Northfield, Minnesota.

Maybe it was good that I was swamped with work. That way I wouldn't be able to think too much.

59

The next evening, after a visit with her gynecologist, Gayle and I were at a table at a place called Anglers & Writers in the Village.

"So what do you have in mind," I said.

"Well, I thought we would get married. I think it's good for the child to have a last name. For he -- or she -- to have a father. Studies show that having a father around is even more important than having a mother."

"And you believe those studies?"

"You don't sound too thrilled, Max."

"Would you consider an abortion?"

"I thought you wanted kids someday."

"Look, I don't know if I can hang around for this. I'm not cut out for bourgeois life. If I was, I'd have been there already. Besides, I'm halfway to being an old fart."

"Keep an open mind, Max."

"Oh, it's open, all right."

"Maybe this will be a good thing for you, have you thought of that?"

"How do you figure?"

"It will keep you young. And maybe it will help your writing."

"Are you saying my writing is bad?"

"Max! I think you're a great writer. You know that. I've always said it. What I mean is that it will reveal new dimensions of life to you. Maybe it will even bring a change of luck."

"That's nothing but an old wives' tale... Listen, what will you do if I walk away? Will you sue me for support? Because I don't have any money, in case you haven't noticed."

She laid down her fork.

"You can go if you want to. I won't stop you."

"I'm thinking about it. I'm really thinking about it..."

"Do whatever you want, Max. You've been with me long enough to know that I'd never try to keep you somewhere you didn't want to be. So don't worry. We'll make it somehow, even if it's without you."

"How do you know?"

"I just do."

Gayle was unflappable. She was serene. She'd always been that way, which was one of the many things I admired about her. I had no doubt that she'd find a way to take care of matters if I was out of the picture altogether.

"So, you sure you really want to bring a new soul into this fucked-up world?" I said after the waitress delivered another Belgian ale to the table.

"You're crazy, Max."

"What have I told you all along? You can't say you weren't warned."

60

I kept thinking that I should split, but I didn't. When my head cleared a little and I was able to think straight, I went back to working on my novel.

One evening Gayle came in and announced, "It's a boy."

"A boy, huh?"

"That's what the latest test says. We'll have to think of a name for him, won't we?"

"I guess so."

"Max, could you be any less into this? I feel like I'm by myself on a desert island."

"Sorry, baby."

She retreated into the bedroom, where I could hear closet doors opening and closing. I sat there in front of the computer screen, my brain frozen into ice.

A *boy*. I began to see him... to picture him in the schoolyard, being called a little bastard because he didn't know who his old man was... having to fight for his life because of the relentless teasing and bullying, if kids still did that sort of thing in school...

No, that wouldn't be good, would it? I didn't want that happening to any son of mine. Maybe Gayle was going to have her way after all. Women usually do...

61

Gayle and I tied the knot on a Caribbean island. We didn't really have the money, she had to talk me into it, but in the end we somehow managed it and it was okay. Far out in the ocean there were no families to deal with, no friends to mingle with, no elaborate arrangements to be made. It was just Gayle and me with the turquoise sea as a backdrop, a lady who brought a spray of flowers, and a priest in traditional knickers who delivered a little speech on the duties and sanctity of marriage.

Like a somnambulist in the grip of fate, I nodded at everything he said. "I do," I answered when he asked if I took Gayle to be my lawfully wedded wife. I made a promise to be faithful. I made a promise to stick it out with her through sickness and health, richer or poorer.

It's a strange, strange moment, the moment of the marital vows. If you're like most men, you feel the cell door clanging shut in your face. If you dislike or even hate the woman you're binding yourself to -- and it must happen a good amount of the time -- it has to be a moment of sheer terror managed only by alcohol or some other substance...

I'd managed to avoid the pit until my forty-sixth year, but at long last I'd succumbed, like all the other dudes who are neither saints nor stones. My only hope was that if I tried to stick it out, it wouldn't be a disaster.

I thought about all the oaths I'd just sworn. Since the beginning of time billions of men and women had sworn them. And billions had ignored them, which allowed me to breathe a little easier. Contracts weren't made to be abided by -- they were made to be broken...

That night there were fireworks all over the island for some unknown occasion.

"It's like a celebration just for us," said Gayle, gazing up into the heavens.

We stood on the pink sand and watched the gaudy explosions overhead. The setting sun, the Roman candles, the blue-green sea splashing a few feet away -- it was all quite beautiful. Beauty cajoles you into thinking that something more, something miraculous, should happen -- but it doesn't. Nothing happens, the moment passes, and beauty, you realize, doesn't mean a thing...

62

The kid was born deep in the heat of August at Lower Manhattan Hospital, the only Caucasian baby among a sea of new Asian-Americans. I stared at him through the glass and could hardly make sense of it. I'd gotten it on with Gayle one night before Thanksgiving after a bottle of wine, and now there was this, something that would change my life forever. It's overwhelming, the awareness that lodged inside your two balls is the power to create life...

Gayle was on a maternity leave from her job, which she'd come to hate. Her boss was a bitchy gay man who spent much of his time surfing the net for dates, and he detested her. It wasn't unusual -- New York is full of homosexuals who despise women. But it made her life hell, and it made me feel guilty that I wasn't doing something to relieve her misery.

I'd recently snagged some extra freelance work as a proofreader at Fetere, Schlussman, Jones, and Bigelow Associates down in Soho. Fetere was one of the prestige New York ad agencies. They handled copy for everything from financial investment to frozen food. The other drones in the unit were allegedly out of the same mold as me. Abby Cohen was an aspiring playwright. C.B. Hiller, too, and he wrote novels as well, one of which had been published by St. Martin's Press. Billy Ray Jones was an actor who was trying to become a copywriter since his theatrical career wasn't doing much. The supervisor of editorial services, Christiane Saint-Mark, was a would-be screenwriter. The atmosphere seemed loose enough, the hourly was decent if not spectacular, and the building was only a one-stop underground ride from my apartment.

Christiane seemed to take a shine to me. One afternoon as we rode the elevator down to the street, she asked if I'd consider coming on board as a full-time employee. The question caught me completely off guard.

"I don't know. I'm claustrophobic. I need to feel like I can get out, you know?"

Then I remembered my wife, bound to her shitty job.

"Listen, you can take the late shift if you want, and use

your mornings for writing. Start after lunch and knock off at nine. I can only offer you thirty-eight thousand a year to start, but the medical coverage makes the job worth a lot more. You just became a daddy, right? You could use that coverage. Please think about it, Max. It's hard to find someone who fits in here, and you seem to get along with everyone in the department."

"All right, I'll think about it," I lied, just to get her off my back. *Fuck*, I thought.

"Great! But if you don't want the job, I've got to offer it to someone else before they take the money away from me. That's the way it works around here, so let me know ASAP."

————————

That evening the kid wouldn't stop crying. My wife had returned to work, and she looked more haggard than usual. The queen she was working for didn't give a damn about the problems she had on the home front -- he wanted results. We'd hired a Guyanese nanny who came a couple of afternoons a week, but it wasn't nearly enough help.

"I got offered a full-time job at Fetere," I told Gayle over dinner.

"So?"

"I'm thinking of taking it."

Her brows crunched up. She looked at me as if I'd just told her I was about to book the first voyage to the planet Uranus.

"Why?"

"Because we need the money, and you need to get away from that asshole you're working for. If I accept the offer it'll take at least some of the pressure off while you look for another job. It won't solve all of our problems, but it'll help."

Gayle shook her head. "You'd be making a mistake, Max."

Maybe she was right, but the schedule would allow me to have the all-important mornings, when I wrote best, to myself. I'd arrive home late at night, when everyone was asleep, which meant I'd avoid the lion's share of babysitting, which bored me, like it did most guys who weren't afraid to admit it.

"Look, honey. Writing isn't working out for me. Year after year goes by and I get nowhere. You know how many novels and stories and plays I've turned out at this point? I can't even count them all. Notice that the mailbox is overflowing with rejections? I can't go on anymore this way -- I just can't. I need a break from all the defeat."

"Max!"

"What?"

"You're not writing for money! We'll get by somehow if you don't take a fulltime job."

"Will we? You've got a kid, a job you can't stand, and you're ready to drop. This is my contribution to the survival of the Zajack family. Look at it this way: you may never get the chance again."

She shook her head. Her tired eyes were full of skepticism.

"Here's something else. Once I get us covered by medical insurance you can work part-time until you find something better.

"Well, okay... I hope you know what you're doing, Max."

"Don't worry. The worst that can happen is that I quit, right?"

63

I took the elevator up to six. Christiane greeted me with a big smile.

"Ah -- finally, a full crew!"

Wherever you went it was the same -- false cheer, then they tried to kill you with work.

"Max, meet the rest of the department. Some of us you've already met and some you haven't, but we're all happy to have you."

This was a little different, I had to admit. They were at least trying to make me feel at home. The problem, of course, was that I didn't want to feel at home.

I was led around the floor to shake hands with everyone. Right, sure, it's great to be here, etc.

The proofreaders' office was a rat's nest. It smelled moldy, like a mixture of unwashed armpits and rancid cheese. In every corner there were stacks of newspapers and journals, books and style manuals in steep, crooked piles. Somehow they'd managed to squeeze five desks into a space the size of a tiny bedroom, so that we were all on top of one another. If one of us rolled his chair back six inches, the others felt it.

"You're over there, Max." Christiane pointed across the room to a computer terminal set against a grimy window. To get to it, I had to climb over the other worker bees.

And, just like that, I was in, a full-timer, an official peon just like everybody else in the world lucky enough to land a nice position. What did I have to bitch about?

———————

The copy piled up in a wire basket just outside the door. Volvo, Swanson's frozen dinners, and Oppenheimer Funds were the major accounts, with several smaller numbers tossed in. You were supposed to go to the basket and pick up the folder on top of the pile, return to your station and proof its contents against all of the backups. It was a dreary routine that often left me with a migraine and aching neck muscles at the end of the night. When occasionally there was nothing to do, you were supposed to sit patiently at your desk and wait for new copy to arrive. No reading, no net surfing, no listening to music. Your idle moments belonged to The Man.

That night my wife wanted to know how it went.

"It is what it is, as they say. But the thought of being there forever, week after week, month after month, year after year..."

"Going back tomorrow?"

"We didn't hit the lottery today, did we?"

64

I had no choice but to succumb to the routine. For eight hours a day and often more I perused copyright notifications through a magnifying glass... I checked the borders around the photos of automobiles... I pored over ads for frozen chicken dinners...

It was crushing. It was deadly. The clients were shelling out millions for our services, but how much of it was I going to see?

"So -- I hear you're a writer too, Max."

C.B. Hiller's voice was a trifle precious.

"Sometimes."

"Yeah? What do you write?" The more he talked, the more he sounded like Truman Capote, complete with the acerbic condescension.

"Whatever I can, pretty much."

"Published?"

"A little. Fifty stories or so in journals and magazines. A couple of micropress novels. A few plays Off-Off Broadway, too. One of my screenplays was optioned, but nothing came of it."

I kept hearing from Christiane about how talented Hiller was. Now I was supposed to ask him about himself. Being around other writers was such a drag.

"So, what about you? I hear you're a genius," I said anyway.

Hiller's eyes took on an otherworldly glint, as if he'd just been waiting for the moment to hold forth on the most important person in the world -- himself.

"Well, since you asked, I won the creative writing award at NYU as an undergraduate, then I won it again at Columbia as a graduate student..."

Shit. Why had I opened my mouth? Now I was going to have to listen to Hiller's entire literary history.

I'd known another guy who'd won a writing award as a student. It was the worst thing that ever happened to him, not only because he no longer wrote, but because it had fostered a very dangerous delusion: he'd actually come to believe that because a professor said so, he was endowed with some kind of mystical talent, was better than others around him, and was destined to become a famous author. He didn't seem to grasp that something far beyond the ability to write a slick sentence was involved in the spawning of a true artist, that it had to do with loneliness, torment, and desperation, not to mention superior perception and originality.

"... and I've had a book published by St. Martin's..."

"Oh, yeah," I said, trying not to sound jealous. "What's it about?"

"It's a collection of spoofs of canonical American writers like Updike and Oates, Roth and Mailer. *I'm what you would call a modern-day Max Beerbohm.*"

"Max Beerbohm -- I see."

"You know him?" he asked. His tone was snooty.

"Not personally. He was a fop who parodied the rich and famous."

Hiller seemed disappointed that I was familiar with his idol. I didn't let on, though, that I'd never read a word Beerbohm had written.

"But I'm really a playwright."

"Ah." This was my cue to inquire about his successes on the New York stage.

"Yes, my work has been produced at Chelsea Rep and the Cherry Lane Theater."

Hiller had done a hell of a lot better than me. I had trouble getting even the lowliest theater companies to consider my scripts.

"But my agent thinks the piece I'm working on now will be my breakthrough. I can't say I disagree with her."

"Is that so?"

"It does have all the elements: it's a farce about the political travails of the transgender daughter of the most powerful senator in Congress, who just happens to want to become the first female president herself."

It was a lot to absorb, but I had to concede that C.B. Hiller's play was a perfect fit for the New York theater. Right there was my problem. Writing a script about a man who turns himself into a woman, or vice-versa, had never once entered my mind.

When he wasn't talking about himself, Hiller spent most of his time on the phone with his TV cable company. He lived in a closet on MacDougal Street, and for some reason the provider had decided to pull Turner Classic Movies from his package. This sparked endless arguments that seemed to never get resolved. Hiller's battles over his TV channels were the most exciting thing that happened in the proofreaders' space...

Then there was politics. Everyone except for me was submersed in the subject, and it was talked about *ad nauseum*.

"What did you think of the Clinton healthcare initiative?"

"It doesn't go far enough!"

"No matter what, we have to crush the right-wingers!"

And so on, and on, and on...

Overnight, something happened. It must have become obvious to everyone that I wasn't playing along. Or maybe it was my refusal to kiss up to Hiller, or maybe Christiane didn't like the work I was turning out, but suddenly the room seemed to go silent whenever I appeared.

I began to spend more and more time out of the office. I'd prowl the Strand Bookstore down on Fulton Street, or Borders at the Trade Center, or I'd thumb the racks at J&R Music or Bleecker Street Records. Sometimes I'd sit in a corner of the employees' lounge, drink coffee and read Raymond Carver, which suited my mood. Anything was better than sitting in that rat's nest of an office, staring at those infernal ads and listening to what amounted to bad talk radio...

65

One afternoon when I was trying to keep myself from falling asleep at my desk, I swung around and asked Hiller if there were any jobs in the basket.

The great artist didn't even bother to look up.

"Nope. Nothing." His tone was sharp. He snorted, got up, and stormed out.

Christiane was beside herself. *"Max! You can't do that!"*

"What? What did I do?"

"You're not supposed to ask C.B. to check the incoming work orders for you!"

"Why not? Who is he, the Duchess of Windsor or something?"

The supervisor's eyes narrowed into angry slits. She swung back to her computer screen.

I turned back to mine and tried to sleep.

_____

When I signed on, Christiane had assured me that one of the perks of the night shift was leaving the office early if there were no outstanding jobs circulating between the editorial unit and the graphic artists. All I had to do was walk around and ask in order to make sure my ass was covered.

Until now I'd never done it, but that night Billy Ray was off and I wanted to catch a revival of *Peeping Tom* at the Film Forum, so I walked around the floor and did a check. According to the graphics guys, there was nothing that needed attention. When no one was watching, I slipped out.

The next day all hell broke loose.

"What's wrong with you, Max? The graphic artists complained that

you went and bothered them about their assignments! Under no circumstance do you EVER bug the artists about what they're doing! They're the most important personnel on this floor!"

It was as if I'd committed cold-blooded murder, or something close. Christiane was all bent out of shape -- again. I was baffled.

I plucked a folder out of the basket, retreated to my desk and sat down. Hatred and hostility crackled in the air. My days at Fetere were numbered, and I knew it. I hadn't even been on the job for two months.

66

The big freeze was on. None of my so-called colleagues in the proofreaders pool would even look at let alone talk to me. Overnight I'd turned into a pariah. The minute I showed my face, a lively conversation went as dead as Abraham Lincoln.

That wasn't all. At every turn Christiane ripped into my work. If there was a single missing comma, or a hyphen wasn't in boldface, she was all over me like stink on a turd.

It was very, very tiresome. I decided to get it all out into the open.

"Meet me in the employees' lounge," I said to the supervisor.

"All right," I said when we sat down out there. "What's the deal? It's no secret that I've turned into an untouchable."

Christiane was incandescent with rage. Instead of giving it to me straight, she shrugged her shoulders as if she had no idea what I was talking about. I waited a few more seconds. Nothing happened. Meeting over.

Later that afternoon I made up my mind.

———————

Billy Ray had the night off. The others had gone home. I waited a half-hour, to make sure none of them would come back for some reason, then locked the door.

The first thing I did was pick up Christiane's job log. I flipped it open and grabbed a fistful of pages. *I'll fuck that sow up good*, I thought to myself. When I was through with her stuff, I'd start on everything else. When I was finished, there'd be nothing left of this outhouse but shit.

Just as I was about to rip out the first bunch of pages, I hesitated.

What the hell am I doing? Did I really want the police coming to my apartment and accusing me of destroying private property? Or worse, arresting me?

I dropped the log on the floor, unlocked the door, and walked out. I rode the elevator six floors down to the street. Then I stepped into the first bar I saw to celebrate my liberation.

———————

The next morning when she was fixing the kid's breakfast, Gayle ducked in and asked me why I was still in bed. Normally I was already up and at the keyboard.

"Today, I'm not in any hurry at all." Then I thought how lucky it was that she hadn't deep-sixed *her* job, because we were going to need the money.

"You got fired," she laughed.

"Not exactly. Let's say I became *persona non grata*. I won't be reporting to work anymore. At least not at Fetere, Schlussman, Jones, and Bigelow."

"I don't get it."

"I'll explain it to you later. I'm too hungover to talk about it right now."

"What did I tell you, Max?"

"You told me I wasn't cut out for a job. I'll be damned if you weren't right."

67

I jumped into the car and drove down to the Atlantic Highlands to audition for a movie being produced by a "major independent artist." I was up for the part of the brutish father of a high school football player. The sides were pretty straightforward.

"You're not gonna make the team now, you fucking idiot... What the hell's the matter with you?... No kid of mine is gonna act like a sissy on the field..." That was the gist of it.

I gave it all I had, keeping in mind Spencer Tracy's advice to thespians: say your lines like you mean them.

"Awesome," said the director, a wide-eyed kid by the name of Vance Portugal, when I was through reading. He couldn't have been more than twenty-two, twenty-three. What the hell was he doing making a movie? What could he possibly know about anything? According to the syllabus, the "major independent artist" was his best friend. Connections counted, all right, and you couldn't ever forget it.

"You're a great actor, Max."

If that's what Vance Portugal wanted to believe, I wasn't going to try to change his mind. But my experience whispered that he was setting me up to let me down. It usually went something like this: *"You're wonderful, you're fantastic... but unfortunately you don't fit the part."*

Instead, Portugal said, "The part of the father is yours."

"Thanks... What's the pay?"

"Deferred."

There was an old saying in the business: *Deferred means never.*

"I'm convinced you'll get your money, though. The executive producer of *The Happy World Of Kittens* is Kent Jones. You know who he is, don't you?"

Everyone who'd picked up a newspaper or watched TV in the past couple of years knew who Kent Jones was. A couple of years back he'd maxed out his credit cards and shot a movie called *Counter Jumpers*, which traced the lives of a pair of slacker convenience store workers. For some unfathomable reason, it had become one of the most successful indie flicks of all time, praised effusively by the critics and transforming its director overnight into their darling for his salty inventiveness and irreverent wittiness. Curious to see what the fuss was about, I'd rented it and watched. Jones couldn't write and he couldn't direct, he had the mind of an eleven-year-old, and yet all of the Hollywood suits went wild over his comedy, which wasn't in the least funny or clever but won him mouth-watering deals that the vastly more gifted would kill for. As usual, nothing about what happened made sense.

"Yeah, I know who he is."

"Great, isn't he?"

"That's what everyone says. If everyone says it, it must be true."

"Kent promised me that if he ever made it big he would bankroll my script and let me direct my own feature. I taught him everything he knows about the technical side of low-budget film. Now he's keeping his promise to me. That's how *The Happy World Of Kittens* got the green light."

"He sounds like a very loyal guy. That's rare."

"He is. Anyway, we start shooting in mid-August. And by the way, Jameson Leigh is in the film too."

"Cool."

Jameson Leigh was a former skateboard legend in the process of becoming a star on account of his appearances in Kent Jones's movies. What skateboarding had to do with acting, I didn't know, but Jones was apparently the ticket to the big time. This time, I assured myself, I couldn't possibly miss.

"Welcome aboard, Max. Our people will be in touch with

the contract and schedule."

The star of *The Happy World Of Kittens* was Florian Montrose. He was another kid, only nineteen, maybe twenty years old. For the duration of filming he was bunking at Vance Portugal's house on the Jersey Shore. Didn't any of these kids have jobs? Apparently not, since I never heard the word "job" uttered once, even as as joke. During rehearsal breaks Florian and I got to talking.

"How long you been doing this, Max?"

I told him.

"Really? That long?"

"I wouldn't lie to you."

"I don't know what I'm going to do. I just graduated from the American Academy Of Dramatic Arts, and I'm trying to figure out where to go from here..."

"Looks like you're off to a good start."

"Yeah, maybe... What do you think I should do?"

"I'm exactly the wrong person to ask, kid. But chances aren't good that you're going to make it as an actor. It doesn't happen very often."

"That's what I think... Soon as this thing wraps, I guess I'll just go home to California and take it from there."

"There are worse places to figure things out."

A week or so later shooting commenced. Cast and crew were assembled on a suburban side street when Montrose was summoned for a take.

The scene called for him to harangue his buddy with some philosophical twaddle as they walked down the street arm in arm. The dialogue was all about life, and how nothing means anything so there's no point in living. Like so much bad writing, it was pretentious and designed to impress the viewer with the writer/director's brilliance.

I watched Montrose move around. He wasn't bad, but he was trying too hard. In front of the camera you want to be very easy-like. In fact, you want it to look like you're doing nothing at all. I was surprised they hadn't taught Montrose that at his fancy academy.

"Cut!"

Luis, the camera operator, a fat guy with sparse black hair on his face, was beside himself.

"You gonna make it, man, you really gonna make it! You gonna be a fuckin' movie star!"

Montrose shrugged. He tried to look unaffected, but he was sucking it all in like a fish. And Luis kept pouring it on.

"No, man, I mean it -- the camera loves you! The camera *loves* you!"

Now that was probably true. Montrose was a pretty boy, straight out of a *GQ* clothing ad. Someone clenching a boom called that he was a ringer for Henry Fonda. His face was smooth and untouched by life. He looked like he'd never put in a hard day's work anywhere. The girls were going to be all over him, if they weren't already. It was annoying as hell.

"So what do you think I should do," Montrose said to me again when the crew was setting up for another shot. "I know I bugged you about it before, but you're a lot older than me, you know the ropes..."

Of course I knew nothing about anything, but people don't

want to hear that. Why this kid regarded me as a voice of wisdom, I had no idea. Maybe he didn't have a father.

"Just keep doing what you're doing. And when you hit the big time, don't forget the peasants."

———————

The Happy World Of Kittens made it into a couple of film festivals, then went straight to video. It was a huge disappointment since Vance Portugal had all the right connections and before it was finished, his movie was assumed to be a legitimate theatrical release...

Maybe the problem was *me*. Even though my part wasn't big enough to matter, it was beginning to seem like whatever I was even remotely connected with was cursed.

———————

Jameson Leigh went on to become the star of his own TV series. Florian Montrose returned to Santa Barbara, got discovered, and hasn't stopped working in movies and TV since. Both shagged the beautiful women and snagged the fat paychecks, and never had to audition for anything. Some guys have all the luck...

After a while I sent a message to Vance Portugal and inquired whether his film had gone into the green and my deferred money was on its way.

No answer.
I waited a few years and tried again. Same result.

68

"Hey Max, this is Kent Jones."

It must have been a year or so after the release of *The Happy World Of Kittens*. In the meantime, I'd been cast in another Crazy Vision film, *Huge Buffalo Gas*, in which I played a series of perverted fathers of young children, a film never released for some murky reason that was never made clear. Kent Jones had recently scored another hit with his follow-up to *Counter Jumpers*, which was called *Hanging Around The Shopping Center*. At the age of twenty-seven, he was rich, famous, and fat, as well as one of the most coveted properties in all of filmdom. Now, unless someone had decided to give my leg a good pull, he was right here on the line.

"Sure, man, sure. Look, I'm a little busy at the moment, okay?"

"No, seriously, it's me, Max. I got your number from Vance Portugal. I really dug what you did in the films I produced."

"Thanks." Maybe it was Kent Jones after all.

"So listen...I just signed a deal to direct a series of soda pop commercials. You're a perfect fit for them, Max."

Visions of money -- the real thing, as in thousands, maybe even tens of thousands -- whipped through my brain. Maybe

I'd make enough that I wouldn't have to work a suck job for a year or two.

"I submitted your name to the casting agency. They'll be calling you."

"Thanks again, man..."

"Don't mention it, Max. It's my pleasure."

Good ol' Kent Jones. Now that was one cool dude. And *generous*! Not too many like him in this business. Never mind that he was short on the talent end. What did talent matter, anyway?

———————

"You wouldn't believe the phone call I got today." I told Gayle all about it.

"That's nice, Max."

It had reached the point where my wife never showed the least bit of excitement over my prospects anymore. There'd been too many fiascos, too many humiliations, far too many defeats.

Nevertheless, the next day I got a call from the Donna Vanella Agency and was told to report to their studio on Broadway on Monday afternoon at three. I was reading for a Kent Jones commercial.

"Sides?"

"You'll get them when you arrive. We don't want you getting locked into a specific interpretation."

Interpretation? This was going to be some soda pop

commercial, all right. I preferred not memorizing anything beforehand anyway, because it gave me an even chance against my competition.

There was nothing to the scene: a guy changes a light bulb in a kitchen fixture while telling his son how great Coca-Cola is. I made sure to inject some life into the proceedings, and afterwards I felt pretty good about what I did.

"We'll be in touch," mumbled the casting assistant when I was on my way out.

I was a little disappointed. Since the famous director himself was the one who had me sent in, I'd nursed a foolish hope that I might be handed the booking on the spot. But they couldn't really do that, could they?

———————

I waited. And waited. And waited...

Two weeks passed, and no call from the agency. No call from Kent Jones either. Maybe they hadn't decided yet? Maybe they needed more time? Sometimes it happened, and decisions were postponed. But if Kent Jones wanted me, if he was the one in charge, what was the hold-up?

I couldn't sit around waiting any longer. I put a call into Crazy Vision headquarters.

"This is Max Zajack calling for Kent Jones..."

"Who?"

"Kent had me in to read for a soft drink commercial a few weeks ago, but I never heard anything. Any idea where that situation stands?"

"Let me see what I can find out," said the girl on the other end. I could hear her jaws working a wad of chewing gum as she thought it over. She laid the phone down. In the background, muffled voices.

When she picked up the phone again, her voice was like a sliver of ice.

"What I've been told is that the executives at Coca-Cola decided to go in a different direction. They didn't think you were exactly what they were looking for. Sorry."

The suits. I'd forgotten all about the suits. And no matter how hot Kent Jones was, he could never trump them.

The suits were the ones laying out money for the commercials. Kent Jones was just their chubby little office gofer.

"Is Kent there?"

Pause. "Uh -- no. He's not available at the moment."

So -- now he was ducking me. Could I blame him?

Those bastard mother-fuckers. I'd never swallow another ounce of Coke again for as long as I lived.

I sat there in the dark, chewing over how the hell another sure thing had fallen through...

69

Hating Olivia -- that's what I was calling the new novel -- was in circulation, but so far, nothing but rejections. An indie

California publisher offered to bring it out, but I'd have to foot the entire printing bill, which came to around seventy-five hundred dollars. No thanks, I said, I'll wait. But what was I waiting for?

I'd never completely forgotten the play about Henry Miller, my old idol. In fact, I'd finally produced a draft I was satisfied with, a three-way Strindbergian death-struggle involving Henry, his wife and her lover. For the most part, *Draco And The Ecliptic* -- I'd named it after one of Miller's never-written books -- worked, it had real drama. But like all plays, it would have to go through "the process" of readings, revisions, staged readings, more revisions, and so on. As usual, nothing would be easy.

Jane Littburg was its first director. She'd been a friend of the producer of one of my shorter plays at a small theater a year or so earlier.

"Don't worry about casting. I'll take care of it," she assured me at our first meeting. She claimed to know every actor in town.

Draco's first reading took place at the director's nineteenth-floor apartment in a tower that stood in the shadow of the World Trade Center -- and only a few blocks from where Miller had worked as personnel manager for Western Union seventy years earlier, just before the events of my play. This, I thought, had to be a good omen.

Jane made the introductions.

"This is Max Zajack, our playwright."

The cast members nodded in my direction.

"And this is Dick Vincent."

I stared at the fellow cast as Henry. He was all wrong in physical type. Brutishly handsome in a Columbo-Peter Falk way, Dick Vincent was fifty where Miller was supposed to be thirty. There was no trace of the intellectual in him whatsoever. What the hell had Jane been thinking?

"Great play," he said to me before we got started.

"We'll see, man, we'll see."

On the other hand, the women, whatever their names were, were lookers –- they were the right fit for the characters of June and Jean. The supporting characters were fine too.

"Everyone's had a chance to look at the script. Shall we get started?" said Sarah.

The second he opened his mouth, it was obvious that Dick Vincent didn't have the "chops" to handle the character I'd written. I was after someone who was both bookish and streetwise -- a tough combination, for sure -- and I'd tailored the dialogue to that end.

Miller had a tendency to use fifty-cent words -- like "empyrean" and "dithyrambic" -- in everyday conversation, and Dick bumbled and stumbled over every one. Apparently it had never occurred to him to consult a dictionary -- if he knew how. Worse, he failed to infuse the character with so much as an ounce of believable life. With all of the spectacular New York actors running around, how had I gotten stuck with such a lump?

Watching Dick Vincent mangle my play was excruciating. When it was over two and a half hours later, I couldn't tell whether the lead character I'd written worked or not. On the other hand, what I'd done with the women and supporting characters was good -- very good. That was something, at least. All was not lost.

The next day Jane phoned.

"What did you think, Max?"

"Not half bad," I said. "But the guy playing Henry was ghastly."

"Dick Vincent is actually a fine actor. I don't know what happened last night. I just wanted you to hear your words, Max."

"The problem is that I *couldn't* hear my words. Vincent swallowed them all."

"Next time around I'll get someone else."

70

In the meantime I tore into the script. I rewrote. I revised. I cut. Wading in with a machete is often the solution to many problems.

Reading number two, which was open to the public, went down in a rehearsal space over a McDonald's on Seventh Avenue. Jane assured me that this time around things would be better. Dick Vincent was replaced as Henry, but the new lead, Lyle Breckman, was even worse. For some reason he was in tears from curtain up. He overacted, he emoted, he gnashed his teeth, all hallmarks of the amateur hambone.

The results were mortifying. As the small audience was

filing out, Jane slipped a few pieces of paper in front of me.

"Sign this when you get a chance, Max."

I glanced at it. It was some kind of agreement. As far as theatrical contracts went, it seemed quite standard -- not that I was any expert on theater contracts. Like an idiot -- and many idiots before me -- I thought I understood it, signed it, and handed it back to the director. A few days later when I deciphered the fine print, I realized that I'd been bamboozled into agreeing to allow Jane Littburg to direct my play *in perpetuity* -- in other words, *anytime* and *anywhere* in the world it was staged. And that she was the *only* one with the privilege.

Witnessing the pair of lousy "Henry Millers" massacre my offspring had robbed me of the capacity to think straight. Now I was going to have to hire a lawyer -- a lawyer I could hardly afford -- to extricate myself from the suffocating agreement.

Draco And The Ecliptic was beginning to turn into just another nightmare.

———

I didn't tell Jane Littburg she was fired. I didn't tell her anything. I just never phoned her again, and when she called me, I didn't return the call.

But whenever she caught wind of a new reading of my play, she sent me a certified letter detailing her eternal willingness -- *and legal right* -- to direct it. Whatever happened now, I was going to have to look over my shoulder forever...

Fuck it, I decided. If she sued, she sued. I couldn't let it stop me from trying to find someone to produce the play. In the meantime, a movie called *Henry And June* hit the big screen, and after all the years of work on *Draco And The Ecliptic*, the Hollywood players had stolen my thunder. Now what? An over-saturation of the market with the names of Henry and June Miller might well be the death knell for my project, which couldn't ever compete on such a grand scale.

Of course I was curious, so I laid my money down and went to see it. Despite the tagline "A True Adventure More Erotic Than Any Fantasy," the movie was a clunker. *The Diary Of Anaïs Nin*, internal and navel-gazing as it was, did not make one automatically think "moving picture." That was just one problem. Another was that the onscreen chatter was cringeworthy. Clichés about "obscenity" and the "inner self" abounded. The acting was okay, but you always expected that.

The so-so quality of the film was a double-edged sword. If a major biopic about Miller and June could be so dull, who'd want to see anything else about the two of them?

My play was in even more trouble.

71

If I felt defeated before, I was feeling positively star-crossed now. And I was right back at square one, where I always seemed to be.

Still, I hadn't completely given up hope that *Draco And The Ecliptic* was going to be brought to life someday. I was just at a loss for how to make it happen.

My luck was about to take a turn. Months earlier I'd given the script to an actress I'd befriended while doing a B film, then forgotten all about it. A few weeks after the film wrapped, the phone rang.

"Max! It's Sharon Mitchelson. I hope you don't mind, but I showed your script to a friend. He wants to play Henry Miller. As a matter of fact, he'd be perfect in the part -- he looks just like him!"

Another one. I thought of Jon Denis. "Can he act?"

"Oh, sure, sure, he's good... *he also happens to be the brother of a very high-up executive at Starmaker Films.*"

Starmaker Films. I didn't have to think twice about who they were: *Noir Dreams. The British Invalid. On The Hunt For Genius.* None of them were very good, but as usual the public had been bamboozled, and they'd raked in hundreds of millions of dollars in profit.

"Would you object if he showed his sister your play?"

"Please -- be my guest," I heard myself say, like any well-seasoned whore.

"How about if he played the role of Henry," she said next.
"No problem."
"I hope there's a role for me in your play, Max."
"I'm sure there is, Sharon. You just name it."

"Max? This is Sandy Bevas."

It was the very next evening.

"I'm the executive vice-president in charge of legal affairs for Starmaker Films. My brother Dolph and I think your play about Henry Miller is great."

Sweet words to the ear, indeed. I slurped every one in like the starving beast I was. Years of deprivation will transform a man into a giant leech.

"Why, thank you," I answered modestly.

"We'd like to meet with you as soon as possible to talk about an option deal -- that is, if you're interested."

"I believe I could be."

———————

Thursday. Six PM. The White Horse Tavern.

Sandy Bevas had long, curly blond hair and a trim figure. For a film company executive, she was strikingly attractive. Her brother, Dolph, looked like a younger version of Jon Denis, the actor who'd planted the seed for the Miller play in my head in the first place. His features were a little too sharp, too Semitic, to play the gentile Henry Miller, but from beyond the lights, maybe nobody would notice.

"I loved your play," Sandy began.

We were off to a wonderful start, all right.

"And your writing," nodded her brother.

We hadn't even downed our first beers before we were talking directors, venues, *movie options*.

Big time, Max, big time, the voice inside me whispered. I'd never been this close.

"There's only one problem," I confided to Sandy. By this time I'd already gotten the firm idea, since she was doing all the talking, that she was the brains of the operation.

"What's that?"

"There's this director who keeps telling me that she has the legal right to direct the play anyplace, anytime. My stupidity, but I thought I should let you know up front."

She waved her slim, elegant fingers. "Don't give it a second thought, Max. Brushing off nuisances is what I do all day long at Starmaker. Remember, I report directly to Abner Bierstein. You know who he is, don't you?"

Of course I knew who he was. Abner Bierstein was one of the most powerful producers in the film industry. He'd had the foresight to found Starmaker Films. He was feared and admired and envied, and would do anything to achieve his ends.

It was like a dream. All my troubles with *Draco And The Ecliptic* had just vanished into the air like a wisp of smoke.

Sandy just happened to have an option agreement with her. She laid the paper on the ancient, rancid bar.

"Take your time reading it."

It was straightforward and simple. In essence, Sandy had a year to do something with my play. After that, I'd get the rights back if the option wasn't renewed.

"Any money involved?" I asked, a benign smile on my face.

"Sure," she said.

She opened her briefcase and pulled out a checkbook.

Then she scribbled something, tore out a leaf, and handed it to me.

It was a good number. Not great, but good. And as usual, I needed it.

We went on spinning plans. By the time I walked out of the White Horse that night, my head was in a puffy cloud. *Draco And the Ecliptic* was actually going to get produced, and produced well, by real players in the business. Now, finally, everything made sense. There'd been a cosmic reason for all the obstacles in my path until this moment. And that was because my play was going to break big. How could it not? A wheel from the hottest film company in the entire world was behind it. What could go wrong?

Power wins, baby.

I wasn't on the losing side anymore -- I'd crossed over the line. Now I was one of the winners.

72

It was about to get even better. The very first reading of *Draco And The Ecliptic* with the new team would happen in front of none other than Bert Olds, a Hollywood director who made *Entangled*, one of only a handful of powerful films I'd caught over the past decade, and one of the only American movies worth its weight in a long, long time. Bert had a bona fide track record: he'd also directed critical hits like *Two-Trick*

Donkey and *Frederic And Steven*. Even better, he was an old personal friend of Sandy and Dolph. Bert Olds was major connected everywhere, in both New York and L.A. If he got interested in my play, really interested, we might even skip the theater leg altogether and jump straight to the sound stages in La-La Land, with the likes of John Malkovich and Madonna reading for leading roles...

I could hardly believe it -- the Bevases had delivered a winner the first time out.

A few days later we gathered in a Union Square rehearsal space. Within seconds, from the first words of Henry's "farewell to America" monologue, I knew I was in trouble: I had another loser leading man on my hands. Dolph Bevas was absolutely devoid of charisma. This boy couldn't sell dog shit to a tree. His acting "talent" consisted of nothing more than reciting my lines in a tedious monotone. He was quickly overwhelmed and outshined by the supporting players, including his friend, Sharon Mitchelson.

Christ fucking Almighty. How could it happen again? Maybe Dolph's performance would improve as we went along? That had to be his trick -- he was one of those artists who needed time to explore and immerse himself in a character. He couldn't get much worse.

When the reading was over, all eyes fastened on Bert Olds.

"You got something good on your hands," he stated unenthusiastically. He checked his watch.

And?

"Keep doing what you're doing."

And that was it -- Bert Olds was a lost cause. He wasn't

going any further on the ride.

Was it my play -- or his actor friend -- he didn't like?

I was never going to know. I'd struck a deal with the devil. If I wanted to keep the Starmaker executive on the line -- and Sandy Bevas was the promise of a wide audience and probably my best shot at getting Draco into a professional theater -- I was going to have to allow her brother to go on playing my lead character.

On the subway afterwards I was assailed by an old, familiar, ominous feeling...

73

Around that time everybody was talking about *Scythe Edge*, which had made Willie Joe Roseton a big Hollywood star. *Scythe Edge* was yet another Starmaker film. It seemed like they couldn't miss. One evening, sitting in her office high above the streets of Tribeca and talking about our next move with *Draco And The Ecliptic*, Sandy said, "You know, Max, one day soon everyone might know your name too."

And I thought: *Not if I'm stuck with a stiff for Henry Miller.*

"Dolph will get better and better the more he sinks his teeth into the part," she assured me. It was like she was reading my mind. "He's really committed to being an actor. He's going to put everything else aside and do nothing but work to turn himself into the reincarnation of Henry Miller."

What else did he have to do, was my next thought. As a so-
called thespian, wasn't that his job? Dolph had no wife, no
kids, no steady job. I'd begun to think that he was living off
his smart, beautiful, successful sister.

A disturbing thought occurred to me. Maybe Dolph Bevas
was a little... *backwards*. I still hadn't seen his résumé. I never
heard him talk about what he'd accomplished as an actor,
or anything else for that matter. All I knew was that he liked
to play tennis, and swim, and hang around the chic bars of
Manhattan. In other words, he was a *boulevardier*. Maybe his
sister felt guilty that she'd made it in life and her brother was
nothing. Maybe she was tossing him a bone in the form of my
play. Maybe she didn't give a damn at all about my work, and
optioning *Draco And The Ecliptic* was all about giving her loser
sibling something to do with all his free time...

———

Nevertheless, things kept moving forward, forward,
forward. Sandy was about to invite a new heavy-duty partner
on board to help with the financing of *Draco And The Ecliptic*.
Ted Bondy was the prime force behind such commercial fare
as *The Dumped Wives Sorority* and critical successes like *Melvin's
Chamber*. This guy apparently knew what he was doing, he was
flush with jack, and after reading it he was interested in my play
too, enough to open up one of his sound studios in midtown
Manhattan for our next reading, which would be attended by
him and other industry "insiders."

"Don't be discouraged, Max," Sandy told me more than once. "This is the business. We're just getting started..."

And so we got ready for round two. A new cast was assembled. Several of the actors in the earlier readings were history, chopped away by Sandy like weeds out of a flowerbed. It made me feel a trifle guilty, especially when she dumped Sharon Mitchelson, who brought me together with the Bevases in the first place. But what could I say or do?

Sandy was in charge now. She was running the show. I was just the writer, and who gave a fuck what the writer thought or wanted?

But the second time around, Dolph's performance was just as bad, if not worse. He did futile battle with my language and was about as animated in his performance as a dead goose. I sat in the dark, tearing my hair out. His sister had sworn to me that her mope of a brother was going to *work* on the fucking part. *And maybe he had.* Maybe he just didn't have what it took, which was exactly what I was beginning to suspect...

"The guy fucking sucks," I bitched to Gayle when I got home that night.

"I'm sorry, Max. Didn't you check his credits before you agreed to let him play Henry Miller?"

"No -- but I should have. But if you'd heard the words 'Starmaker Films', what would you have done? Would you have insisted, 'Let me audition your brother Dolph first'?"

For once, she didn't have an answer.

"This was my shot. This was my big shot, baby."

"It's not like it's over already, Max."

She was right. It wasn't over yet.

74

I waited for word about what was going to happen next. In the meantime I revisited Hating Olivia, cutting away more and more fat until the prose was as sharp as a razor. Then I sent it out again, but again nothing happened. There was no interest in the novel, and there wasn't any interest in my new stories, either. Maybe I'd end up a playwright after all. There were worse things. It's always better to be something instead of nothing...

———————

Now both Sandy and Ted Bondy were making decisions about my play. But we were still without a director. Sandy launched a search among her show business contacts for someone to help develop the project. She sent out feelers to Broadway legends, Off-Broadway phenoms, movie stars turned theater directors -- a list of names I could never get near on my own. Then suddenly, without warning, her producing partner disappeared.

"What the hell happened?"

Sandy wasn't exactly sure. Ted Bondy was in the process of getting separated from his wife. His mother had been diagnosed with terminal cancer. He liked *Draco And The Ecliptic*, but he couldn't possibly stay on as a partner, given all his personal crises.

"I'm a bit baffled myself, though," Sandy admitted. "I thought he was in for the long haul."

Since I hadn't had a single decent lead actor, I nursed fresh doubts about what I actually had in *Draco*. Maybe, after watching Dolph Bevas in action, Teddy had either seen enough of him or he couldn't decide on the quality of the play itself. I could only hope that once a production was mounted -- hopefully before -- the powers that be would come to their senses and recognize that he couldn't cut it as Henry Miller and would move him out of the role.

Sandy remained undeterred. Nothing seemed to daunt her... A couple of weeks later, she came up with a new combination director/producing partner. Brooke Samson was the founder and former artistic director of a renowned play development unit on Theater Row. Stage and movie stars had been her repertory regulars. Now she was running the creative arm of the Cherry Lane Theater (where Henry Miller himself had seen shows in his youth) and she too claimed to be infatuated with my period piece.

Well, there it was -- a fresh vote of confidence. Just what I needed.

75

There were more readings of *Draco And The Ecliptic* but the quality didn't improve. The weak link was always Dolph.

Brooke and I began meeting privately, behind the closed door of her office at the Cherry Lane.

"Maybe, if we can somehow move Dolph to a supporting role where he won't be able to do major damage to the play ... like maybe Doctor Cohen? He could certainly pass for Doctor Cohen..."

Brooke was doing the talking, but the idea had occurred to me too. It seemed strange to be plotting without Sandy. I felt a little sleazy about it.

"A very good idea. We'll say we want to try out different actors in different roles, shuffle things around a bit. How can Sandy argue with that?"

Early the next afternoon the phone rang. I was walking around the apartment with a cup of coffee, hoping it wasn't my supervisor wanting me to report to work earlier tomorrow.

"Hi, Max..." It was Sandy. "I know you won't want to hear this, but we've decided not to renew the option on *Draco*."

"You're right, I don't want to hear it. In fact, it's the last thing I want to hear."

"It hasn't worked out, Max. We gave it a good shot and we couldn't make a go of it."

Suddenly Sandy sounded very cool, almost uninterested, like we'd never even known each other. Overnight all of her fight and enthusiasm had vanished.

She had nothing else to say. She couldn't come right out and admit that she'd seen the writing on the wall, could she, that she'd heard the whispers after every reading that her brother sucked as Henry Miller. In the end, she couldn't stand by and watch him be forced out of the cast. Blood is always thicker than water. Dropping the option on the property was the easy way out.

But I was just guessing. Maybe after hearing it so many times, Sandy arrived at the conclusion that my play was shit.

Now here we were. It had been a whole year. An entire year of meetings, rehearsals, readings, critique sessions and revisions, and it had all come to nothing.

"I have no doubt you'll find someone to produce your play, Max."

That's what they all say.

"But stay in touch, okay?"

"Sure. Sure I will, Sandy..."

That was to be our last conversation. After Ms. Starmaker had blown all that sweet smoke up my ass, it was finished, just like that. Kaput. Over. *Dead*. I was free to do whatever I wanted with my goddamned play.

I hung up and stood there, shell-shocked. When it sank in all the way, I'd be devastated. I'd had one of the world's premier film companies on the line and it had somehow wriggled off the hook. How could I replace it? I couldn't. It was impossible.

I realized I was holding an empty coffee cup. I turned, went into the kitchen and dropped it into the sink on top of the other dishes. I didn't know what else to do with myself, so I stood there staring out the window at the gray river below.

I no longer had to walk around wondering whether *Draco And The Ecliptic* was star-crossed. Now it was a fact.

76

Any other clinically sane person would have run up the white flag. Not me. I wasn't a quitter. I was a fighter. Max Zajack was made of something else -- rage, madness, guts, something you couldn't put into words. He was also one dumb fuck.

"Why don't you give it a rest for a while, Max?"

Gayle seemed to never tire of trying to talk sense into me.

"That's not the solution to everything. The time to forge on is when all seems hopeless."

"What about your Zen philosophy? Going with the flow and all that?"

"It's nice on paper, but not in reality. This is New York. Zen doesn't work here."

"All right, have it your way."

I took the play and dropped it off at the Rattlesnake Theater on Waverly Place. Later that week I got a call that it had been accepted into their development program. This was a very pleasant surprise after the collapse of the Starmaker deal. Did I have a director in mind?

Well, that could be something of a problem. I thought at once of Brooke Samson, but why would she want anything to do with me now that Sandy Bevas and Starmaker were out of the picture and I was no longer "connected?"

But I called her anyway, since I had no one else to call.

"The Rattlesnake is a great little theater," said Brooke. She sounded surprised that *Draco* was still breathing. "The play will be actually get mounted in a near-full production, complete with sets and costumes. It's a development workshop production, but you can't do better than the Rattlesnake, Max. And the heavy hitters will be in to see it for sure. You might even pick up a review in the *Times*."

It was a real chance for redemption, something to take the sting out of the Starmax debacle.

"I'll take care of everything, Max. Don't you worry about a thing."

I knew from experience that Brooke preferred doing the nuts and bolts activities, like casting and rehearsals, on her own and out of the writer's presence. I had no problem leaving her to her own devices.

It was a huge weight off my shoulders. The name of the play and its author -- Max Zajack -- went up on the theater's marquis. After all the anguish and woe, Henry and his ladies were finally going to stride the boards.

"Excited, Max?"

Gayle and I were lying in bed. For a change, the kid was sleeping. The next day *Draco* was scheduled to move into the Rattlesnake for dress rehearsals.

"I'm cool. Course, I'll be more excited when I see what Brooke Samson's done with it."

I got up and dressed. That day I didn't have to be at some company or other, proofreading. I wandered around the apartment, made coffee, took the elevator down to the street and grabbed a newspaper.

When I got back upstairs, the phone was ringing. It was Adrian Closter, head honcho at the Rattlesnake Theater. He was frantic.

"What's going on with your director? I've got a slew of calls into her but haven't heard a thing back!"

"What?"

"Yeah! So what's the deal?"

"Brooke Samson told me she was taking care of everything," I responded lamely.

"Is this how she normally operates? In secret?"

"Supposedly she can be relied on. At least as far as I know."

"Supposedly? Well, let me know the minute you hear from her. I'm getting very nervous here! And that's not supposedly!"

I hung up and immediately dialed Brooke. I got the same result that Closter got -- an answering machine. I hung up and rang again. And again. Brooke Samson was nowhere to be found. There was a new bad feeling in my gut.

I phoned every fifteen minutes. When after a half dozen times I got no answer, I ran over to the Cherry Lane Theater, but the doors were shut up tight.

I had no clue where Brooke Samson lived. What the fuck was I supposed to to? My hands were tied. I went back across the river. The phone was ringing and wouldn't stop.

"I CAN'T AFFORD TO HAVE THIS THEATER SITTING DARK FOR A WHOLE WEEK, ZAJACK! I COULD HAVE HAD ANOTHER PRODUCTION IN HERE! THIS IS FUCKING BULLSHIT!"

Adrian Closter was beside himself with fury. When he got tired of ranting and raving, he slammed the phone down.

Draco And The Ecliptic's opening night came and went. According to Closter, this fuck-up was going to cost him his position as producing director of the Rattlesnake's development program.

I was dazed. I was embarrassed. Then I was so enraged I could hardly see straight. Brooke Samson never returned any of my calls. It was like she'd disappeared from the face of the earth. I didn't even know if the bitch was alive.

But what did it matter now? It was too late for everything. *Draco And The Ecliptic* had been pronounced dead, and was officially in the grave.

77

For her birthday, I took Gayle out to a Brazilian bistro on Bedford Street. Months had passed since *Draco And The Ecliptic* had bitten the dust, and though I still sometimes boiled over what had happened to my ill-fated baby, it no longer came back and plagued me all night long.

The waitress had left a shrimp starter on the table. We'd just started in on a second glass of Portuguese red. I slipped my hands between Gayle's legs.

"Happy birthday, baby."

"Thanks, Max! It's nice to be out with you tonight! We need a good time for a change!"

I happened to be facing the narrow street through the long window when suddenly there she was: Brooke Samson, my tormentor, a scruffy little mutt tugging the end of her leash, looking for the world like she'd never done anything shady in her entire life.

I couldn't believe my eyes. I couldn't believe her gall, appearing on the street. I jumped up from the table, rattling the cutlery and sloshing the booze out of the glasses.

"What is it, Max?"

"I'M GONNA GO OUT THERE AND KILL HER! I'M GONNA BREAK HER FUCKING NECK, THEN MURDER HER DOG WHEN I'M FINISHED!"

Gayle jumped up and grabbed me. "Max -- sit down! What's wrong with you?"

"WHAT'S WRONG WITH ME? SHE'S THE ONE WHO FUCKED ME OVER! HER -- *BROOKE SAMSON!*"

"Max! Please! Calm down! Get a hold of yourself!"

"I've been waiting for months to get into that whore's face!"

"I'm begging you again -- please! It's my birthday!"

"But this is my chance! I may never get another one!"

"Think about me for a change, Max! Just this once!"

The waitress had come running out from the kitchen, alarm on her face.

"Is something wrong?"

I shook my head. "No. Everything's fine..."

Brooke Samson passed out of sight, and I dropped back into my chair. Gayle took a long swig of her wine. "My God, Max! Chill out! You didn't really want to make a fool of yourself, did you?"

"Brooke Samson already accomplished that for me. Once you've been made a fool of, what's one more time?"

———————

A few years later Brooke Samson would be convicted of bilking a famous show-business father and son team, as well as a prominent theater company, out of hundreds of thousands of dollars. She would be sentenced to five years probation, ordered to repay what she stole, and banned for life from working in the professional theater world.

It was small consolation to me. Everything I'd done to wrestle *Draco And The Ecliptic* onto the stage had ended in disaster. All the wind had finally been sucked out of my sails. And a sailor in a hurricane can only survive for so long.

78

"There goes Max Zajack. He's a great writer, but he's a fucking prick, too."

I was making my way along Hudson Street on a beautiful summer evening when those words stopped me dead in my tracks, especially the part about being a great writer.

I hadn't seen Dick Vincent in months, ever since he'd butchered the role of Henry Miller in the very first reading of *Draco And The Ecliptic* and established a pattern. He was sitting in front of a schooner of golden brew at an outdoor cafe.

"Hey, man, what happened to that play of yours?"

"You don't want to know, believe me."

"That's too bad... Come on and sit down here and drink with me."

I've always been cursed with an inability to waste time, but I had nothing better to do. I ordered a beer.

Dick started bending my ear about his life. He was an out-of-work actor back from fifteen years in L.A., where instead of making it big in the movies or TV he'd ended up driving a hack or collecting unemployment. He went on and on about how he hated Hollywood, how he'd been screwed over time and again for parts, and how he got sick and tired of sitting on the beach in the sunshine every goddamned day.

In other words, we were both paddling the same boat.

After that evening Dick and I spent lots of time hanging out together. He was the kind of guy who always told you how great you were. It was incredibly seductive and impossible not to fall for. Even if you didn't believe him, you needed to hear it when the rest of the world kept telling you that you were a piece of shit.

Before I knew it, Dick Vincent had me going to parties all over town.

"Look, Max, this is how it works -- you've got to *schmooze*. You might have more talent than anyone including Da Vinci, but nobody knows who you are. If you don't go out there and rub shoulders and kiss ass you'll never get anywhere..."

Was he right? Probably.

"But I'm not into it, man. All that shit isn't me. I don't give a fuck."

"Then you shouldn't be in this business!"

Right again. But out of curiosity and boredom I went along for the ride. Dick knew scads of people and was plugged into all of the gossip, who was screwing who, who was into snorting coke, who liked to suck cock, etc.

We were sitting in a Soho loft one night watching the beautiful people come and go when he elbowed me in the ribs.

"See Eileen Larkin over there?"

It was her, all right. She looked just like she did in the movies.

"That's one kinky bitch, Max."

"How's that?"

"She likes to stick her tongue into dudes' assholes."

"No shit."

"That's why her husband divorced her. He caught on that

252

she was cheating on him all over town..."

"And there's Rachel Gilnick."

"Wasn't she in -- "

"Yeah. Remember she screwed the ears off Don Hoit in that one movie?"

"Right! Isn't she like a hundred years old?"

"A hundred and one. Her thing is gay muscle-heads. She always has two of them hanging off her arms. She offers to suck them off, but they won't let her."

"Shouldn't she be at home in a rocking chair?"

"Are you kidding? That old tart would crawl to the opening of a phone booth if there was a chance she'd be noticed."

That's what we were there for, too. We all wanted to be noticed. We sat around trying to figure out if we recognized one another, or if someone on hand could do something for us. It's called networking, but it just seemed very sad to me, and I was very sad being there.

At one of these shindigs, Dick tried to hook me up with Maureen Mayer, the powerful ICM agent who handled all the hot playwrights, TV writers and novelists in town. According to Dick, she had a thing for underage boys. She was outside smoking a cigarette when he collared her.

"Maureen, this is Max Zajack. He's a really good writer. He's somebody you should know..."

She took one look at me and turned up her nose, as if she'd caught a whiff of excrement. Then she ran back inside to do another line of coke.

"It doesn't always work, Max. But that's okay, there's

always somebody else to meet."

Three years later Maureen Mayer was dead of an overdose...

79

It was rather pathetic: Dick Vincent and I had somehow gotten inducted into the army of losers wandering the vast, indifferent metropolis, lost souls on the margins who would more than likely never amount to a pile of donkey shit, grown men frittering away their time on pipedreams. Dick had already turned fifty, and I was just about there. Worse, we were getting even *older*. Whenever I thought about it for too long, I felt more than a little embarrassed...

In the fine weather we'd sit in the little park on Sixth Avenue and Bleecker Street and try to figure out how to pull ourselves out of our quagmires. Dick had a wife he no longer cared about, and like me, a young kid.

"You know, Max, you should let me run around town with your material," he suggested one afternoon after we'd polished off our pepperoni pizza slices. A greasy wad of cheese had dropped onto my shirt, leaving a spot. I dabbed at it with a napkin, but instead of disappearing, it spread.

"Be my guest."

"Seriously, you're a damned good writer."

"Maybe. But if that's the case, why can't I ever sell anything?"

"What do those bastards know?"

And so we started laying down plans. More accurately, Dick regaled me with what he was going to do for me. I'd learned a long time ago that actors will tell you pretty much anything in order to snag a part. But hell, if he wanted to hustle my work, I wasn't about to stop him. It was like having my own personal agent.

That's how he connected me with Mike Dulle. They met drinking down at the old Shark Bar on Spring Street. Dulle was a location manager and aspiring director who'd graduated from the film studies unit at NYU, where all the hot young prodigies came from. He had big plans for himself, but his problem was that he couldn't write. For some time he'd been on the lookout for an original screenplay to shoot, but whatever he saw hadn't knocked him out. Dick suggested me. Max Zajack had good scripts.

Our first meeting took place at Dulle's office on lower Fifth Avenue. I brought three screenplays for him to look at. Then we went out and talked over lunch. He picked up the tab. Whenever someone pays the bill, I'm impressed.

A week later he called.

"I want to shoot your script."

"Which one?"

"*Something Under The Surface.*"

It was the last project I thought he'd want to tackle, since it was the most complicated and ambitious of the scripts I'd given him, set as it was both in Manhattan and on a wild, desolate river in an unnamed northern forest. But Dulle liked the story, which was about an uptight, overachieving Wall

Street executive who decides to run off for a quick holiday with one of her underlings, a mysterious guy who intrigues her. I'd hatched the plot after observing the high-powered but frustrated women in all the offices I'd passed through.

So... things were looking up again. But of course I'd believe there was actually going to be a movie when I saw the finished product, complete with credits.

I held the phone to my ear and listened. The would-be director launched into a convoluted explanation of how he was going to make the movie. He'd use underwater cameras and build special contraptions to secure them and he'd hire a quality actress for the lead. Big names -- Coppola, Spielberg, Scorsese -- flew around like guided missiles. When he was through making *Something Under The Surface*, Mike Dulle would be mentioned in the same breath as those figures. It would be smashing.

These fucking film guys, I thought -- even the ones who haven't accomplished anything -- all they ever want is to hear themselves yap. Nothing about the writer, nothing about the story itself, nothing about what I'd tried to inject into the script -- it was all him, him, him.

"Before I agree to anything," I said, "we have to talk about the option."

This was, as always, the tricky part. Whenever I mentioned the green stuff, I came down with the jitters. It was the result of a long history of rejection. It came from losing. It came from being devoid of confidence. How could you have any confidence when you were always beaten down? Goddamn it! I hated myself when I groveled and didn't make demands like all the other no-talents.

Then I reminded myself that Mike Dulle was nobody too. All he had was some money, right? So what was there to be afraid of?

"Negotiate with me, Zajack. That's what producers and writers do -- they negotiate."

The last thing I wanted was to negotiate with *anyone*. I wasn't a businessman, I was supposed to be an artist. Dick Vincent was always reminding me that to make it as a writer I had to be tough, and when it came to dollars and cents I wasn't tough at all. But there was another side to the story that he didn't get at all. You had to be tough as nails to get up day after day and face a blank sheet of paper, especially when the world couldn't care less and everybody was telling you no. When it came to that, I was Hercules.

My fear at this moment was that I'd make an outrageous demand and price myself straight out of the deal.

"You can think about it if you want," said Dulle.

"I think it would be better if we settled it right now." I knew how much I'd be okay with, so I'd go higher in the event he balked. It was a shot in the dark, but what the hell.

"Twenty-five hundred."

Silence on the other end. *Well, that's that*, I thought.

"I can do two thousand."

I heard the kid crying in the bedroom. Two grand would mean that for a couple of weeks I wouldn't have to break my ass at a job. It would also be the biggest payday I'd ever scored for my original work. There wasn't much to think over.

"It's a deal."

"All right, Zajack. We're in business."

Dulle wasn't finished jabbering. He had a budget of around forty grand. I'd get two grand up front, another installment when principal photography wrapped, then another payment when the film was purchased for distribution.

I was immediately perplexed -- troubled, even. Forty grand was nothing, a spit in a bucket. When it comes to making films, an anemic sum like that could disappear in *one afternoon*. *Something Under The Surface* would take at least four, five times that much to complete, and that was on the cheap.

I decided not to say anything. *Take the money and run* was always the best approach. Dulle swore that he had a solid plan, and it was all written down. When he produced his rough cut, investors would flock to him and the finishing funds would magically appear.

But I was taking nothing for granted. Until the upfront money was in my bank account, I wouldn't even believe anything was going to happen.

80

The director/producer showed up at my apartment the next evening and handed me a check. When he walked off, I waved the oblong slip of green paper at Gayle.

"Can you believe it? I'm going to deposit this thing and I'm not going to touch it -- if it doesn't bounce, that is. I call it blood money, because I shed blood for it."

"What are you talking about, Max?"

It was hard to explain. Earning money from my own creative efforts made the compensation different from what I earned when I sat in a cubicle or swept floors or drove a truck. It was more *valuable* somehow, even if the sum was paltry, because that was where I poured my guts and heart and soul.

To my surprise, the check cleared. Immediately Dulle began phoning me every day. Whenever he had an idea of any kind, he picked up the receiver. First, he wanted me to expand the original script by fifteen or twenty pages. Sure, I said, no problem. And maybe if I threw in a little more sex.

"Hot women having sex sells tickets, man."

And he wanted me in on everything else -- casting, rehearsals, the shoot itself. He was going to tackle the outdoor sequences during summer on account of the better weather. He was determined to push this thing, and he was going to push it hard. Damn near everyone he'd graduated from film school with had already made a name for himself as a director, and here he was, still scouting locations. He had to get a move on! And blah blah blah...

Dulle ran the auditions for the principal roles in one of the classrooms of an ancient, smelly grammar school on the lower East Side. It was as hot as hell. There were flies everywhere. As I watched the parade of emoting contenders, I wondered how any kid could actually bear sitting there all day long. Then I remembered where I went to school as a kid, and it didn't seem so bad...

The more I was forced to deal with Mike Dulle, the more I disliked him, and I realized what a steep price I was going to have to pay for that measly option money. He was always bitching and moaning and whining about how he was going to lose all of his hard-earned dough on this project if it didn't work out, and how the actors he'd seen weren't all that great, and how tough it was being both producer and director. Worst of all, he had no sense of humor whatsoever about any part of it.

"Maybe," I said -- keeping in mind that by contract my option money was non-refundable -- "it would be better if you waited awhile to start making this movie. Maybe if you try and bring some other investors on board first it'll be easier on you."

No, he insisted, he was going to realize his vision, come hell or high water. Nothing was going to stop him! The time was now! He'd make his forty grand stretch as far as it possibly could, he'd make it stretch as far as the goddamned moon if he had to! Others had done it, hadn't they? Kent Jones had forged a Hollywood career on a thirty thousand dollar movie and zero talent, so there was no question it could be done...

Before long all I wanted was for him to shut up.

Finally the cast was set. We agreed on our leading lady, Laura Faulkner, an attractive blond who could project a range of emotions without the benefit of dialogue. The plum supporting role of a cop, the part Dick Vincent had been after from the beginning, went to the director's best friend, Brad Ashton. Dick, who'd put Dulle and me together and should have received an assistant producer credit, was relegated to playing a bartender in a single scene. But Dulle didn't want him in the film at all.

"He's a shitty actor," Dulle sneered. I liked Dick, but he was way over the top, undisciplined, a scene-chewer who only succeeded in making himself look like an amateur. It was all on account of his worship of the late-career Al Pacino, but he refused to take suggestions or criticism. It was no wonder he'd gotten run out of Hollywood and had trouble landing work in New York. But out of loyalty I lobbied for him to get the bartender role.

Dulle eventually capitulated. "But it's on your head if he sucks," he threw in with a dash of acid.

I also pushed for Swain Wilson to play the male lead. Dulle was dead-set against him too.

"He's full of himself, and he's got the acting skill of a log," he snapped.

"Yeah, but the character is supposed to be something of a cipher. Mostly all he has to do is strike poses and look good, and he did that pretty well during the auditions."

What Swain Wilson couldn't quite pull off effectively was projecting an air of menace and danger when the script called for it, but none of the other hopefuls could either. The way I saw it, he at least *looked* the part. And maybe by the time the cameras rolled he'd learn to act -- though that hope had crashed in the case of Dolph Bevas. The problem was that Dulle's production schedule made it impossible to go on looking for somebody else, and we'd been through a hundred actors already.

There was one part left to cast -- the bloated corpse that

gets pulled out of the river. The person who desperately --
and mysteriously -- wanted it was Dick's buddy, Marty Barker.
Marty's real name was Muhammad El-Birshibi. He was a
Syrian-born computer whiz who'd changed his name when
he came to America in order to fit in. Or maybe he was a
terrorist waiting for his orders. He and Dick had become tight
out in L.A. when they were driving cabs. Marty paid Dick's
way whenever he was out of work or had a falling out with
his wife -- which was every other week. When Dick needed a
place to crash or a free meal, Marty was there. A con man by
nature, Dick sensed that his pal was an easy mark, and Marty
complied because he was lonely, overweight and unattractive.
It was a weird, symbiotic relationship, but for Dick it had its
perks, especially now that Marty had moved up in the world:
he was making a killing on Wall Street, where they couldn't
seem to operate their computers without him. To boot, he
had no compunction about springing for prostitutes when he
and Dick needed them, and he owned a big SUV that he'd
use to transport us to the location up in the Adirondacks. If
he was so starved for attention that he'd lie in the freezing
water and play dead for no pay, who was I to say no?

81

For ten days the cast and crew of *Something Under The Surface*
were going to be stranded at a broken-down compound in

a godforsaken spot called Eagle Lake. According to Dulle, it was once a resort for the rich and famous before people quit vacationing in the Adirondacks a hundred years ago. It included a ramshackle house and lodge, but little in the way of amenities.

Marty, Dick and I drove up on the third day of shooting. Marty took one look at the chaotic and filthy living quarters and shook his head.

"I gotta have my own private bathroom," he grumbled. Dick and I were welcome to join him at the cabins down the road, on his dime.

Hell, yes, we were on board for that. All of us were too old for a communal shithouse.

The Eaglet Cabins were small and tight, but the showers worked and the water gushed hot out of the nozzles.

We soon got word that the first three days of shooting had wrapped without a hitch. Everything was cool. We sat around and had a couple of beers, then hit the sack.

Sometime after midnight a frantic rap on my door jarred me out of a coma.

"What? What is it?"

"Max Zajack? Telephone!"

I pulled on my shorts and tee shirt and ran over to the office. The lady at the desk pointed at the receiver. It had to be Dulle, calling to bitch about something. I was wrong: it was my wife.

"It's Ray." My three-year-old son.

"What's wrong?"

"Max, it happened practically the minute you left! I was

giving him a bath like I always do, and when I reached for the towel, he slipped and cut his eyelid on the spigot. I had to rush him to the emergency room and sit there waiting while he bled. It was horrible."

"How bad was the cut?"

"A dozen stitches."

"Ouch."

"But I called in a plastic surgeon so any scarring would be minimized."

"Good thinking." Suddenly I felt guilty because I wasn't there. Wives and kids have a facility for producing that effect.

"That's not all. I had to undergo an interrogation while we waited."

"What?"

"They thought I might have done something. You know -- abused him."

"Oh, fuck."

"Anyway, I just wanted you to know. Luckily Dick let his wife know where you were, since you weren't picking up your phone... Weren't sleeping with a hot young actress, were you?"

"If I could find one, I would. By the way, there's no cell service up here... So, is the kid all right?"

"He'll live."

82

The next morning Marty was up early and in the makeup chair over at Eagle Lake. They worked on him for hours, transforming him from a human being into a decomposing slab of meat. Playing a corpse made Marty feel important. He became the center of attention, a movie star. When his makeover was finished, he looked like the ugly cousin of the Frankenstein monster...

Later that morning a caravan of vehicles moved out of Eagle Lake to a remote bend on a river where some of the crew, along with their underwater equipment, had already set up. I got out of Marty's SUV, walked down to the water and stuck my hand in. Early August and it was as frigid as a glacier.

I felt bad for Marty, but Dulle needed a corpse, and he was willing. The director ordered him to plunge in and assume his position. Like an obedient soldier, he followed instructions and didn't complain once about the bitter cold. It was a whole hour later when Dulle called for action.

"How long are you going to make him stay in there?" I asked between takes. "The poor bozo might have a heart attack or freeze to death."

"That's his tough luck," Dulle snarled. "If he wants to be in my movie, he'll stay in the goddamned water until I tell him he can get out!"

There wasn't much for me to do, so I hitched a ride back to

the cabin. That night Dulle stopped by with a video camera. We sat on the edge of the bed and he switched it on.

"It's a fucking disaster," he bellyached.

He tilted the viewfinder towards me. After hours in the water, Marty looked like a giant, overripe tomato. What he didn't look anything like was a dead man. In every close-up it was obvious that he was shivering or that his teeth were chattering. I thought it was hilarious, but I didn't laugh.

"And that's not all the problem. I'm stuck with a goddamned mummy for a leading man," Dulle moaned, referring to Swain Wilson, who, he reminded me, was my choice. "I don't know what the hell I'm going to do."

I didn't know what he was going to do either. And I had to admit that in the footage Wilson did look about as animated as a two-by-four. I'd been wrong about him after all. But shit, I wasn't a casting director -- I was just a writer.

Barring a miracle, Dulle just might be fucked.

I decided to encourage him anyway. "You've got to hang in there. Maybe things will improve. And the footage isn't all bad. Maybe some of it can be salvaged."

I had my own agenda, of course. I wanted Dulle to plow through, no matter what. I was thinking of the money I stood to make if he could manage to finish *Something Under The Surface*, though by this time I'd begun to realize that he was the wrong person to direct what was really a subtle psychological drama. I'd coveted recognition and money, and now I was paying for it. Greed -- even on a small scale -- will always exact its revenge.

On the other hand, the history of the film industry is

littered with rubbish -- some of which goes on to win awards -- so who was I to cast judgment? Maybe, in the end, *Something Under The Surface* would find its audience, no matter how it turned out.

After his scenes were wrapped, Marty took off for his gig back in the city, which left Dick and me in our prepaid cabins. Since Dick wasn't scheduled to shoot his scene until the final night, we were free. Lost in the immense park with only the moon, the stars and the calls of wild animals for company, we were quickly bored shitless.

"Why don't we hit that roadhouse we passed on the way in?" Dick was a guy who couldn't sit still or stay away from the bottle for long, and he made no secret of it.

"Why not? It's a lovely evening for a walk."

Since Marty had driven his SUV back to Manhattan, we had to make the trip on foot. When we reached the Eagle's Nest a couple of miles away, the parking lot was half-filled, mostly with trucks adorned with gun racks and the names of contracting businesses stenciled on their doors. Loud blasts of cock rock -- Hendrix or Zeppelin -- came from inside.

"Hottest joint in town," Dick laughed.

Sure enough, every seat at the bar was occupied. When the door slammed behind us, all heads turned in our direction.

I poked Dick in the ribs. "So where are the ladies?"

There weren't any. Not a single one. Apparently there were no stray females in Eagle Lake. We commandeered an empty table in the corner. Dick shuffled over to the bar. As he waited for service, I took in the other patrons. They darted hostile glances at both of us -- or so I thought. But then I'm naturally hypersensitive and paranoid.

"Interesting crowd," I whispered when Dick banged a squat glass full of amber liquid down in front of me.

We sat there sipping our whiskey in silence. The voices of the boozers at the bar, which were subdued when we walked in, seemed to have grown louder, rowdier, bolder.

"If I'm any judge of tone, the mountain men all sound very pissed off at something," I said to Dick without looking up. "Maybe they think we're a couple of fags. That would not be a good thing."

I began to wonder whether we could fight our way out if it came to that. Nah... We wouldn't be able to do squat against these guys -- they were all super-macho types and there were only two of us. And if we couldn't psych them out, then we'd have to call someone, like the cops, for help. The problem was that the Eagle Lake Chief of Police was probably sitting right there at the bar.

The atmosphere grew even more hairy. Now they were talking about somebody who "*needed to be taught a lesson.*"

I knocked back the rest of my drink. "Know what? I think we should get the fuck out of here."

Dick wasn't about to disagree. We got up and skulked towards the door.

We hadn't made it far on the road that would take us back to the cabins when we heard the squeal of tires.

"What the fuck...?"

"*Shit!*"

A pick-up with ridiculously oversized wheels was bearing down on us, the rubber screaming bloody murder.

"DUCK!"

A flying bottle narrowly missed my head. There were whelps of laughter from inside the truck.

"I'M GLAD YOU THINK IT'S FUNNY, YOU STUPID SHIT-KICKING HILLBILLIES," Dick shouted at the pickup's tail-lights.

"Shut up, man!" I yelled at him. "You want to get us shot?"

The vehicle swerved, backed up, and turned.

"*JESUS FUCKING CHRIST!*"

The beast hurtled towards us, its gigantic headlamps making us look like convicts trying to pull off a jailbreak.

"DOWN! *HIT THE GROUND!*"

When I dove onto the shoulder I got a mouthful of gravel. I looked up just in time to see one of the yahoos waving a rifle out the window. There was a popping noise, pings and pangs off the asphalt. Goddamn it. The hayseeds were actually *shooting* at us.

More whooping and hollering. I didn't hear a word out of Dick. I looked around. *Where the hell was he?* Maybe he'd been hit. I stayed flat against the ground until the truck roared off into the blackness.

Finally it was quiet.

"*Dick! You all right? You alive?*"

After a few seconds he staggered out of the brush, shaking the mosquitoes and ticks off.

"You fucking believe this shit?"

I rolled over and felt myself up and down to make sure a bullet hadn't hit me. Then I jumped to my feet and began jogging toward the Eaglet Cabins. I heard Dick puffing behind me, trying to keep up.

83

Gunshots.

They were trying to kill me again.

More angry gunshots.

"No... no... no... No, NO!"

Where was that voice was coming from?

It was me, screaming in my dream.

I lifted my head off the pillow and fumbled for my watch. *6:40.*

What the fuck? It had to be morning... My eyeballs were sore. My temples throbbed. I had a hangover from a lousy double shot of rotgut.

My hay fever kicked in and I started sneezing. As I began to come to my senses, I realized it wasn't shots I'd been hearing. Somebody was punching the door. I threw back the sheets and opened up.

Mike Dulle.

What the hell did he want at this ungodly hour? Without a word he pushed his way in. He launched into the same old lament, with a few new wrinkles. Now, in addition to pretty much everyone in the cast, he also hated everyone on the crew. They were a bunch of worthless turds, totally and completely incompetent, and he had a good notion not to pay them even a penny of their salaries.

Whew. It was much too much to deal with so early in the morning.

But what he was really worried about was tonight. The big scene. The *key* scene of the film, the one that demanded the most complicated set and camera setups.

"Zajack, everything rides on tonight! Whatever else happens, it *has* to come off because half of what I've already shot is unusable..."

"Don't worry man, it'll be okay..."

While playing cheerleader I pulled my clothes on. I was half-sure that it would be okay, because the scene was well written, if I did say so myself. Swain Wilson wasn't part of it, and Dick Vincent had little to do but stand there and deliver a few words. Our leading lady had proven herself to be a fine performer, the shining star of the cast, and there was no doubt whatsoever about her ability to carry it. That left Brad Ashton, who was playing the cop. I'd not seen him in action yet, but the director swore by him.

"The best actor of the lot," he'd declare vehemently whenever Ashton's name came up.

It was a whole hour before I was able to maneuver Dulle out the door. By that time my headache had gotten worse. *What a fucking asshole.* How did I always manage to get entangled with assholes? What was it about me? Or was the world just filled with assholes and it was unavoidable?

I was exhausted but couldn't get back to sleep. I walked over to Dick's cabin, then we hiked into the village and sucked down plates of bacon and eggs and home fries at a greasy spoon. When we got back, I took a long, luxurious shit, then watched Dick smoke Marlboros and pace his cabin while trying out his few lines several different ways. Later I stretched out on my bed, read Jim Thompson, sipped a beer, and fell asleep, until we got picked up and driven to the set...

Dulle had rented a veterans' club for the occasion. The interior was as hot as a corner of Hell, what with all the lights, the stifling summer heat and the absence of air conditioning. It had only been a few days since I'd been up in the forest and I already felt like I'd been through a war. I was covered with mosquito bites, and chigger bites, and who knows what other bites. Being shot at didn't help.

I collared a chair and observed the goings-on. The hall was still being dressed to resemble a wilderness inn. The DP was taking light readings. The other crew members were running around doing whatever it is they do. Dick took his place behind the bar and began twiddling with the bottles and glasses, making himself feel at home. Dulle darted here and there in a state of near hysteria.

Brad Ashton was holding court, and everyone was listening. Like his pal Dulle, he had a nasty attitude. He'd supposedly been around. According to him, he'd pulled daring stunts like driving antiquated school buses from Minnesota, where he hailed from, all the way down to Guatemala, where they were purchased by the government and used for public transportation. There he'd slept under the stars, like a true vagabond, oblivious to the dangers of being alone and unarmed in a so-called developing nation...

All this was very impressive. Whenever someone did something a little out of the ordinary, no matter how stupid, we were all supposed to be dazzled.

When he wasn't acting, according to Dulle, Ashtonbuilt

furniture and was engaged to a beautiful girl from a very wealthy family. The director thought he had rugged good looks and couldn't understand why he wasn't a big-time movie star.

Ashton, the virtuoso performer, was passable in his cop uniform, but he wasn't at all what I had in mind for the part. Too smug. Too scrawny. He looked a little like a weasel. I'd wanted a laconic type with some heft in body, mannerism and persona, the kind of easy-going, veteran civil servant you'd find in a remote outpost. I didn't see Ashton's acerbic, contrary style going over up in the north country. Hell, Dick Vincent was a much better fit for the part. But as usual, the guy with the money had final say.

Ashton plopped his bony ass on a barstool. One of the wardrobe assistants, a pretty young thing I'd had my eye on all week, rushed over and began fixing police officer's stripes on his shirt.

There was lots of barking back and forth between cast and crew. *Everybody in place? Cameras are ready to roll!*

"Twenty minutes!"

"I need twenty-five!"

I watched Ashton thumb through the script. He kept shaking his head. This captured my attention. I was curious about what was bothering him, but I didn't want to interfere with his "process." You never mess with an actor's preparation.

As usual, our leading lady was ready and waiting. I liked people who were prepared. So much of what happens on a movie set is nothing but an enormous waste of time and energy. Laura Faulkner was different. She was always ready.

She was very attractive, in an understated way, sort of like Gayle...

Dick asked Ashton whether he wanted to run the scene, just the three of them, before "action" was called. Ashton shrugged -- he couldn't care less. What the hell was this about? Dick cranked up his dialogue, but Ashton refused to pick up his cues. Within seconds it was obvious that he knew none of his lines -- not a single goddamned one.

Dick looked at me and threw up his hands.

"What's the problem?"

Ashton made a face. *"I can't say these lines."*

I glanced at Dulle, who was waiting to shoot the big scene. "Which lines are you talking about?"

"These." Ashton flicked the script with disgust.

"What do you mean?"

"I mean I can't say these lines the way they're *written.*"

I looked at Dick. Dick looked at me. We both looked at Laura Faulkner, then at Dulle. Nobody knew what to say.

It began to sink in. *This third-rate nobody thought my script was trash.* It was so beneath his contempt that he refused to memorize his part of it. And now he was throwing a diva fit.

It was unbelievable. Any two-bit hack would have been ready to work. Swain Wilson, weak as he was as a performer, had his lines committed to memory within a couple days of landing the part. Even Marty had known which way to roll in the water.

I grabbed Dick's script and silently reviewed the scene. I couldn't find anything wrong with it. The writing was serviceable, the conversation natural. I tried reasoning with

Ashton, but he would have none of it.

It was absurd. It was insane.

Dulle, who'd turned away to confer with the sound unit, came over to see what was going on. Ashton laid it out for him. He wasn't going to deliver his lines as I'd written them, and that's all there was to it.

Instead of trying to get something on film, we all stood there with our thumbs up our asses. A war of attrition erupted over Ashton's intransigence. I quietly insisted on my lines, the actor resisted. Back and forth it went. Instead of doing what he'd signed an agreement to do, Ashton tossed out random words and phrases that didn't make sense and fit the scene. But the most maddening thing of all was that his buddy the director had suddenly lost his tongue.

Finally I pulled him aside. "This fucking dick-head is going to destroy the scene if he insists on holding out. If he comes up with something better, I'm all ears. But I haven't heard anything yet."

Dulle was flummoxed. He didn't seem to know what to do except allow Ashton to mutilate my words until he found another way to say the same exact things I'd written. It was the most ludicrous thing I'd ever witnessed.

"Don't tell me you're afraid of this douchebag? What does he have on you?"

"He's got his own way of working," Dulle mumbled sheepishly. "Just give him some time."

The production of *Something Under The Surface* ground to a complete and total halt. Valuable time was being lost. Most of the crew were scheduled to leave for other commitments in the morning, but nobody but me seemed to give a damn.

Ashton went on fiddling with my script. An hour passed.

"Just say the fucking words," I swore at him finally.

"I can't do it, man."

"Fine. Fuck it. Say whatever the hell you want to say. What do I know? I just wrote the goddamned thing."

I stormed off and watched from behind the glare of the lights. Finally the director gave the command to get ready for a take. Apparently he was going to waste precious film on a spontaneous performance from Ashton.

The crew roused itself.

"Action!"

"Uh... mmm... *agh...*"

It was both farcical and painful. Ashton stumbled, hemmed and hawed through the scene in some half-baked attempt at imitating Brando. It was after three in the morning when I decided I'd had enough, and walked beneath the black sky back to the cabin...

84

The remainder of *Something Under The Surface*, the segments set in New York City, were supposed to be filmed soon after the wilderness section wrapped, but, strangely, nothing happened.

Then Dulle phoned one day, inviting me to a Chelsea

editing suite to observe while he worked on the footage that had been shot upstate. When I got there, the director was his usual surly self, complaining about anything and everything.

"I'm telling you, Zajack, the movie business is a fucking money pit!"

I sat with a cup of coffee while he peered into a monitor and ran the same sequences from *Something Under The Surface* again and again.

What I saw didn't do much for me. The footage wasn't exactly awful. In someone else's hands, it might even have had potential. But at this point it was nothing more than mediocre. Flat. Lifeless. Was the problem my script, or what Mike Dulle had done with it? Impossible questions to answer.

"So what's the deal with the rest of the movie?" I asked anyway when he took a break.

"The rest of the movie? Man, this is all I've got to work with. And I'm broke. I spent every cent I had in the world on these forty minutes."

"But I thought that by now you'd have figured out how to finish shooting -- wasn't that the strategy?"

"I've shown what I've edited so far, and I've not been able to lure a single new investor... Hey Zajack, if you have any spare cash, I'd be happy to use it towards shooting more."

"Me? I'm in this to *make* money."

I was crestfallen. Every idiot knows that when shooting a film you have to move fast. Momentum dries up. Actors move away, or their looks change, or, if they're lucky, they land other gigs. Sometimes they even die, then everyone involved is screwed.

"The problem is that we only have half a movie," I

pointed out to Dulle, as if he didn't already know it. "What good is half a movie? You can't do anything with it. It's like having nothing at all."

He shook his head. He was going to use what he had to keep hitting up suckers for more funds. If I didn't have any money myself, did I have any flush contacts?

No, I didn't.

Right then and there I knew I was never going to see another penny from Dulle. With all of its shortcomings, there was no way a choir of angels was going to happen along and rescue *Something Under The Surface*. Dulle had fatally miscalculated and blown it.

And there it was -- another setback. Another big setback. It appeared that I wasn't cut out for the film industry, either.

Seconds later I was on the street, swimming among the other lunatics, heading for the subway, thinking about how yet another golden opportunity was going to come to nothing.

Which is exactly what happened.

85

Between the crashes of *Draco And The Ecliptic* and *Something Under The Surface*, I felt like I'd been hit with a wicked overhand right, followed by a devastating left hook. I was wobbly. Punch drunk. I might not be able to stay on my feet. All of the fiascos I'd endured had forced me to question everything about myself. How could I not?

It was morning. I lay in bed hoping for something to happen, some kind of revelation, something to tell me which way to go. There were sounds coming from elsewhere in the apartment -- probably Gayle making herself something to eat before shoving off for work. A few feet away the kid lay sleeping. Today it was my turn to watch him. Outside, the sun was throwing platinum over the Manhattan skyline.

I kept waiting and listening, but God didn't appear and tell me what to do. No inner voice made itself heard. If I stayed there on my back, nothing would ever happen: I would just stay there on my back. *That was the great revelation.*

Finally I rolled out of bed, careful not to rouse my boy. I slipped into the next room and switched on the computer. The latest story I'd written was waiting for me there. I started fiddling with it, hoping to get a few pages polished before he woke up.

When Ray got out of bed, I fed him and we walked over to Hudson Park, where *On The Waterfront* was shot a long time ago. He rode the slides, climbed the monkey bars, and scurried through the jungle gym, all without a care in the world. The kid made me laugh and forget myself, and everything else, at least for a while...

"Max Zajack?"

"You got him."

"We'd like you to read for one of the leads in our film *The Road To Chaos*. When can you come in?"

"When do you need me?"

Just like that, I was back in action.

———————

"Max, I thought you were coming to Arizona with us!"

It was just before the Christmas holidays. I'd promised Gayle that I'd go with her and the kid to visit her family in Tucson.

"I know I did, but this audition came up."

"Can't you tell them to work around your schedule for a change?"

"It's for the lead in a film, baby."

"But you know how these people are. They change things around at a moment's notice and leave you hanging."

"Right... but what if this is the one that -- You have to admit I'm due for a break. A colossal fucking break. My luck has to turn sometime. Maybe the time is now."

She rolled her eyes, shook her head and disappeared into the bedroom. I had to wonder sometimes why that woman put up with me.

86

I rode an elevator high up a skyscraper on Fifty-seventh Street and read for the lead of *The Road To Chaos*. The casting people sat there and watched me with their jaws hanging open. Whether it was because they thought I was great or god-awful, I didn't know...

The wife and kid took off for Arizona. I stayed back East, waiting for a callback for *The Road To Chaos*, reported to my various gigs, and froze my ass off. There were blizzards, ice storms, howling winds. In Tucson there was warmth and sunshine and palm trees. What the hell was I doing?

A few weeks later, long after Gayle and the kid returned to Hoboken, there was finally a message on my machine.

"Max, could you please call us..."

It was the business office of *The Road To Chaos*. Maybe for some reason there'd been a delay in the production. Maybe I wasn't out of it yet.

"We start shooting in a week. We'd like to offer you the part of the janitor, if you're interested."

"The *janitor*?"

"Yes, it's a brief scene. No big deal. If you're not interested, we'll call someone else."

"I thought I was up for one of the leads. What happened?"

"Oh -- the team decided to go with someone else. That's the business."

"Pay?"

"Deferred. You'll get a contract."

"Right."

———————

When it was completed, *The Road To Chaos* somehow made it into rotation on a major cable station. It was one of the cheesiest, junkiest pieces of crap I'd ever seen, so dismal across the board that it was impossible to even begin to pinpoint where it had all gone wrong. I was too embarrassed to even tell anyone that I was part of it. The good news was that my performance was natural, better than everyone else's. The bad news was that I spoke only two words and was on screen for all of fifteen seconds...

87

Back in the fall I'd taken a small role in a no-budget flick called *Out Of Sync*. It was shot around the corner at the Hoboken courthouse, where Henry Miller married his notorious second wife, June, way back in the 1920s. Since I didn't have to travel, it only set me back a few hours.

The scene was a loony one involving FBI agents on trial. I played a prosecuting attorney who made a fool of himself every time he got up to say something. I didn't know what the movie was about, but it didn't matter. I looked at it as nothing but an item to add to my credit list.

The director, Herman Fernandez, lived on the other side of Hoboken, and occasionally I'd bump into him on the street.

"How's that movie coming along?" I'd ask whenever we ran into each other.

"Getting there!"

There was something a little nutty about Fernandez, it was evident from the goofy expression in his buggy eyes. Maybe he'd suffered some sort of breakdown and been institutionalized. Maybe he was challenged in some way. It was okay. Look at Warhol. Look at Dali. Many outrageously successful artists were on the eccentric side. Maybe this Fernandez dude had what it took.

Months passed, and I forgot all about *Out Of Sync*. What was one more waste of time? All I'd done for years was fritter time away. If the cliché that the definition of insanity is doing the same thing again and again without learning a lesson from it, then I had to be more than ready for the straitjacket...

The apartment was quiet. A light snow was falling over the Hudson, making the island of Manhattan look like a magical painting, and creating the momentary illusion that all of the ugliness had been blotted out. Just then the phone rang.

"Max. It's Herman Fernandez."

"Hey, man. Is that goddamned movie of yours finished yet? I thought I was supposed to get a copy?"

"That's what I wanted to talk to you about. You remember Clay Netherland?"

"Yeah, I remember him all right." The guy had played the lead in *Out Of Sync*. Nice actor. I'd enjoyed what he was doing.

"Well, he's left us high and dry."

"What do you mean?"

"We shot damned near seventy-five percent of *Out Of Sync*, and he's suddenly decided he doesn't want to finish."

"What? Can't you force him?"

"It's not in the contract. Besides, he was working for deferred pay, like all of the actors. He's decided he's going to quit acting, and he's moving back to France."

"Too bad. Sounds like you're fucked."

"Tell me about it... Max, can we get together and talk?"

"What's wrong with right now?"

"It'd be better in person."

"As long as you don't want money from me and it doesn't take too long."

Fernandez laughed. We made an appointment to meet the next evening at the producer's apartment on the north end of Hudson Street.

———

The basement of the brownstone belonged to Danny Gabarza. All three of us, Gabarza, Fernandez, and me, sat at a long table in the dining room.

"Thanks for coming, Max."

"No problem."

Gabarza was staring at me. He was thickset and had the

eyes of a hog. I wondered how he'd managed to get himself in charge of *Out Of Sync*.

"So listen, Max," said Fernandez, "we were wondering if you'd be interested in taking over the lead role in our movie."

This was a stunner. It was the first time it had happened in all the years I'd been chasing parts.

"Danny and I have decided to re-shoot the entire film with a new actor, someone who will hang around until it's really and truly finished."

"Huh." I slugged my water.

"We really liked you as the prosecutor in the courtroom scene, Max. We think you can carry this film, we really do. And the completion money is there."

My ears pricked up.

"Does that mean there's a salary?"

Fernandez and Gabarza glanced at one another.

"Well, not exactly. But you'll get it on the other end, once we secure a distributor. And at that point we can negotiate the contract any way you'd like."

I'd heard it all before, of course. But this time the camera would be focused on me in every single scene. If the flick was a winner, I had everything to gain and nothing to lose except for more time.

"Here's the revised script," said Fernandez, pushing a sheaf of paper towards me. "Why don't you go home, read it and let us know what you think -- and whether you'd like to play Steve Borden in *Out Of Sync*."

———————

That night I stretched out on the bed with a cup of coffee and read the latest version of *Out Of Sync*. It was a quirky idea having to do with a guy who gets stupidly and mistakenly involved in a murder as he attempts to make an indie movie of his own. It wasn't Bergman. It certainly wasn't Kurosawa. It wasn't even Joe Eszterhas. But it had something, a batty sense of humor that kept me laughing with each new scene. And I couldn't say I didn't identify with the character of Steve Borden...

I closed the script and shut my eyes.

If these two weirdos could manage to actually finish *Out Of Sync* this time around, it might just finally be my ticket -- to something. Maybe, if I turned in a solidperformance, I'd at long last attract some attention and --

I had to face hard, cold facts: I was almost out of time. I was just south of fifty, and I could make out the scenery over the hill. Nobody was going to discover a fifty-year-old has-been wannabe. Work for guys my age would go to lifers with a legit track record, and there were plenty of those around...

Unless something happened. Unless I made something happen. Once in a while a man got lucky -- didn't he? Even the worst batter eventually gets a hit, doesn't he?

"I'm going to do this film," I told Gayle that night when we climbed into bed.

"Max! Not again!"

"What else do I have?"

"But a no-budget home movie shot on Super 8?"

"They all can't be seventy-millimeter epics."

"And how long is this going to take?"

"I don't know."

"Max -- it could take months -- a year. Do you really want to tie up all of your time working on a movie that nobody's ever going to see?"

"It's the chance I have to take."

"Don't forget I met that guy Fernandez too. It doesn't look like the elevator stops at all floors in that building."

"That's the way it is sometimes for genius. Hitchcock couldn't stop eating. Van Gogh sliced off his ear. Einstein used to walk the streets of Princeton without shoes."

"Genius? Fernandez is lucky he made it out of grammar school."

"So was Edison."

In fact I had no proof that Fernandez *had* graduated from grammar school. All I knew was that he and Danny had a crew and equipment and a script.

That was enough for me.

88

It started all over again. A new round of casting. Rehearsals. Wardrobe meetings. More script revisions. Guerilla shoots in Hoboken, Brooklyn, Jersey City, Weehawken, Manhattan, the suburbs of Bergen County. Then reshoots. Day after day, week after week of work. The weeks turned into months. The scenes accumulated. A year later, only two were left to be shot. We were standing just short of the finish line. Everybody involved felt pretty good about what had been captured on film.

Besides Fernandez and Gabarza, the single constant was me. Even the crew changed sometimes on a weekly basis.

One night when I was waiting to find out when and where the final scenes were going to be set up, the phone buzzed.

"Max. We have to talk." It was Herman Fernandez. His voice was unusually subdued.

"I'm right here."

"Listen, I don't know how to tell you this, but... the movie's dead."

"Wh-what?"

"*Out Of Sync* is history."

Okay -- I got it. Fernandez was pulling my chains.

Crazy guy. I started to laugh. "That's a great joke, man. That's funny. *Really* funny."

"It's not a joke, Max."

"Don't tell me that, Herman. Don't tell me that or I'm going to come over there and kick your fucking ass into the Hudson River."

"Look, man, it's not my fault! But it's all over and there's nothing that can be done about it."

"HERMAN, DON'T TELL ME AFTER I WORKED A FULL FUCKING YEAR *FOR NOTHING* THAT I'VE WASTED ALL MY TIME! BECAUSE I DON'T WANT TO HEAR IT!"

"I tried, Max, I swear to God I did! Danny and I had a major falling out over it, screaming and yelling and cursing and all the rest of it."

"What the fuck are you talking about, Herman? You sound like a crazy man! Two days ago there was no problem whatsoever between the two of you! So start talking some sense here!"

"There's something you didn't know, Max. All the cash for *Out Of Sync* was coming from Danny Gabarza's old man. Now he's getting a divorce and spending all his pesos on alimony and some Dominican bitch with a big ass. Night before last he took a look at the *Out Of Sync* footage and decided that he wanted to pull the plug on it before post-production, that it's not going to be another *King Kong* or *Star Wars*, and why should he waste all of his hard-earned money on a bomb?"

"Of course it's not fucking *Star Wars* or *King Kong*! But it's not going to be a bomb either! It can make noise on the festival circuit or in the art houses. The movie has something."

"I agree with you, Max. But I can't even look at that motherfucker anymore! Danny Gabarza is a spoiled cunt who lives off his father and never worked a day in his life!"

"And you're telling me all this shit *now*? Why don't the two of you work something out? We're two scenes from a wrap!"

"I can't do it, Max. I can't work another second with that bastard!"

"So what about me? What about all the goddamned work I and all the other actors and the crew put in?"

"The problem is that Danny Gabarza and his old man are the sole owners of *Out Of Sync*. We signed a notarized contract. Aside from writing the script and directing, I have no stake whatsoever in the project. There's not a thing I can do."

"No, no, no, no, no, no, no," I heard myself groaning.

"I'm gonna kill Gabarza. Then I'm gonna kill his old man."

"I wouldn't try anything like that, Max. Gabarza senior is *connected* -- it's common knowledge on the street. *He's a member of one of the families*. You could get yourself into some real trouble. You got a wife and kid, right? And your wife hasn't kicked you out yet? Count your blessings."

We went over the same ground again until it finally sank in.

I slammed the phone down. Mother-*fucker. I'd been had again*. I couldn't believe it.

I staggered over to the cupboard where the liquor bottles were stashed, opened it and grabbed the first thing.

"What happened, Max? I heard you ranting."

Gayle had thrown open the door of the bedroom.

"I don't want to talk about it."

"All right. I won't force you."

Five minutes later I broke down and told her, repeating the contents of my phone conversation with Fernandez like a zombie.

"So there you have it. Go ahead and call me a simpleton. Call me a fool. I won't argue with you."

"Want something to eat?"

"I don't have an appetite. I'm going to drink instead."

"Okay, Max. But don't get too drunk. I need you to make a run to the store. Ray is out of milk."

Gayle never rubbed it in. She was very good that way. She knew when to leave me alone. And she probably really loved me.

89

Like so many times before, the phone went dead.

Forever there was nothing, not a single call for anything, including extra work. It was like they could all smell the defeat wafting off my carcass. When finally I got summoned to read for something, the material was flat-out terrible. The scripts seemed to be concocted by cretins incapable of a single line that made sense. I often had the impression that the writers and directors -- mostly they were the same -- wanted to see what quality of actor they could lure in hopes that they might somehow improve their drivel...

The boy was about to turn four and my wife was unhappy in her latest job. The apartment on Hudson Street had grown very tight. Three people crammed into one bedroom on the tenth floor was getting to Gayle, not to mention that we were wedged between a pair of five-story parking garages where angry drunks leaned on their horns at three in the morning.

"Max, we have to get out of here before I jump out the window," she said one evening after supper. "Not only is it as noisy as Times Square, but the rent keeps going up. It's almost twice what it was when we moved in."

"Yeah, I know."

It was a discussion that always made me feel guilty, since what I brought in wasn't nearly enough to ease the pain.

"If we move further away from the city, we can get a mortgage on a house for half of what we're paying here."

"But once we're gone, we're probably never coming back."

"Has it been all that great for you?"

"You know the answer to that."

"Maybe you'll have better luck somewhere else."

"Like in the middle of nowhere?"

"North Jersey isn't exactly Kansas. It's actually a vast city."

"But at least here I meet people on the street who are actually in the business."

"A lot of good it's done you."

It was the truth. Could I argue?

"What do you think, Max? If it doesn't work out, we can always move somewhere else, right? It doesn't have to mean we'll be stuck out there forever. We can try California next. My family would be happy to have us around."

"I'm not going. I'm not going out into the hinterlands to mow lawns and drive to the fucking mall and coach soccer."

"Have it your way. But don't forget that Ray will be ready for kindergarten soon and the public schools here are horrible."

"I'll keep that in mind. But I'm still not going."

90

Near the end of summer we packed up and moved out to the suburbs. A few days later, the World Trade Center and its occupants were blasted into rubble and dust.

91

I was miserable out in Montfleur, but then that was my typical condition. It is said, and the fancy psychological studies have shown, that writers are prone to depression at much higher rates than everyone else in the population, more even than other artists. Whether it's the constant rejection, or the solitude, or the self-doubt, or something that drives a writer to write in the first place, maintaining one's sanity is a war without end. It's best for the writer to stay self-contained, and not check his mail too often, and not fret over the success everyone else seems to be having. Because even if they have it today, they'll be fucked tomorrow. It's a way of life that produces very few winners, and the winners aren't anywhere as great as they think they are...

————————

After auditioning for a slimy B flick about a gang of thugs who knock over a check-cashing business, blow away the proprietor, then hole up at a brothel, I was sent away, then called back to take one of the lead roles when the original choice didn't work out.

The shoot lasted a couple of weeks and featured cameos by an aging Hollywood legend and a Hispanic actor famous in south of the border films. Good, right? When the movie was cut, I didn't like what I saw. My performance was wooden and indifferent for a man whose life was in danger of ending in a hail of bullets. A paunch hung over my belt. I was starting to look... old.

Gayle had been right after all. Turning myself into an actor in order to bring attention to my writing had been a bomb. When I hadn't been paying attention, twenty years of my life had evaporated and I had nothing whatsoever to show for it.

92

I didn't say anything to anyone, but I was finished.

One afternoon, just to get out of the house, I drove over to the local Barnes & Noble. I spotted a rack full of the latest "Best Of" series, which had just been released. I grabbed the literary and mystery editions and found a chair in the corner. I'd been writing stories for decades and had never come close to being cited for anything, despite the fact that by this time I'd gotten a good deal of them published -- no small feat in itself. I remained utterly baffled by how a writer's work actually got noticed, since it always seemed so maddeningly beyond my grasp.

As usual, no one who made these decisions had noticed my so-called "literary" stories from the year before. I wasn't surprised or disappointed -- I'd expected it. I dropped the fat book on the carpet and picked up the mystery volume. The big winners' names were familiar: Oates, King, Grisham, etc. Nothing new there. I was just about to toss it when as an afterthought I flipped to the back pages... and there it was, under "50 Other Distinguished Mystery Stories of 2000": *The Man In Unit 25*, by yours truly, published in the *Pacific Rim Review*. At first I thought I was dreaming. I rubbed my eyes and looked again. No -- it was real.

I went back to the introduction and learned that over three thousand stories had been considered for the volume. My name had been misspelled, but it *was* there, and that was the only thing that mattered.

I'll be damned -- *someone had finally noticed*, and it had nothing to do with acting. Maybe I was some kind of writer after all.

Soon afterwards *Hating Olivia* was published by a small press in England, and to my shock and amazement it attracted some notice, as much notice as a novel can attract in an overcrowded, indifferent world. After damned near thirty years of work, something had finally happened.

I didn't have to kill myself trying to be something I wasn't after all.

93

"Mister Zajack?"

"Yes?"

"We have a principal part for you in an upcoming episode

of *Crime Files*. It shoots next week in Allentown, Pennsylvania."

The call came in at the end of July. By this time I hadn't given acting a thought for nearly a year.

"Do I have to read for it?"

"No. We had your headshot in our files. You bear a strong resemblance to the character you'll be playing. In addition to your pay, you'll be provided with a copy of the episode, which will be titled 'Two In A Million.'"

I might have retired, but as soon as I heard the word "pay," my will weakened.

"Day and time? Oh, and don't forget to send the directions."

94

The shoot had gone seamlessly. I played a wealthy California airplane mogul and father of two who is murdered with the rest of his family after arriving home from a weekend vacation. I'd done a damned good acting job, if I did say so myself. And I had the bruises on my forehead, after falling to the floor dead for fifteen takes, to prove it.

September 15 was the big night. "Two In A Million" was scheduled to air for the first time on national television. Max Zajack would at long last be exposed to millions all over the globe.

The kid was already asleep. Gayle and I sat with our drinks in front of the tube and waited. After the background of the case was set up by the baritone-voiced narrator, it was time for the reenactment of the crime.

My character, Wesley Sortin, pulled his Mercedes into the carport.

"Pretty good so far, eh?" I nudged Gayle.

"Nothing's happened yet!"

"Don't worry -- it's coming, it's coming...!"

After sitting in the car for a moment, I got out, and when I moved into the eye of the camera, my face was... *pixelated*. And it was pixelated when I walked into the house and discovered my wife and daughter shot to death... and nothing but a blur when I tried to revive them, and a blur when I phoned 911, and a black hole as the camera trailed me through the rooms in the long seconds before I was blown away from behind, execution style.

"What happened to your face, Max? What did they do to it?"

Fuck if I knew. I sat there speechless, staring at the screen. It didn't make sense -- it didn't make any sense at all. Whoever had blotted out my face hadn't done it to any of the other actors.

My wife and I looked at one another.

"What did I tell you, Max?"

I started to laugh.

Then she started laughing too.

Once we started, neither of us could stop.

We both had a big laugh, a huge laugh, hah hah hah, hah hah hah -- over all of it, everything that happened from the

moment I decided that I was going to become an actor.
There was nothing else to do but laugh -- nothing.
And we kept laughing.

T H E   E N D

Lightning Source UK Ltd.
Milton Keynes UK
UKHW012041210919
350164UK00001B/71/P